CATHEDRAL OF BONES

AN ELA OF SALISBURY MEDIEVAL MYSTERY

J. G. LEWIS

CATHEDRAL OF BONES

AN ELA OF SALISBURY MEDIEVAL MYSTERY

by J. G. LEWIS

For my mother, Mardie Gorman, who instilled in me a love of books and history from a very early age.

ACKNOWLEDGMENTS

I owe many thanks to Mark Armstrong, Betsy van der Hoek, Anne MacFarlane and Judith Tilden for their careful readings and excellent suggestions. Thanks also to my wonderful editor Lynn Messina. All remaining errors are mine alone.

CHAPTER 1

*S*alisbury Cathedral, Sunday March 8, 1226
My deepest condolences!
Cut down in his prime!
Such a horrible shock!
Our most heartfelt sympathies!

Dazed and weary from three sleepless nights, the newly widowed Ela Longespée, Countess of Salisbury, heard their words and even managed to murmur the appropriate response as she traveled through the crowd of barons and knights. Most were damp from the insistent rain, some having ridden hard all the way from London to be here this morning. Their furrowed brows, wan faces and the occasional red rimmed eye reminded her that some of them would take his loss almost as hard as she did.

The service was over. He'd been laid to rest. And now she had to endure the rest of her life alone.

This is what the aftermath of a battle must feel like.

Smoke from censers thickened the air and stung her teary eyes. All the whispered words—we're so sorry!—rose high into the stone vaulting of the new cathedral where they seemed to multiply before descending again like a fresh rain of arrows.

The first person to be interred in our cathedral!

Ela felt like a traitor leaving William in that wooden box. If this were a battle they'd at least carry him home, but his flesh and bones would remain here forever and ever. Tomorrow she'd meet with the stonemason about the likeness on the lid. A stone carving befitting a king's son, another king's brother.

Her own dear husband.

Ela wished she could lift her head and wail like a Saracen. Just once she'd like to let the ear-piercing shriek of her pain travel up to those high vaults and ring hard enough to shatter the high glass windows.

But she knew her duty too well. She stepped out of the scented smoke and back into the drizzle.

"Your horse, my lady." Gerald Deschamps, deputy commander of the garrison troops, held the reins of her big gray mare. Rain hung like tears in Freya's long mane. Deschamps helped her up into the saddle, and she turned to ride the grim road home.

She'd never felt so alone. She wasn't alone, of course. Not with eight children and countless attendants and servants and the king's garrison stationed around her castle. A procession of a thousand people she must now lead back to the castle.

She turned to make sure her children were being suitably mounted behind her. The youngest might need their ponies to be led if they were too distracted with grief.

Her eldest son, Will, rode up beside her. On the brink of manhood, he was named for her husband and bore his impressive height and handsome countenance. "Did you see how the candles stayed lit the whole way, despite the rain?" His taut lips quivered slightly as he closed them.

"Did they?" She didn't know what he was talking about.

"Like the time Papa saw a light at the top of his mast before he was saved from the shipwreck." She could tell that he too was trying not to cry, and it made her chest ache. "It's too cruel, Mama. Why was he saved from the shipwreck and then home with us only a month before he was taken from us?"

She'd asked herself that question a thousand times. And that just in the past hour.

"Your father stands with God now and we must be brave without him."

"I am brave, Mother."

"I know, my heart." Her son was fearless in the hunting field and on the tournament ground. Her pride in his valor often mingled with fear for his safety. A mother's lot. "Come up here, my love, and lead the procession with me."

People lined the streets of New Salisbury. Shop owners, servants, apprentices, young and old. Most of them likely just here to watch the pageantry of the knights and their fine horses. They stared, silent mostly, some whispering among themselves.

Was this how it felt to lead a defeated army back home?

She saw the edge of the town and the open fields with relief, glad to leave the gawpers and the smoke and barking dogs behind, when a man came galloping across the field to her left. She tightened her grip on the reins as her horse stirred in response.

He reined his horse to a spattering halt, hastily bowed to her. "My lady—I—there's been—" His red face and wide eyes alarmed her. Had he just seen her husband's ghost?

"What?" she demanded, panic flaring in her chest.

"A body, my lady." He glanced about, as if looking for someone more suitable with whom to share his urgent news. Deschamps was riding back behind her children.

3

"A human body?" She recognized the man as a local baker.

"A dead woman," he spluttered. "Frozen into the ice near How's Bottom. All this rain has melted the ice and…and—" He looked back at Deschamps, who was already leaving his place in the procession and riding toward them.

As sheriff her husband would have taken charge. In his absence—he was often away fighting or on other royal duties —Deschamps would take command in his stead. But things were different now.

Her husband wasn't coming back. As countess, she was now the castellan of Salisbury and acting sheriff of Wiltshire. "I'll come at once."

"But—" He looked behind her at the growing funeral procession making its way back from church to castle, which was now bunching up behind her.

"My husband is with his creator now. Sir Gerald will lead the procession back to the castle." She shot Deschamps a look intended to silence any protest. "Where's the coroner?" She glanced at the crowd behind her, searching. A knight, he would have attended the service and was sure to be in the procession. "We'll need a stretcher and cart to remove the body to the castle."

"Yes, my lady." Deschamps's countenance revealed no emotion. He turned and called out for the coroner in a booming voice.

Some stirring farther back in the crowd led to a man on a bay horse riding up alongside. "At your service, my lady."

"Please attend us, Master Haughton. A body has been found."

"Lead the way." She urged her horse away from the procession and up to the interloper's roan pony, which steamed in the rain.

"I'll come, too." Her son Will followed. She didn't have the strength to argue with him.

4

The baker led them across the soggy field and up the old track toward the river at a brisk trot. "I'm so sorry about your husband," he called, face still red as a beet. "My lady."

She could tell he felt awkward and had no idea how to address her now that her husband was dead. No doubt he wished Deschamps was with him. "You're Peter Howard, the baker, aren't you?"

"Indeed I am, my lady. I was on my way to town to stand with the crowds and pay my respects—" Most likely he was seizing the opportunity for a little Sunday morning fishing, but no matter. "Then I saw her there in the water. I'm so sorry to interrupt, but I wasn't sure what else to do."

"You did the right thing. Did anyone stay with the body?"

"My apprentice. I told him to watch her—the corpse— while I went to raise the hue and cry."

Ela could already hear the thudding hooves of others coming behind them. She'd heard the coroner call for jurors to attend, and no doubt there were some at hand in the crowd outside the cathedral. She spurred her horse, wanting to see the scene before it was disturbed.

At the riverbank, the baker gallantly jumped down and held her horse while she dismounted and handed him her reins. Will was already clambering down the riverbank and out of sight. The baker's apprentice, wide-eyed at the sudden arrivals, held his horse.

"She's young," Will called from below.

Ela approached the riverbank with trepidation. The water was swollen with spring rain and the ice from the recent cold snap almost fully melted. She suppressed a gasp as a sodden, rust-colored garment came into view. The body lay tangled in a thick stand of rushes that wove into the woman's dark hair.

Will was already in up to his knees, pulling her garments away from the grasping stems.

The coroner half-stepped, half-slid down to the gray water. "We must get her up onto the bank," he said to Will. "You take her arms."

He and Will freed the woman's sodden garments from their marshy tomb. With considerable effort, and no little backsliding, they managed to heave her wet and heavy form up the muddy riverbank and onto the thin spring grass.

Ela swallowed a wave of revulsion at the odor that rose from the woman's body. The corpse was not fresh. She didn't have a lot of experience with dead bodies, but she had enough to know that this woman had been dead at least a few days, maybe longer given the preservative qualities of ice.

She approached, half-holding her breath. The dead woman's gray eyes stared up at them, unseeing as a stone effigy. Her lips were mauve and seemed stuck in a ghastly cry for help. Her dress was made of good wool, not torn or ragged at the hem. One foot was bare and one still encased in a water-shriveled leather boot.

"She's pregnant," Ela breathed as the poor girl's swollen belly registered in her mind. "Hail Mary, full of grace, blessed art though amongst women…" She raised her hands to her mouth as she muttered the familiar prayer, shocked at herself that it took the evidence of this poor woman's dead baby to remind her that a human soul needed their urgent help.

"Amen," murmured the men gathered around her.

"She might have fallen in," said Will.

"Or there might be foul play." Ela leaned in to peer at the dark bruising that bloomed out of her hair near her left ear. "She bears signs of force."

"She could have banged her head on a rock in the river after she fell," said Howard.

Ela looked at the coroner, who silently closed the dead

woman's eyes. Questions crowded her brain. "Can a body bruise after death? Once the blood had stopped flowing?"

"No, my lady." Giles Haughton's quiet response told her everything she needed to know.

"Do any of you recognize her?" The young woman's face didn't look familiar, but her features were swollen and misshapen so it was hard to even tell what she'd looked like in life. Young, though, as Will had said. Not yet five and twenty, with her face unlined and no silver in her hair. Poor girl. Someone must be missing a daughter, a sister or a wife.

She turned to the group of soldiers now gathered around the body.

"Bring her to the castle and have her laid out in the armory." She didn't want this body whisked away and hurriedly buried before all evidence had been examined. How had she been dead for days or even weeks with no word reaching the sheriff? Did she fall in or did someone drown her?

It was her duty to make sure this girl's death was investigated with the same thoroughness and care as if her husband were still alive.

Ela studied their surroundings for hints of what might have happened. Any traces of footprints or activity on the bank had unfortunately been obliterated in their rush to remove her, but Ela had a feeling the girl had entered the river somewhere upstream. The clump of rushes grew in a lazy bend of the Avon and might have held the body fast during the ice and snows of February. Every puddle and stream had been frozen since late January.

The soldiers fashioned a crude stretcher out of woven branches, and they heaved her sodden form onto it as gently as possible. Ela said a silent prayer as they carried her up from the riverbank. The drizzling rain grew more persistent as they remounted, and Ela led this small, grim procession back to the castle.

* * *

The funeral party from the cathedral had reached the castle before Ela did, and she arrived at the gates into a flurry of horses and attendants and gifts being unloaded from pack animals. She rode in and climbed down from Freya. The porter swept her cloak from her shoulders, which was a relief since it was damp through to the fur lining and heavy as lead.

The great hall was abuzz with voices. How William would have loved to see his friends gathered here altogether!

"Wine, my lady?" Sibel, her personal lady's maid thoughtfully hurried over with a silver cup. Ela took a small, bracing sip. How was she to play hostess to half the knights and barons of England when all she wanted to do was retire to her solar and sob into her pillow?

Ellie and Nicholas, her littlest ones, hurried toward her through the crowd, Ellie holding fast to her brother's tunic. Bright eyed and flushed, they looked relieved to see her. She'd lost her own father at age nine and knew that sense of terror that something—anything—could happen to your remaining parent. "I'm here, my loves." She bent down and embraced them.

"Was there a dead lady?" Perceptive Nicholas always asked the hard questions.

"Yes, my love."

"Is her soul resting with God like Daddy's?" asked Ellie.

Ela hesitated. She had a policy of not lying to her children, not even a small fib. The poor girl had no doubt died unshriven. A tiny shiver of despair roamed through her. "We must pray for her. Remember her in your prayers tonight."

"I will, Mama," said Nicholas. She knew he would, too. He

never forgot anything. "I'll pray for her and Papa every day this week."

"Me, Mama," said little Ellie, pulling her tiny bone-bead rosary from her sleeve and pressing it to her pink mouth. "I'll pray for her every day for a month."

"With so many prayers she's sure to be welcome in heaven." Ela kissed the top of Ellie's curly golden head, still damp from the rainy ride back from her father's burial.

"Do come close to the fire, my lady," urged Sibel. "You're shivering. You'll catch a chill riding out in the wet like that. And after such a shock on an already difficult day, too." She ushered Ela past the children—and past the clamor of barons looking to offer their condolences—to a chair within the heat of the great blaze.

"You're a treasure, Sibel." Sibel had cried longer and harder than she had at William's death. She'd been with them since before Ela's children were born and loved them all like family. Ela sipped her hot spiced wine and the heat of the fire began to stir some warmth back in her limbs. Her daughter Isabella came and wrapped her arms around her neck. "I can't believe he's gone, Mama. We only just got him back."

"I know, my sweet. It's too cruel." He'd spent much of Isabella's life—and hers—away on one adventure or another. "At least he arranged your betrothal before he passed." She was engaged to one of William's wards, thus ensuring that the ward's estates and income would stay in the family. Ela intended to plan the wedding as soon as possible before another earl or baron could petition the king for the wardship now that her husband was dead.

"I don't want to leave you." Isabella clung to her mother. "And you need my help with the little ones."

"It's your duty. We must all do our duty." She sipped her wine. Many would think it her own duty to marry again as soon as possible. Ela's mother was currently with her fourth husband.

But right now she had other concerns.

She rose from her seat and handed her cup to Sibel. The hall was thick with nobles from the funeral procession who'd returned here to share her grief or perhaps just to drink at someone else's expense. And a feast would soon be served on the trestle tables set up for the occasion.

Some of them turned to look at her as she rose. What did they see? A tragic widow? A forlorn mother of eight father-less children? A great heiress with a fortune ripe for the plucking? She was all and none of those things.

She made polite conversation with several of her husband's close companions, then cornered Deschamps. "Is the young woman laid out in the armory?"

"She is my lady. The coroner went home to change his wet clothes, but he'll be back to attend her as soon as possi-ble. I've sent for a shroud. She'll have to be buried outside the walls, of course."

Ela bristled. He assumed the girl had no right to a Chris-tian burial. "She won't be buried until we've determined who she is. We don't know the circumstances of her death. Perhaps she has every right to a burial in the cathedral churchyard."

Every person no matter how low—or how high—had a right to justice.

Her husband had a right to justice. She drew in a breath and steadied herself as a wave of anger shook her. His killer was beyond the reach of justice—since he dispensed it.

* * *

Ela swept out of the hall, glad to leave the din of so many voices, and into the adjoining armory. Swords and shields decorated the walls, hung and stored in geometric patterns on the whim of some distant ancestor. The long table in the middle, used for sharpening, polishing and the like, now bore the girl's body and its fetid aroma. Her sodden gown hung down to one side, dripping insistently into a dark pool on the stone floor.

Two guards stood in the corners of the room. They were always there, safeguarding the garrison's weapons, but now she found their presence disconcerting. She needed to remove the girl's clothing to examine her body. She could wait for the coroner, but on reflection she'd prefer the gentler hands of another woman on her own corpse. "May I have a knife?"

The guards stared at her for a second, then one pulled a small knife, the kind used for eating, from his sheath. She thanked him and cut into the woman's gown, starting at the hem and working up the side of her torso to the neck. It seemed less invasive than trying to wrestle the garment off over her head.

The white and blue embroidery at the neck was simple, unlike the gold-threaded finery Ela had worn to bury her husband. Her head was bare, but her head coverings could have come off in the water. Her gown was good quality, made with tightly woven wool, but some wear around the hem and cuffs suggested that she wasn't wealthy.

Ela pushed the damp wool back from her chest, and cut her linen chemise from neck to hem, conscious of the eyes of the soldiers on her. She returned the soldier's knife with thanks. "Is Giles Haughton arrived yet?"

"I'll go check, my lady." He exited the room. She wished she could think of a reason to get rid of the other, to give this poor dead girl a modicum of privacy. "Could you fetch me a bowl of water and some rags?"

His startled expression revealed that he felt this task beneath his notice, but at least he showed deference enough not to protest. With him out of the way, Ela pulled back the

11

sodden garments to reveal the stark pale skin of the girl's small breasts and swollen belly. She was about six months along in her pregnancy, maybe more. Her breasts showed no sign of having nursed a previous infant, and the scars from her skin stretching, which rose around the lower part of her belly like thorns, were fresh and livid. This was likely her first pregnancy to come this far.

Ela let out a sigh and whispered a short prayer. This poor girl wasn't much older than her daughter Isabella. Perhaps Isabella was right to be so afraid of marriage. Even if her husband didn't beat her or crush her heart by taking a mistress, she might die in childbirth with any pregnancy.

The door opened and coroner Giles Haughton entered flanked by two palace guards. Ela quickly covered the girl with her cut clothing, and Giles, perceiving her concern for the girl's modesty, turned and told the guards to leave them for now.

"God be with you," she greeted him.

"And with you, my lady. It was a moving service today." He approached the body and crossed himself. Ela followed suit, then pulled the girl's clothing apart again.

"Yes, praise be to God. And now another tragedy." She struggled to maintain her brave demeanor.

"A young, pregnant woman, found in the river," murmured Giles. "No obvious signs of strangulation. Bruises at her temple could be from a fall or a blow." He grasped her firmly by the chin and tilted her head first one way, then other, parting her hair. "No cuts or puncture wounds, but look at this ear. It's swollen. She might have sustained a blow to that side of her head."

"The swollen ear is on the opposite side from the bruises. Can you tell if she was dead before she entered the river?"

"If we cut her open. There would be water in her lungs if she drowned, and no water if she didn't."

Ela recoiled at the thought of cutting into the poor girl's flesh. But if she intended to be sheriff of Wiltshire—and she did—she must be capable of the least pleasant tasks associated with that duty. "Go ahead."

Giles pulled a sharp knife from his scrip and cut a deft incision down the center of her chest.

Ela felt her own blood drain from her body and for an instant she was sure she'd faint. She gripped the edge of the table and willed herself to recover, offering a quick prayer for strength to the Virgin Mary, who'd bravely borne the cruel public death of her own son.

Thankfully, she rallied—in time to press her hand to her mouth, retching, as he pulled the flesh apart in a way not so different from how she'd parted the dead girl's clothing.

Ela was no stranger to seeing bodies laid out and prepared for burial, but she'd never witnessed one being rent open before.

The guard returned with the water and some coarse linen, which Giles used to clean his knife before asking him to wait outside.

With the neat precision of a trained butcher, Giles sliced in between her rib cage and exposed the exterior of her lung. Ela had spent many hours poring over medical texts composed by her personal heroine, Trota of Salerno, and learning the various points of interior anatomy. Giles cut carefully into the lung—a fleshy bag, not unlike a leather money bag—with his knife. She expected water to spill out, but to her surprise it was solid inside, a bag filled with a thicket of vessels. She couldn't tell if there was water in there or not.

Giles made several more cuts and palpated the patterned tangle of veins while Ela steadied herself on the table and tried not to be overcome by the freshly awful smell or the grisly sight of the poor girl's innards.

"No water. She was dead before she was thrown in."

Ela was grateful to Giles for not patronizing her with pleasantries. "So she was murdered?"

"Very likely, yes." He pulled her torn garments back over her ravaged chest. "Who is she?"

"No one seems to know. It's a shame her features are so swollen." She shuddered at the thought of showing the woman's cleaved body to one of her relatives for identification. "Perhaps I can make a drawing of how she might have looked in life and we can circulate it around the villages. She might be from quite far upstream."

"Someone knows she's missing."

"Her killer."

"It's usually the husband," said Giles, with a hint of apology in his voice. "In my experience."

Ela nodded. "We'll find him. I have no intention of letting this crime go unpunished. I am taking on my husband's role as sheriff."

Giles paused and stared at her for a moment. Her chest tightened. Did the idea seem so preposterous to him?

"I have experience since I've served unofficially in the role when my husband was abroad and his deputy traveling with him."

"You are a credit to your late husband and to Salisbury, my lady. I can think of no better sheriff to serve us."

She suspected he was just offering lip service, but for now that would do. She'd prove her worth to him over time. "Do her hands show signs of a struggle?" She ignored a tiny frisson of revulsion and picked up the poor girl's cold right hand.

"Sometimes a victim will have torn nails or cuts from fighting off their attacker."

Small calluses where the victim's fingers met the palm suggested a life of labor rather than ease. Her hands were swollen and her nails discolored, but she saw no signs of tearing.

Giles looked at the other one. "Some dirt under the nails, but that could be from the river or just from normal life. No tearing or abrasions."

"So she didn't struggle with her attacker?"

"Which suggests that it was someone she knew."

CHAPTER 2

*E*la stared at the dead girl's swollen and discolored features. "We must find out who she is so we can question her husband." If she had a husband. She wore no ring, but that was hardly unusual.

Giles Haughton tilted her head in one broad hand. "I suppose she might have been killed by a stranger if she was taken by surprise. Hit from behind. There's bruising on the side of her skull here, near the front, but let's check the back." Her dark hair was drying in snakelike tendrils, which he parted gently. "There is some bruising to her skull. I feel an indented area here, which would be from an impact."

"Can you tell what kind of instrument made the marks?" Her husband had told her of a case where the abrasions caused by a very particular set of fleur-de-lis iron fire tongs had identified their owner as a murderer.

Giles peered closer. "Nothing sharp. The skin isn't broken." His fingers roamed through her hair like he was looking for lice. "And no hard edges to the marks. Inconclusive, but something with blunt edges and not too narrow."

"Like a wooden club."

Giles looked up at her. His pale blue eyes twinkled with amusement. "As if anyone still carried a wooden club in this age."

Ela regretted her fanciful suggestion. "An ogre perhaps." She shot him a grim smile. She wasn't entirely humorless.

"But, yes, a blow from an object. I doubt she could have simply fallen and hit her head at such an angle."

Ela made mental notes of the details of the scene, with a view to sketching the body once she returned to her room. She wanted the particulars seared into her brain in case her killer's trial was months from now.

They checked the whole body over, her legs, back, arms, feet, all waxen and devoid of compelling evidence. "Is there anything else we should study?" Ela was growing desperate for fresh air.

"I can say with confidence that this is the most thorough inspection I've ever seen performed on a corpse." Giles shot her a glance with more than a hint of his irksome amusement. "Your attention to detail is a credit to you."

She wasn't sure if he was making fun of her or not. "I don't intend to let her down. We'll find her killer and bring him to trial. God go with you."

"And with you." He nodded soberly.

Ela turned for the door, ready to run from the awful stench that filled the room, but not wanting to betray her weak stomach. Outside the door, the soldiers lolled, restless and sullen.

"Please see to it that her shroud is prepared and sewn, except around her head, and have her moved to the mortuary. We'll need her relatives to see her face when we find them."

"Yes, my lady."

Ela swept away as fast as she decently could. No doubt there was some particular person who should perform the unpleasant task of sewing the shroud, but surely the guards could figure that out and summon the person themselves.

The foul air of the windowless armory seemed to follow her into the great hall, where the servants were bringing out platters of food for the funeral banquet. She now realized why the mortuary was an outbuilding far from the hall. Another lesson learned the hard way.

* * *

Guests crushed close along the benches pulled up to the long tables spread with crisp linen cloths. The floors were strewn with fresh straw and herbs that released their aroma under the heels of busy feet. Friends and cohorts of her husband filled the hall: squires and knights and barons in all stages of life who'd come to pay their respects. Men who'd fought with him in the Crusades and more recently in France. The king himself would have been here if not for a pressing engagement. The reassuring sight rallied her.

She took her seat at the head of the table nearest the fire, amid a murmur of sorrow at her husband's death and exclamations over the beauty and vigor of her children. "William would be sad that his funeral feast must be during Lent," she sighed, feeling rather sheepish at the spread of pastries filled with vegetables and nutmeats, tureens of meatless soups and platters of artfully arranged fish. "I'm sure he'd have preferred to be wished farewell around a fat suckling pig and a brace of freshly killed pheasant."

"No doubt he would, my lady." William Marshall raised his cup, and they joined him in a toast to her husband. "A man who loved life and lived it to the fullest. Now he and his brother John shall feast again in heaven!"

Ela paused with the cup at her lips. It was hard to be confident that King John was enjoying a place at the right hand of the Father after the way he'd quarreled with the pope and managed to excommunicate the whole of England, but she smiled politely. "God willing, my lord."

"What drew you from the procession?" asked Ralph de Tosny. "By the time I found my way out of the cathedral you were gone."

"A body was found in the thawing river." Ela decided now was as good a time as any to try to get these barons on her side. "As sheriff of Wiltshire it was my duty to put the needs of our people before my own grief."

"Quite so," came the responsive murmur, but she felt—or imagined—a cross-current of shock and alarm under it.

"Sheriff, you say?" The Baroness Delamere raised a plucked eyebrow. "Surely young Will shall be sheriff."

"He's not yet of age, I'm afraid." Ela was grateful for the excuse. "And he's soon to be married. When he's settled I look forward to seeing him assume his father's many roles."

"Ah." The baroness peered at her with suspicion. "Who is he to wed?"

"He's betrothed to Idonea de Camville."

"How appropriate for the families of two great women to unite," chimed William Marshall. "Idonea's grandmother has been castellan of Lincoln for decades, and sheriff as well. Didn't she hold the castle against a siege from your husband?"

Ela managed a smile. "It's a long story. Suffice to say that Nicola de la Haye is pleased that her granddaughter will be marrying our son. And I'm grateful for the precedent she set as a female castellan. I need hardly worry that people will be scandalized by me following in her footsteps here in Salisbury."

Ela wasn't at all sure that Nicola didn't hate the lot of them. Her granddaughter's great estates had been enriching Ela's family, not Nicola's, because the girl had been William's ward since her father died. But she hoped to win Nicola as an ally when the dust settled.

"I can't believe she's still holding Lincoln castle. Isn't she nearly eighty?"

"I think she's closer to seventy." Ela did hold fond hopes that the proud old woman might be persuaded to step down to make room for her son, leaving Ela to hold sway in Salisbury without dissent. So many plans needed to fall into place, and so fast.

Where was Will? Her younger children gathered about Bill Talbot, the kind knight who gave the boys lessons in swordsmanship and gentlemanly deportment during their father's recent absence.

Will wasn't with them, though. She scanned the crowd and saw him laughing and drinking with Herbert FitzMaurice and Robert Lemains, two noisy young men with more bluster than sense. She'd have to work hard to keep Will on the right path until he gained the wisdom and maturity to balance his bravura. Too much power too soon had ruined many a bold young man.

* * *

It was late into the night by the time Ela finally felt able to leave her guests and climb the stairs to her solar. She was used to sleeping alone since her husband traveled so often, but since his death a different, grimmer kind of solitude hung in the spacious room, almost palpable as the tapestry hangings.

Wiping her tired eyes, she moved to her writing table and spread out a fresh piece of parchment. Her husband had teased her for the amount of money she lavished on parchment and vellum and colored inks, but it was one of her few indulgences and she didn't begrudge herself, especially since most of her drawings illustrated prayers and Psalms she copied for her children.

Now she hoped her skill at drawing would come in useful in a more earthly way.

She planned to draw the woman as she would have looked in life, standing and with her arms at her sides in a natural gesture. She carefully sketched the features, generalizing them on account of the swelling that obscured their exact lines. She drew the waves of her dark hair, her narrow shoulders and small, high breasts, then the outline of her pregnant belly under her long robe.

She drew the pointed leather shoes that she'd retained on one foot and her small hands with their rather delicate, curved fingers. She painted in the rust color of her gown, then replicated the design around the neck of her robe as carefully as possible. She couldn't know what detail might jog someone's memory.

Next to the drawing she made notes in a careful hand. Today's date—as if it weren't engraved on her heart for all eternity—the time of day the body was found, who found it and exactly where. She detailed the physical findings, including a small sketch of the woman's poor swollen face, with its bruises and the swollen ear. She didn't want to rely on her overtaxed mind to retain the important details. When she was satisfied, she closed up her inks and rinsed and dried her pen.

She knelt at her carved oak prie-dieu with a sweet sense of relief. At the end of a long day she could take refuge in prayer and remind herself of the many blessings she enjoyed. If life was to be harder now without her husband, she'd just have to be stronger and face it, with God's help.

After her prayers, she washed her face in the copper bowl Sibel had left for her and dried it with a fresh scented cloth, then removed her robe. She'd stayed up so late that the fire Sibel had set was dying out, and a typical March chill had descended on the room. She could call the boy to replenish the wood and stoke it, but he was probably fast asleep at this late hour and she didn't feel like waking him.

It would be morning soon enough. Sibel had closed the bed curtains, so she lifted them apart and climbed in. Then she pulled the heavy, quilted covers over herself and nestled deep into the soft fabrics, willing the heat of her body to warm the chilly bedding.

Ela resented these dark, cold hours when she had ample time to regret each moment she'd spent chastising her husband for some infraction or absence that seemed quite meaningless now. She'd tried to apologize for her own short-comings and failures, but in those last hours before he died he'd been delirious and likely hadn't heard a word of her frantic mumblings.

She was sure he'd been poisoned. He'd fully recovered from his past injuries, then had sickened to death so hard and fast when a strong man like him could fight off any small cold or fever or ague.

And no one else in the household was sick with similar symptoms.

As the shock of his passing ebbed, hot fury replaced it. It boiled in her belly and seared her mind. She longed to yell from the ramparts that her husband had been murdered and that she knew exactly who'd done it.

But she was a mother and had a responsibility to raise her children to adulthood and see them settled safely in their own lives. Maybe then she'd place her neck on the block and tell the truth about everything she suspected and avenge William's death.

Until then she sought to cool the rage that burned in her veins and would seek her redress in finding justice for others.

* * *

Like the servants, Ela rose with the dawn, splashed her

face with water and dressed without help, though she did let Sibel pin her veil to her barbette and place her pleated fillet on top of the veil.

She began the day with a quick tour of the inside of the castle. "Michael, please sweep the hearth again and spread the ashes on the path outside." She'd learned that attention to detail made a huge difference in the day-to-day running of the castle, which was—in its own way—like a stationary army that must be kept polished and ready for battle or fall into disarray.

"Becca, please remove all the soiled straw from around the tables. And top up with fresh herbs. It smells like an alewife's kitchen in here."

The girl smiled. "Yes, my lady. They certainly were enjoying themselves last night." Then she paled. "I didn't mean— It was a very sad occasion."

"Don't worry, Becca. I know exactly what you mean. I'm glad that the men were entertained. My husband would want them to enjoy our hospitality and everyone in the household did honor to his name by making the occasion a success."

Becca breathed again. "Yes, my lady. I'll be sure to scrub and polish the tables again to get the spills out."

"Excellent. Thanks for being so thoughtful." Becca was a kind and hardworking girl, the daughter of a local potter, who'd joined the castle staff when she was fifteen. It would be a sad day for them all when she finally got married and went to run her own household.

In the castle yard, two boys were shoveling manure deposited by all the visiting horses. "Joseph will be glad of that dung for the kitchen gardens," she called. "Don't waste a scrap. It'll be planting time before we know it." They all knew what to do but it didn't hurt to remind them. Every now and then she found a shirker dumping manure in the moat or covering soiled straw with a layer of fresh herbs in the hall.

Over the years she'd stripped away some of the layers of command at the castle. She liked to deal directly with even the lowliest members of the household. They'd learned they could talk to her, too, and alert her to anything she should know about. There was far less waste, corruption and mismanagement this way.

Her mother had been scandalized by Ela's attention to the minutiae of the household. She felt it was beneath her daughter to share tips with the pot boy or the swineherd, but she had her own affairs to attend to and thus only got to be scandalized a few times a year. In the meantime, Ela enjoyed the benefits of sparkling pots and well-fed swine, balanced books and the security of knowing that all important tasks were well in hand.

In the kitchen, she congratulated the cook and her staff for preparing a hearty and visually pleasing feast within the constraints of the season.

The cook grunted. She was a gruff old character who'd been there since before Ela was born. Ela had no idea how old she was. Possibly older than the castle walls. "Spring can't come soon enough for me, my lady. I'm that tired of dried this and pickled that. I'd give my last tooth for a fresh strawberry from the garden." She grinned, showing that last tooth.

Ela smiled. "A few more weeks—God willing—and your wish will come true."

"Ground's hard as iron, yet."

"The thaw's coming." A vision of the murdered girl, floating in the reeds, swam in her mind. "Spring can't be far behind."

* * *

After a breakfast of stewed oats and dried apricots with her children, Ela asked Gerald Deschamps to summon Giles Haughton and the jurors to the castle for a meeting to discuss the dead girl.

"You are aware, my lady, that these are men of business and may well be detained by their affairs. Perhaps my men could pass a message to them instead?" He lifted a dark brow.

Ela stiffened. She didn't want Deschamps trying to insert himself between her and the men of the hundred, who could be called to form a jury. Perhaps he thought that he might be made sheriff since he'd commanded the garrison in her husband's absence. "I prefer to meet in person with them as a group. Arrange for them to arrive here shortly after Vespers. The day's business should be in hand by then."

She'd set her three oldest children, Will, Isabella and Petronella, to copying the drawing she'd made of the woman's body. Even with their younger siblings pestering them over the ghastly details and—one of them—begging to see the dead woman's body, they worked quickly and carefully. They each made copies—in dark ink on parchment—so she could give them to the jurors to circulate around the villages. Hopefully, they could get people talking and they'd learn her identity.

Shortly before midday she took a copy and asked Will to accompany her into the town on foot. She told herself she didn't require the presence of a six-foot-tall man, but it didn't hurt, either.

They stopped first at the pie shop, one of the busiest establishments within the outer walls. The stout woman behind the counter was bent over her display and started extolling the virtues of the newest pies fresh out of the oven before she even raised her head.

"I'm afraid I'm not here to buy pie."

The woman glanced up and immediately dusted her hands on her apron. "Oh, my lady, I didn't even half look at you! Of course I know you and the young master. We're all that sad to hear of your husband's passing. Won't you both have a pie on the house?"

"How very kind of you." Ela was genuinely touched and had to steady herself against a wave of emotion. "But we already broke our fast." Will looked as if he was going to protest that he still had room, so she shot him a stern look. "I'm afraid we're here on another unfortunate matter. The body of a young woman was found floating in the Avon yesterday, and we're trying to identify her." She unrolled her drawing and thrust it forward.

The pie woman peered at the image. "This her likeness, then?"

"As close as I could make it. She had long dark hair and her age was somewhere between twenty and twenty-five. And she was pregnant."

"Oh dear." She crossed herself. "How tragic. Goodness. She could be half the young wives in the town, though, couldn't she?"

"Slim build, a little shorter than myself. Have you heard of anyone who's gone missing? She might have been gone for weeks. She was frozen into the river ice."

"Can't say I have heard of anyone going missing." She screwed up her weathered face. "Though I suppose if she was in the river she could have come from miles away."

"Indeed. We're out spreading the news in the hope that someone will know who she is. If you hear anything please call on me at the castle or have a word with one of the jurors. We believe she was killed and we must find the murderer."

The old lady's mouth closed into a small O, and she crossed herself again. "To be sure, my lady."

Ela thought it unlikely that anyone would be bold enough to traverse the intimidating ranks of garrisoned soldiers and actually come to call on her personally, so the jurors would be crucial intermediaries, as would putting herself out here where she might hear gossip or news in their midst.

She rolled up her drawing and headed to the dairy stall,

where people went daily for fresh butter and cheese, then the butcher and the chandler. Finally, she went to the baker, Peter Howard, who'd found the body.

The day's baking was done, and Howard and his apprentice were busy scrubbing down the work surfaces and baking trays. She showed him her drawing and explained her plan that the jurors should spread the news throughout the district, including neighboring towns and villages, in the hope that someone could identify the girl, or at least knew of someone who'd gone missing.

"I'd say that at least half the people in town know by now and the other half will by the end of the day. But if she was from here, inside the walls, we'd have identified her by now. She must be an outsider."

"But even someone from the countryside must come to town for market day from time to time. Someone will know her. Talk to everyone you encounter, and I'll do the same."

* * *

Will had grown quiet during their last few encounters, but as they picked their way back up the slippery hill toward the castle walls, he found his voice again. "I'm old enough to be sheriff myself, Mother."

"In good time, Will. You shall be sheriff and Earl of Salisbury, but not until you reach your majority."

"My grandfather invaded England from France at age fourteen," he protested.

"Only because his mother was leading the army." His great-grandmother was Empress Matilda, and her fiery young son would later be crowned Henry II.

"She let him fight."

"She made a number of questionable choices. You have strength and courage, but you need wisdom to keep the peace. You shall learn the duties of sheriff at my side as my deputy."

"Deschamps is the deputy. Besides, Father didn't raise me to be a squire. He raised me to be a knight."

"Would that he had lived to see it happen. And it will, in due time. You must earn it first." She sighed. "You must never forget that we are all in service to the king, the more so since he's your first cousin."

"Half first cousin. Don't forget that Papa was the king's bastard."

"Will!" She looked around to see if anyone had heard him speak so crudely of his father. Two guards loitered nearby but gave no sign of having heard. "Mind your words. You're not young enough to throw them around like a child with his toys. Your father was very close with his royal brothers, be they half brothers or no. When King John was alive your father was rarely home. Sometimes it felt like they were attached at the hip."

"And now they're both gone." His voice was mournful. "Perhaps I'll die young, too."

"Don't talk like that! You must pray for a long life to fulfill your duty to your king and country."

"Yet be ready to die on a battlefield for them on any given day." He lifted a brow, and she was relieved to see a glint of humor in his pale blue eyes.

"Indeed. 'Tis a man's lot to risk his neck for honor and a mother's lot to spend hours on her knees praying for his safety."

"Why is Papa dead? I'm finally ready to fight with him and he's gone." His abject misery pierced her heart. "How are we to go on without him?"

She drew in an unsteady breath. "We must do our duty to the people of Salisbury. Right now that entails finding out who killed this young woman who lies dead in our mortuary, and I must focus my energies on that. Do you hear me?"

"Yes, and I'll do my best to assist you." She could hear the resentment through his polite words. Why did young men think themselves so much more capable than their elders and betters?

"I'd like to compete in the upcoming tournament at Winchester. I'm old enough."

"How can you think of tournaments at a time like this?" She wanted to remind him of his responsibilities to the family, which included not getting killed for sport or badly injured for a few moments of glory. But scolding him wouldn't help. It would just make him sulk.

"I've been training hard. Bill Talbot says I'm ready."

"We'll talk about it later."

* * *

Sibel took Ela's cloak as they entered the hall. She was glad to see the rushes on the floor refreshed. The foul smell of the body now overwhelmed the smell of spilled ale, which was not an improvement.

"My lady!" Albert, the elderly porter, came shuffling toward her. His red face and unsteady breathing alarmed her.

"What's wrong, Albert?"

"There's…" He glanced behind him, and her eyes followed him but the great doors remained closed behind him. "There's a man here to see you."

CHAPTER 3

"*W*ho?" Ela felt the hairs rise on the back of her neck. Surely he wouldn't have the gall to show himself here when her husband's body was barely cold in the tomb?

"A man from down the town, my lady. A rather coarse sort. I told him he can't just march up to the castle and speak with you, but he insists."

"Speak with me about what?"

"He says his daughter is missing."

Ela paled at the thought of having to show that decomposed corpse to the girl's father. She swallowed hard. "Show him in."

She removed her cloak, and Sibel took it away. Ela walked to the sturdy oak chair, raised above the floor on a low wood platform, where her husband used to sit while greeting people for official business. A sense of being an imposter rose inside her as she settled herself into the worn leather seat, but she told herself she was here in the pursuit of justice, and had nothing to apologize for.

She sat there for a moment, wondering where the visitor

was. Then one side of the tall doors opened and the porter returned with an old man. His grey hair was wild from the March winds and his clothes were unusually soiled and ragged. She could see why Albert had paused before letting him in.

But a good reason for that appeared in the big, gnarled stick he carried in his right hand and that he held a few inches ahead of him as he tapped his way—blindly—across the stone flags of the floor.

His sightless eyes stared skyward as he made his way down the length of the hall with agonizing slowness, with Albert at his elbow.

"I am Ela of Salisbury," she announced as he drew closer. She wanted to ask how he'd made his way here from the town without help, but it didn't really matter. He'd done it, and he didn't need to be cosseted with platitudes.

"Robert Harwich," he rasped. "At your service, my lady." He paused, wobbled alarmingly, and bowed. "My regrets on the loss of your lord."

"Thank you, Master Harwich." She blinked, praying that the dead girl wasn't his daughter. "What brings you here?"

He shuffled a few steps farther and Albert halted them both at the edge of the platform. "It's my daughter, my lady." His grimy face scrunched into a strange expression. "Gone missing, she has."

"When?" If she'd just gone missing then she couldn't be the body, which had been dead and in the water for some time.

"Some weeks ago." He shook his hoary head. "Used to come visit me every few days. Then one day she didn't come any more."

"What's her name?"

"Katie. Katherine."

"Where do you live?"

31

"In the new town. I have a blacksmith shop. Been there since the town was but a crossroads, but since I lost my sight nigh on five years ago I'm reduced to making buckles to make ends meet."

"And Katie lives near you?"

"No, my lady. She lived out across the fields on a farm. That's why I haven't been able to go look for her. It's a frightful long walk across the water meadows and boggy, too. I could barely make my way here on the beaten track in my condition."

"Who does she live with?"

"Her husband." He squeezed his sightless eyes shut, and his black-filled wrinkles deepened.

Ela's concentration focused. "And who is her husband?"

"Alan Morse," he rasped. "Never liked him. Told her not to marry him."

"Why?" Ela tried to avoid asking questions that suggested a particular answer.

"Rough man." His blind eyes seemed to stare right through her. "Never was kind to her."

"Why did she marry him?"

"Who can say?" He shrugged. "Women have their whims, don't they?" His words hung in the air for a moment. "Not yourself of course, my lady." His sightless eyes stared right through her with a look that could be taken for insolence. She tried not to take it that way. "I can't say what she saw in him, but she was all bright eyes and blushes from the moment she met him. I could still see well enough back then, so I saw it with my own eyes. He were big and strong, I'll give him that."

Ela could easily imagine a young girl living at home and waiting hand and foot on her gruff and testy father being bowled over by the attentions of a muscular young man who promised her a different life. And if she was used to a man who didn't mince words or waste time on niceties, she'd be all the more susceptible to putting up with another one.

"How long have they been married?"

"Nigh on seven years." He rubbed his face with a gnarled and grimy hand.

"So they have children?"

"Nope. No children."

Ela frowned. Did he even know his daughter was pregnant? "And would you say they had a happy marriage?" She hated the false note that crept into her voice. He'd already half-told her the answer to this question, but she didn't want to put words in his mouth.

His guffaw still startled her enough to make her jump, and she was glad he didn't see it. "Happy? If walking on hot coals and being poked with the devil's pitchfork could make you happy, then maybe so. But no, she weren't happy." He paused and drew in a breath long enough to make his lungs rattle. "He beat her, of course."

"Of course?"

"Hardly a surprise, given his temper."

Everything he said pointed the finger of accusation more firmly at her husband. But there was one important question. Was the girl in the armory actually this man's daughter? And since he was blind, how could she even find out?

"What color is your daughter's hair?"

He pursed his lips. "Oh, blackish, I'd say. It's been a few years since I've seen it."

The dead girl's hair was a dark brown that might appear black to some.

"And how tall is she?" She struggled to use the present tense. She didn't want to confirm that his daughter was dead until she was sure.

"Oh, about yea high." He held his hand level just below his nose. So the girl was about Ela's height, slightly taller than average. Robert Harwich was a big man who must have been tall before he grew old and bent.

"And her eye color?"

"No color really. Grayish like mine. At least like mine used to be. I don't know what they look like now."

The white veil of blindness had crept over both of his eyes, obscuring their original color, but she'd seen the dead girl's gray eyes staring up at her from the riverbank.

She readied herself to break the news. "I believe your daughter is dead."

"Aye." He shoved a hand into his matted hair. "I thought as much when they told me a body were found in the river. She'd been missing that long, and—" He trailed off and hung his head.

"I'm so sorry." Ela wished she could offer solace beyond mere words.

"I suppose she fell in the river and drowned." He wiped his nose on his sleeve. "The banks have been that slippery of late."

Ela hesitated. "Actually we have reason to believe she was dead before she entered the river."

"What? You think she were killed?" His big paws tightened into fists. "Why I'll take that bastard in my bare hands and tear his head off! Blind and all, I'll do it, just you watch me!"

"Master Harwich, calm yourself." The guards nearby rose and put their hands on the hilts of their swords. "Do not take justice into your own hands. That only compounds the crime. Rest assured I intend to identify your daughter's murderer and seek justice for her."

"You?" Surprise temporarily smoothed his wrinkles, leaving the black lines of dirt exposed on the surface of his skin. "But you're—"

"A woman. Yes. I'm aware of that." She paused to get the

better of herself. There was nothing to gain by being sarcastic. "And I worked closely with my late husband on matters of justice. I have been Countess of Salisbury since my father died, and it is with that authority and the wisdom gained from my thirty-nine years on this earth that I intend to assume the role of sheriff and all its responsibilities."

"Begging your pardon, ma'am. I didn't mean to offend."

"I'm far from being offended. I simply want to reassure you that justice will be done."

"I do hope so, ma'am. My own daughter! Dead!" Tears formed at the corner of his blank, staring eyes, and sorrow clutched at her heart.

"She's with God now, Master Harwich. She can't suffer anymore."

"Lord knows she suffered enough at the hands of that bastard."

Ela now faced the most unpleasant task. "Would you be able to identify her—by touch, I mean? We have her body here at the castle."

She could swear he turned pale beneath his layers of grime. "Her body? Oh, I—" He wobbled on his feet and as she reached out to steady him, she noticed how torn and worn and soaked-through his ancient leather boots were. In fact,, all of his clothing was threadbare and inadequate to the March weather.

"Perhaps you need to rest and gather strength first. Elspeth, please bring hot milk and some pie." She led him to a nearby table where the soldiers sat to eat, and those there quickly rose, bowed to her and made themselves scarce.

As the old man ate, she congratulated herself on having so much news to present to the jurors after Vespers. She now knew, with almost total certainty, the girl's identity—Katherine Morse—and that her husband, Alan, was a violent man.

It was odd that Katherine had no children after seven years of marriage but that she was now pregnant.

She sat down opposite him. "I'm so sorry for the loss of your grandchild."

"Grandchild? I ain't got no grandchild. Katie were my only one still living, and as I said she never had no babies."

So he didn't know she was pregnant. "She was with child."

"What?" Crumbs fell from his open mouth. "She never said nothing. Perhaps she didn't know yet."

"Perhaps not," said Ela slowly, knowing that Katie would have been very much aware of her advanced pregnancy. Why had she not told her father about it?

Another mystery to solve.

"That just makes me want to kill him all the more. With my bare hands!" he growled. Harwich spread his big, callused hands flat on the table as if to demonstrate how well they were built for the task. "He killed my own grandchild! It's enough to drive a man wild with grief." He shook his tangled head and squeezed his sightless eyes shut.

The sight was affecting. Ela dreaded having to place his hands on his daughter's rapidly decomposing body. "Rest assured that justice will be served."

"Thank you, my lady. That's one thing I can hold on to. If there's anything I can do to help, I shall, though I'm not sure how much use an old blind man is to anyone. It's all I can do to keep body and soul together in these hard times."

"I've summoned a meeting of the jurors, and we'll bring her husband in for questioning. Is there anyone else who might have reason to kill her?"

"Kill my Katie? Why would anyone want to kill her?"

Ela was puzzled that no one at the riverbank had recognized the girl. Yes, she was altered by death and her time in the water, but surely if she'd grown up nearby she would be known to them. "Have you always lived in this area?"

"Not always. Moved here nigh on nine year ago. Built the blacksmith business up from scratch just in time to go blind and find myself hanging on by my fingernails."

"Was Katie ever involved in your business?"

"What? A girl in a blacksmith shop?" He emitted a sound somewhere between a laugh and a snort. "She worked in a dairy, and that's where she met her husband." He hissed the last word with disgust. "He were one of the farmers served by the dairy. She'd milk his bloomin' cows and churn butter all day long...all for a pittance, mind you. I suppose she thought she moved up in the world marrying a farmer with land and all. But I told her for nothing he was no good."

Once again Ela's heart went out to the poor girl, caught between a cruel father—who had no place for her in his life or business and had sent her out to make her own living—and a brutish new husband. Ela had no choice in her husband, though fate had been merciful and given her a kind man she could love. Many women—most even—weren't so lucky.

"How did you know her husband before she married him?"

"Shod his horse, didn't I? And forged bits and bobs for his farm. Always one to dicker over price."

"When did you last see him?"

His grimy face scrunched up even tighter. "Oh, I couldn't say. Some months at least. Now I can't shoe his horse he won't give me the time of day."

"So your daughter would come alone?"

He hesitated. "Mostly, yes. She had a heart to care about her old father even if her husband didn't."

"A caring child is a blessing indeed." She sighed. This poor old man was now blind and alone in the world with no one to care if he lived or died. She resolved to make sure he was provided with alms and assistance in a way that wouldn't offend his pride.

"And now she's gone…." His words trailed off and he sat back in his chair as if bracing himself. "I'm ready to see the body now."

Two guards led their grim procession around the castle's inner walls to the mortuary, where the body now lay. There, they parted the partially sewn shroud to reveal her face and placed the man's fingers on her cheek.

With a shaky intake of breath, he moved his big, dirty fingers around slowly, taking in her eye sockets, her brow, her nose and her mouth. "Aye, that's my Katie." His gruff voice was on the verge of breaking.

"May God give you solace and comfort," murmured Ela.

"For all the good they'll do me on a cold winter's night." He rubbed his hand over his face. "But thank you, my lady. I appreciate your kindness."

"The guards will find a cart to give you a ride home." She looked them in the eye to make sure they were paying attention. "And I'll be in touch as the investigation progresses."

Ela watched as the guards escorted him out to the stable yard. What a rough old character. She closed the shroud over the poor girl's pale, lifeless face. "Please have the shroud sewn closed. I'll speak to the Bishop about her burial."

Burial was an urgent matter. The arrest could wait because a man with cows to tend wasn't going anywhere. This body was decomposing and even now she was in an outbuilding the stench of lingering death would swirl around them until she were interred.

* * *

It was afternoon, the pale sun already descending toward the treetops, when Ela dismounted her horse outside the newly built bishop's palace near the grand new cathedral. She drew in a breath and called on her ancestors to give her strength. There was no love lost between her and Bishop Richard Poore.

One guard took her horse and another rapped on the polished wood door with its new-forged iron studs. Only the best for his excellency.

A manservant answered the door and hurried away to find his master. Ela took in the rich details of his new residence, built to replace the supposedly insalubrious conditions of the old bishop's palace inside the castle walls. Poore had rankled for years about noise and disruption from the garrison's soldiers. He'd complained about the poor quality and insufficiency of the water and had whined endlessly about the bracing winds felt high up on the castle mound.

Good riddance to him, though it had pained her deeply to see the old cathedral, where her ancestors had worshipped and where the venerable Osmund himself had served, deconsecrated and dismantled so its stones could form rubble in the walls of his new cathedral just a few miles away.

The manservant returned and led them into a large chamber with new carved oak furniture. A deep-colored tapestry with a hunting scene covered one wall, and tall silver candlesticks ornamented an antique table.

If a bishop was supposed to renounce the frivolities of worldly life—as St. Bernard of Clairvaux had proposed— then Richard Poore was doing a pretty rotten job of it.

"My lady." Poore swept into the room on a wave of gold brocade. His silvered hair framed the plump pink face of a man who enjoyed his victuals. "Once again, my deepest condolences on your tragic loss. I apologize that my humble service was inadequate to the occasion."

"Your words were and are deeply appreciated, your excellency. My grief is assuaged by the knowledge that your prayers for my husband's soul accompany mine to heaven."

She hoped her insincerity didn't show in her voice. He'd

39

once publicly called her husband godless as part of his campaign to get the cathedral moved outside of the castle walls.

"Your piety is a credit to you and your husband, my lady." He took her hands and squeezed them, and she felt a trembling of forgiveness in her heart. He had prayed fervently with her husband during his last hours, and given him such comfort as could be found by a dying man in fear of his soul. He'd never attacked her personally and he was always kind to her children, even young Will, whose wayward and arrogant behavior—such as striding in late and wet for church services—were met with warm indulgence. "His memory will remain with us as long as his body lies in our blessed cathedral."

Ela wasn't at all sure how her husband would feel about that. He'd bitterly opposed the cathedral being moved, seeing in it a loss of power and authority for the castle. Since he'd left explicit instructions for her to found a monastery in his memory, moving his tomb to it in future was a definite possibility. But that was a matter for another day.

"I'm here about another untimely death, I'm afraid."

"Oh dear." Poore frowned and led her toward two elegantly carved chairs. She settled herself into one and took the cup of spiced wine offered by an elderly manservant. "Did a member of the household catch your husband's illness?"

"My husband's illness was not contagious." She met his gaze, wishing she could say more. "The body of a young woman was found tangled in reeds in the Avon. Her father has identified her as Katherine Morse, the wife of a local dairy farmer. I seek permission to bury her in the churchyard."

He frowned. "Katherine Morse? I don't know the name. Who is her father?"

"Robert Harwich." She rather hoped he didn't know of him.

"The old blind beggar?"

"He is indeed blind but I believe he's a blacksmith."

"He does live in the blacksmith's shop, but I'm not aware of any smithing having occurred since I've lived in town."

"He is blind and no doubt in need of alms at his advanced stage of life." Ela bristled.

"Alms are certainly available to those who ask. We pride ourselves on—"

"Pride is a sin, and no doubt his own pride prevents Master Harwich from asking for alms. He is indeed a testy character. I know nothing of his daughter except that her body lies moldering in my castle and I am in urgent need of a suitable burial place for it."

"I didn't know he had a daughter." Poore twisted his jeweled ring. "Are you sure she really is his daughter?"

"Why would he lie?"

Poore shrugged and something like amusement sparkled in his water-pale eyes. "Who can say? The motivations of men can be mysterious."

"Naturally we are pursuing the matter of her untimely death, but that doesn't solve the question of where she's to be buried."

"The paupers grave outside the castle walls seems ideal." A large sapphire sparkled in the ring on his right hand. "Unless her family is prepared to buy a burial place."

"Her husband is our chief suspect, and she has no other family."

"That is unfortunate." He lifted his chin. "Perhaps a wealthy benefactor—or benefactress—could intervene." His eyes twinkled with amusement.

"No doubt." She had to admire his gall. "So if the coin

could be found to pay for a quiet spot she could be buried on the cathedral grounds?"

"The Lord is merciful."

"Indeed he is." She decided to consider this progress. She'd ridden here half sure that he'd refuse the girl's body outright.

"And how much coin buys enough mercy for a slender shroud about five feet and five inches long?" She maintained a placid expression.

"We are in receipt of a quote for seven pounds to create a new door for the rood screen."

"Seven pounds! The Lord's mercy comes dear in New Salisbury."

He shrugged apologetically. "And fine workmanship, of a type to honor the memory of your good husband, is not found cheap, either."

"My husband was a good man." She'd never forgotten what Poore said all those years ago.

"He was indeed a fine fighting man and an honored friend and cohort to our crown." He crossed himself. "God rest his soul."

She crossed herself, too, saying a quick prayer for all the souls in urgent need. "You broke his heart by moving the cathedral from within the castle walls."

He leaned forward and took her hands. His palms were ridiculously soft for a man. "My dear lady, I know it was your heart I broke, but I did it for the good of our holy brothers and the future of the holy church in Salisbury. You must admit this is a more salubrious location."

"I admit the supply of water is more steady, though perhaps the entire area is subject to inundation under the right circumstances."

"We have taken measures to ensure that all excess water flows to where it can be usefully employed, and the cathedral itself is on a high gravel bed and will stand for a thousand years or more."

"God willing." She tugged her hands back and cursed herself for wishing to see Bishop Poore's hard work floating away on a surge. She knew her family pride was a burden that impeded her soul's progress. "Though I'm sure you miss the fresh air high on the castle mound."

Now he laughed long and steady. "May I never feel my bones rattle with the morning chill like that again. You and your family are made of stern stuff, my lady."

"And I don't intend for us to soften, even though we currently enjoy the luxury of peace and prosperity." She shot a pointed glance at his gaudy ring.

"Admirable, my lady. Your piety and devotion to your family are a beacon for us all." Then a peppered brow lifted. "But I hear that you intend to become sheriff of Wiltshire?"

"Why not? My husband was sheriff. I am his heir, much as I was once my father's heir to the castle and titles that come with it."

"No doubt you will soon find a suitable lord to pair with."

Ela rankled. Why did such men assume a woman needed a man at her side? She had money and power and influence. She'd borne eight children. What did she need a man for?

But she was not fool enough to utter such thoughts aloud.

"In time I intend to take holy vows and retire from the world." That should silence him. "But now my foremost duty is to my young children. I do not intend to marry again."

If he were to spread this rumor he'd do her a great favor. No doubt men across the south of England were already considering how they might link their fortunes with the superior ones of the Earls of Salisbury. The prospect of their endless visits, and the polite and expensive entertaining they would require, exhausted her.

"Once again, your piety is a credit to you. But should a

woman who wishes to retire behind the veil take an active part in the affairs of our cold and brutal world?"

"If she wishes to see that world operate according to the principles of the Ten Commandments, then, yes, she should."

"Thou shalt not kill," he mused. "And if thou hast, then thou should be swiftly brought to justice and punished according to the laws of the land."

"Exactly. I am thirty-nine years of age, with all the life experience that age implies. My husband entrusted me with his thoughts and invited me into confidences about the cases he has dealt with as sheriff. I am more thoroughly prepared to assume the role than anyone else in Salisbury."

Bishop Poore sipped his wine, regarding her over the gilded rim of his cup. "You will find enemies, even among your friends."

"I was not raised to lie in a feather bed and congratulate myself for it."

He laughed. "You are a credit to your parents, and your husband."

And you hate me for it. She realized that her visit here had as much, or more, to do with convincing Poore of her fitness for the role of sheriff as it did with securing a final home for the dead girl's body. He'd already proven the extent of his power and influence in spiriting their cathedral away —with the king's and the pope's permissions—and his opposition to her new role would undermine her authority in ways she couldn't afford.

"Can I count on your support as I seek peace and justice among the citizens of Salisbury?"

"Of course, my lady." His tiny smile suggested that he even found pleasure in the idea. She decided not to ponder the reasons for his enjoyment.

"Seven pounds is a high price to pay, but if it will secure this unfortunate woman a peaceful repose, it shall be paid."

"Wonderful." His smile broadened. "And in more good news, Hubert de Burgh has promised us a fine illustrated prayer book in your husband's memory."

"What?" The news shocked and chilled her.

"A most welcome gift for our new cathedral. And he's made a generous donation toward the almshouses I hope to build for the poorest among us."

Ela struggled to keep her composure. "How magnanimous of him. Perhaps you can find a place for the poor dead girl's elderly father in these almshouses."

"Indeed! He's just the type of person we'd like to provide for."

"I'll arrange for the seven pounds to be delivered forthwith." She wished she could truly speak her mind, but she'd been raised from birth to consider her words and their impact carefully, and she'd never needed that skill more than now.

She rose, desperate to get outside. Not that she could scream to the four winds like she craved, but at least she could contemplate the possibility in peace.

The dead woman's body couldn't be buried without her husband's consent. He might even have plans of his own for her burial, though those could be in jeopardy if he were to be taken into custody. But at least now they could send the body to the cathedral and the poor girl wouldn't lie decomposing in her mortuary or at risk of being buried outside the walls like refuse.

She took leave of the bishop and exited his grand new palace into a light drizzle. The soldiers hushed their chatter as she emerged, and one helped her back onto Freya.

The days were still short and she'd have to trot the whole way to be home before dark. She didn't want her children to worry. She was all too familiar with that sense of insecurity that followed the death of one parent.

She led the way onto the road back to the castle with her guards in tow. The grand old oaks loomed against the iron-gray sky. Some of them were likely older than the castle. Maybe some of these venerable trees even remembered the men who'd led rituals at the nearby stone henge that dominated the landscape. She was just one more in a procession of frail humans to ride under their spreading branches.

They passed a number of people on the road, mostly laborers, masons and carpenters returning home on foot from their work on the new cathedral. Most people in the area still lived in the town within the castle's ancient walls, but household by household they were moving down the track to the new town growing around the cathedral.

New Salisbury's straight streets lacked the organic coziness of the old village lanes that meandered around the castle, where the houses sometimes looked as if they'd sprung out of the damp earth like so many thatch-roofed mushrooms. But what the new town lacked in quaintness it made up for in space, tidiness and—the bishop was sadly right—a more reliable and palatable water supply.

Approaching the grand walls of the castle across the open fields, she could almost imagine the day when all the ordinary tradesmen and housewives and villagers would be gone, and there'd be no one left inside the outer walls except the family, servants and the garrison soldiers.

She trotted across the bridge and in through the arched entrance, glad to see the welcoming lights of the torches and the bustle of soldiers preparing for a change of guard before the evening meal. At least for now the castle and its surrounds still teemed with life. One day she really would leave it for the sanctuary of a religious house, but she intended to hand the castle and its inhabitants down to Will in a condition as close as possible to that in which her husband had left it.

Ela dismounted and patted Freya before handing her to the ostler to go enjoy her evening oats. She ordered the removal of the dead girl's body into the bishop's care, and no one dared to suggest that the journey could wait until morning. They could all smell the urgency of the errand. Ela headed into the hall and Sibel's kind ministrations with relief. She looked forward to stretching out before the fire for an hour or so with her children before vespers and her meeting with the assembled jurors.

CHAPTER 4

*T*he jurors and Giles Haughton all arrived promptly before Vespers. She greeted them and ushered them into the chapel that did service for the residents of the castle in the absence of their once-loved cathedral. She was glad they'd all arrived early enough to spend some time contemplating their duties in the presence of the Lord.

And their attendance here was a sign of respect to her. Or at least she decided to take it that way. If it was a sign of respect for her late husband that was just as good.

She led the way into the great hall, always a rather bustling environment and no less so now. The servants had laid out a supper of roasted salmon with parsnips and carrots, and they filled a cup for each man as he took a seat at the long table. Ela sat at the head.

"I think I can smell our urgent matter," said Peter Howard, the baker who'd found the body. His apologetic tone contrasted with the sparkle in his eyes.

"Indeed. I have made arrangements for her to be buried in the new churchyard now that she's been identified. She's been removed to the cathedral close already, but her scent lingers."

"You know who she is?" Howard looked surprised.

"Her father visited me today. His name is Robert Harwich, and he's a blacksmith who lives in the new town. He's blind but he identified her body by touch. Her name is Katherine Morse and her husband is Alan Morse, who farms cattle."

It was the jurors' duty, as respected members of the community, to learn the facts of the case and verify them so they could serve usefully during the trial.

"Her father cast much suspicion on her husband. He said Alan Morse was a violent man who treated her poorly. Our first course of action should be to interview Morse and likely take him into custody. Does anyone know where Alan Morse lives?"

"Aye." She recognized Thomas Pryce, a fortyish man of neat appearance, and racked her mind to remember exactly what he did for a living. "I know where he lives. I replaced the roof on his barn two years ago." Thatcher. "He has a small, mean house out near the bottom fields but a good spacious barn where he houses his cattle in the winter when the river rises and makes the land too wet to use."

"Excellent. You can lead us there tomorrow. Have you been able to form an opinion of his character?"

Pryce shrugged. "He paid me on time. Can't say he was friendly. Seemed prosperous enough, at least judging from the condition of his cattle."

Ela nodded. "Anyone else know him?"

No one did. Which was strange when you thought about it, since he lived only a few miles from the castle. He must be a man who kept to himself. Farmers were rather like nuns and monks, in her experience, and liked to spend their days quietly worshiping in cathedrals framed by oak branches and staffed with quiet cattle. Farmers in town for market day often looked a bit lost and out of place like they'd just arrived from an earlier time, when things were quieter and simpler.

"Did any of you know Katherine Morse? Or Katherine Harwich as she used to be called?"

Again, silence. But beneath their quiet she could feel the pressure of questions building inside them. No doubt they wondered why she was leading this investigation and not her husband's deputy, Gerald Deschamps, who sat quietly, not eating or drinking, at the far end of the table.

"Master Pryce, did you see Mistress Morse when you were thatching the barn?"

"No, my lady. Never saw no one. Just Morse himself and the cows."

Almost like she's invisible. And it was a shame because it would be reassuring to get a firmer identification of the dead girl before they buried her.

"She was pregnant." Ela looked from one to the next. "And although she and her husband had been married for several years, they had no children."

"How far along?" asked Deschamps abruptly.

All the men turned to look at him as if he'd cast a spell on them.

"At least six months, I'd say, based on my experience." Only some of the men turned back to her. The others remained fixed on Deschamps as if relieved he'd finally taken over.

She couldn't allow that to happen. "Tomorrow morning we must question her husband."

"We'll know where to find him if he has dairy cows to be milked," chimed in Stephen Hale, the cordwainer who made shoes for her household. "He'll either be milking them himself at home or he'll be at the dairy down the road from his farm."

"I know where that is, too. I repaired the roof of their barn three years ago," chimed in Pryce.

"Good," said Ela. "And we can wait until the cows are milked before accosting him. If he's arrested his cows can be driven to the castle for safekeeping and milking, since it doesn't sound like there will be anyone left to look after them."

"Good thinking," said Paul Dunstan, a miller.

"Thank you, Master Dunstan." She kept her tone cool as she didn't want to encourage the men to patronize her. "Since none of you know the people in question, any further discussion would likely be idle speculation at this point. So I'll adjourn our meeting until we've interviewed Master Morse tomorrow."

"We could save the trouble of riding out there and have the soldiers bring him to the castle," said Deschamps.

"The coroner and I prefer to ride there ourselves with a retinue. We wish to see the place where he lived with his wife and watch his reaction when he learns of our purpose. Do we have two volunteers from the jury?"

The men froze. No doubt they all had business obligations and weren't anxious to venture out into the countryside on what might prove to be a dangerous encounter with a killer.

"You can count on me, my lady," said Peter Howard. "I'll be done with my baking by dawn."

"Me too," chimed in Hugh Clifford, a comely young man who'd recently become a partner in his father's trade as a wine seller.

"If you need more, I—" The thatcher and two or three of the others now stirred.

"Two will be quite adequate to provide witness. And I'll bring soldiers, who can take him into custody. I thank you all for coming out after dark on a cold night. Please take the time to enjoy your supper."

They all murmured how it was no trouble, etc. This was largely true since as far as she knew they all still lived inside the outer walls and had only the briefest walk back to their houses. That was part of the reason they'd been chosen as jurors in the first place. In future, it might make sense to select at least some men from the widely dispersed population, including the new town and some of the nearby villages.

She left them to eat and talk among themselves, though a couple—one of them Haughton—did leave immediately, no doubt hurrying home to dinner with their wives and families. She didn't leave the hall as she had no desire to give them an opportunity to discuss her apparently audacious desire to become sheriff among themselves. She took up her seat on the wood platform from where she could listen without seeming to eavesdrop, while sipping the cup of wine that Sibel brought her and attending to her children.

Ela was used to living her life in public, surrounded by an audience of soldiers and local squires and visitors and servants. She rarely felt a burning need for solitude. Sometimes it tired her to be the object of prying eyes—especially in a time of worry or grief—but mostly she bore it as her duty.

* * *

"Mama, cook says that one of the guests brought a gift of spices," said Nicholas, his bright eyes sparkling. "And that we can have spice cakes tomorrow."

"A kind gift though plain fare is preferable during Lent, my love." She'd have to speak to the cook. The celebrations over her husband's return and now the funeral festivities had enriched their meals far past the requirements of piety. She didn't want her children getting spoiled. "Easter isn't far off and soon we'll celebrate the rebirth of our Lord with all the rich food he graces us with."

Speaking of being graced with riches, gifts were piled in one of the storerooms off the hall. Many of William's friends and comrades had brought tributes to lay at his tomb. She'd have to write them all thank you letters, a prospect which made her heart sink.

On the other hand, the correspondence might be a good way to quietly announce her new role in Salisbury. "Sibel, can you arrange for St. Germain, the silversmith, to visit me tomorrow afternoon? I'd like to have a new seal designed."

She tousled Nicholas's hair as he sat leaning against her chair, playing with his whippet. He looked up at her with his curious, long-lashed eyes. "What will happen to Papa's seal?" He frowned. "Since he can't use it anymore."

A wave of sadness swept over her. His clothes still filled the chest in their chamber, and Sibel had not dared to suggest removing them. "We'll keep it to remember him by. We must cherish our memories and honor them."

Her son's lip quivered and he bravely bit it to stillness. She knew that deep sense of loss too well and still missed her own father in a secret part of her heart, though she could no longer recall the details of his face.

It was hard to believe that such a vital man as her husband had been cut down in his prime. She could have borne it more bravely if he'd died on the battlefield. He'd been alive and here, warm in her arms, after all the months of gossip and rumor that he was dead in France.

Then he'd been snatched from her so fast. Before she'd even had a chance to become pregnant again. One last child might have consoled her. Even her baby was now a young man learning his letters and chasing hounds for sport.

Then again, it was better that she didn't have a babe in arms. It would give the men an excuse to say that she was preoccupied and couldn't lead the forces of justice in Salisbury.

She looked across the hall to where the jurors were eating and talking. No raucous laughter or drunken hilarity, just a group of mostly middle-aged men who probably wished they were home in their beds. Did they care about justice?

A door to the hall flung open, admitting a gust of wind that caused every candle in the room to gutter. Albert the porter hurried in. "My lady, wonderful news." His flushed face and startled eyes rather belied his words. "Your mother, Mistress Alianore, and her entourage are riding in through the arch."

"What?" Ela stared. Her mother had sent word that she was too ill to attend the funeral. Why would she suddenly arrive in the night without a word of warning?

"Sibel, please speak to the cook about food for the party." She flew to her feet and commanded for two more trestle tables, recently set aside after the funeral, to be erected and set with plates, goblets and good wine.

"Grandma Allie!" exclaimed Nicholas with a grin. "I wonder if she'll bring her poodles."

"Of course she will, darling. Can you imagine grandma without her poodles?"

"Nope." He grinned. He picked up his little whippet. "I hope Pharaoh won't chase them too much."

"You must make sure he doesn't." Goodness she was tired. It had been a long and taxing day and now, most likely, she'd have to stay up late into the night and use Matins as her excuse to retire. She wanted to run to her solar to splash her face with water and put on a fresh veil, but from the sounds of it they were about to come bursting through the door so she decided she'd better not.

Her mother entered amid a gaggle of servants and poodles, her dark red velvet cloak sweeping out around her.

"Mama!" Ela hurried forward and hugged her mother, whose expensive scent did battle with the aroma of horses and the fatigue of travel.

"Darling, I'm so sorry we missed the funeral and all the festivities. I was tied to my bed racked with fever all last week. Today was the first day I felt strong enough to travel."

"You shouldn't be riding across the countryside in the dead of night."

"The roads were deep and slippery so we couldn't go as fast as we planned." Her husband, Jean, entered behind her. A tall man and handsome—he was her mother's fourth husband and twenty years her junior—he came and kissed Ela on both cheeks. "We're devastated by your loss. William was a great man whose memory will live on among us."

"I know." It was a sudden relief to be surrounded by family. People who were older than her and had borne their own burdens. Her mother had buried three husbands before Jean.

"We were so shocked to hear of his passing. Was it the coughing fever?" Her mother handed her wet cloak to a servant.

"It wasn't like any fever we've seen." Ela hadn't shared her suspicion that he was poisoned and certainly couldn't now, in the crowded hall. "He was raving and sweating and then he lost consciousness completely." There was no need to mention the relentless vomiting and bloody emissions from his bowels.

"Oh, my darlings!" Ela's mother lavished kisses on the heads of her children, as they crowded around their grandmother and petted her dogs. "Are you taking good care of your mama?"

"Yes, we are, Grandma," said Richard with solemn seriousness. "Though she's been busy."

"Has she, my dear? Well, keeping busy can be a good thing when you're dealing with grief."

"Do come sit down and eat." Ela ushered them to a new table the servants had erected. Deschamps had left and the last of the jurors were now making themselves scarce which avoided the awkwardness of necessary introductions. Her mother was a grand lady of the old world and was not likely to be interested in common tradesmen, no matter how good and true they were.

"She's very busy being sheriff of Salisbury," said Stephen brightly. "She just had a meeting with the jurors."

"Don't talk nonsense, my cherub. Your mother has far more important duties."

Ela bit her tongue. "Will you have some of this lovely roulade?" The kitchen staff were rushing out with dishes made for Ela and the children's' dinners. Luckily, they knew from long experience to always cook for a crowd. She didn't know what was rolled up in the light pastry crust, but it was bound to be good. "And a big salmon will be out in a moment."

"Oh, goodness, I'm not sure my digestion is up to such indulgence," Alianore protested. "Especially during Lent. Perhaps a thin barley gruel would do."

Ela asked one of the servers to order a barley pottage. The cook would be sure to throw up her big, red arms in dismay at yet another order, but who knows, maybe she had a vat of it going already. She had an almost magical ability to produce what was needed in record time despite her constant grumbling and protestations.

"My dear, this roulade looks wonderful." Jean carved it into slices and passed some out to the children before taking a couple for himself and pouring thick almond sauce onto his plate.

Ela was glad there had been no more mention of her new

role. "I'm sorry we don't have more vegetables but you know how it is at this time of year. There's a leek and parsnip pottage, and these fried onions look tasty. The cook has a way of making them so sweet and crispy."

With the fire roaring and her family gathered around her enjoying the modest feast, Ela took a moment to be thankful for the blessings she enjoyed. The dogs hovered around the table, their faces hopeful, pouncing instantly on any scraps that happened to come their way.

"Is Deschamps to be sheriff?" asked Jean between mouthfuls. "Or perhaps young William?" He shot a bright smile at Will, who was busy stuffing his face at the far end of the table.

"Will is still too young." Ela stuck a spoon in her pottage.

"I'm not," he protested, with a full mouth.

"I intend to hold the role until such time as he's ready to assume it."

"I know it's too soon to talk of marriage—" Her mother peered over her wine cup. "But perhaps your next marriage will remove you from Salisbury altogether. Young Will needs to—"

"If I married again, my husband might command the title and estate of Salisbury for himself, thus depriving Will of his inheritance entirely." She looked her mother hard in the eye. "Luckily, this is not a risk since I do not intend to marry again."

She wanted to forestall endless discussions about just which recently widowed baron had the right credentials. No doubt her mother already had a list as long as her forearm. "The Magna Carta states that no widow shall be compelled to remarry, as long as she wishes to remain without a husband. William Longespée was my husband, and he was all the husband I shall ever want or need. When all of my children reach majority I shall take the veil. Until then I intend to manage my household, and my earldom, as I see fit."

She knew her face was flushed by the end of her speech. She looked from her mother to Jean. She could see her mother's mind whirring behind her blue-gray eyes. "You can't be sheriff, my dear."

"It's really not a subject for discussion." Ela kept her voice calm, trying not to let her bubbling anger spill out in front of her children. "Since none of his heirs have reached majority, I have inherited the entirety of my husband's estate and responsibilities, to hold in trust. William kept me in close confidence. During our long marriage I have witnessed and participated in countless meetings here in this hall and abroad. I have experience and authority, and I intend to use them to maintain peace and order in Salisbury."

"Well." Her mother had stopped eating and now flapped a linen napkin in front of her face as if it could provide her with desperately needed air. "That was quite a speech."

Jean looked amused. "I admire Ela for making it. She's a brave woman."

"A reckless one," hissed her mother. "A woman's duty is running her household. If she tries to do a man's job it will just invite the ire of other men."

"Are there any particular men that spring to mind?" She spoke mostly out of pique, but her mother did have an ear for gossip.

"Hmm, let me see—" Her mother pursed her lips. "Oh, all the barons. And—" she cast her eyes skywards where a couple of birds roosted up in the rafters. "All the earls and dukes and knights of the realm and perhaps even the king himself."

"Then let them come talk to me. My house is open to friends."

"And enemies?" Jean asked, his characteristic easy smile still evident.

"Sometimes admitting enemies can't be avoided, more's the pity," Ela said wryly. She hoped Deschamps wouldn't become her enemy. It was too early to tell.

"I ran this household myself as a young woman, don't forget." Her mother lifted a brow. "It's no small feat." She glanced around at the soldiers who stood in the doorway, along the walls and who sat at the table furthest from the fire. "All these rough garrison soldiers are as essential as they are irritating. I remember wondering how the country housewives in their tiny cottages felt, sitting down in front of their own cozy fires with no one to tend to but their nearest and dearest. It's our lot to tend to a town and our nation as well as our own families. Your father would be proud of you for all you've accomplished."

For once Ela couldn't hear any censure in her mother's voice. She allowed herself a moment to bask in the thought of her father looking down fondly on her from heaven. Sometimes she forgot that her mother was mistress of this house once.

"I thank you and my father for raising me with a full awareness of my responsibilities as heiress to Salisbury. And I thank my beloved husband for guiding and protecting us through turbulent times. It's bitter to face the future without him, but I won't let him down."

"What on earth is that smell?" Her mother's nose tilted skyward.

Ela tried not to glance in the direction of the armory. The body was gone but the stench still lingered, mingling with the smoke from the fire and the aroma of roasted fish. "Since you're keen for a wedding, you can help me plan Will's and Isabella's. I intend to have them both married by this summer."

Her mother looked surprised for a moment. Then her familiar knowing look returned. Her mother knew that wealthy wards were not a prize to risk. "How lovely! Isabella, you must be so excited."

Isabella looked like she wanted to cry.

"William de Vesci is awfully handsome, my love! I'm great friends with his grandmamma. We took the boat back from Normandy together last summer. It is a shame that he's called William like almost everyone else in this family, but I'm sure you can find a pet name for him." She turned to the other young William, who was seated next to her, and patted his knee. "And Idonea de Camville is a lovely young girl. I'm sure her grandmamma will forgive your father for all the trouble he's caused her." She winked at Ela.

Ela wasn't so sure, but she wasn't going to let that stop her folding the castle of Lincoln and its attendant manors into her own family. All part of the great chess game of life. At least the attention was off her and onto her children.

"It's a good idea to get Will settled with his wife before he reaches the stage where serving girls start to look pretty to him."

"Indeed." Ela shot a pointed glance at Will, who had the decency to redden. Ela didn't mention that she'd had to send one poor girl away just after Christmas because she was worried he'd sully her virtue. It was unfair that the girl's family should suffer the loss of her pay due to Will's foolishness. "He's more than ready for marriage."

"I shall have a new sword made for you, befitting a young man who'll soon be a knight." Will brightened at the prospect. Then she turned to Isabella. "And you'll be the most radiant bride in England. I know a man who sells the finest silk brocade from Italy, my dear. We shall order some for your dress, Izzy. A yellow gold, perhaps? That would bring out the gold highlights in your dark hair. Your weddings shall be glittering occasions that will bring smiles back to our sad faces."

Isabella glanced at Ela, who winked at her. Isabella managed a brave smile for her grandmother.

They chattered about musicians and food and which guests to definitely invite and which to keep away. If she could keep her mother and Jean up late enough perhaps she'd be able to sneak out tomorrow before they noticed she was gone. She certainly didn't intend to explain to them that she intended to enter the house of a suspected murderer.

* * *

In the morning Ela dressed in a dark-green gown and asked Sibel to add extra pins to her wimple and fillet so they'd survive a windy cross-country ride. She hurried through her morning rounds and ate a light breakfast before the children—and more importantly, her mother—were even awake. Giles Haughton and Hugh Clifford were early. When Peter Howard arrived, flour still clinging to his tunic, she mounted Freya and they set out, with two guards in tow.

"I know where the house is," Hugh reassured her. "My mother grew up out that way."

"Have you asked her if she knew Alan Morse?" Ela wanted to know everything she could before they encountered him.

"I did last night. She remembered him as a boy from when his father kept cows there. She said he was pale and sickly but didn't know that much else about him. His parents had an older son who was supposed to inherit the farm but he was killed in an accident years ago."

"What kind of accident?" Had Morse murdered before? Or was she now seeing murder everywhere she looked?

He shrugged. "She wasn't sure. She's lived here in town twenty-five years or more and hasn't been back out that way since her father died and her mother moved in with us going on twenty years. She told me the best route to get there, though. She said to avoid the river because it will be boggy at this time of year. She said we should go the hilltop route even though it's longer."

"Please thank her for her advice." Ela led them onto the suggested path, which took them past a flock of sheep grazing on the first tiny shoots of spring grass.

The morning was bright and dry and they made good progress across the fields, through a dismal hamlet and into a small knot of still-leafless woodland where they watered their horses at a stream. There was no trace of ice left anywhere. Ela wondered how long Katie Morse had been missing from her home and hoped they'd learn the truth.

The track to Morse's house passed along the side of a field with a large bull in it—they could see it over the hedgerow—and another field with a fine herd of brown dairy cows. Morse's barn was a big wattle-and-daub structure, with a neat thatched roof, that towered over the small cottage nearby.

The cottage itself looked in poor repair, the thatch dark with age and missing in patches. The daub had washed off the walls in some places, exposing the woven wattle beneath. Morse clearly took better care of his cows than his wife or himself. A thin trickle of smoke rose above the roof, suggesting that he was at home.

Ela drew in a steadying breath as they approached.

CHAPTER 5

"*P*'raps it would be best if one of us knocked, my lady," said one of the guards, a big jovial fellow who'd been chattering away to his companions the entire ride.

"I shall announce myself," she responded. She doubted they'd need to knock. Morse must be deaf if he hadn't heard the approach of six horses in this remote valley. As expected the unpainted front door flung open and a man appeared.

He had a broad build and stood at medium height. His dark hair was thinning on top. His tunic was soiled and he wore no hose or shoes, despite the still bitter weather. He looked like he was about to start yelling but when he saw the entourage of armed guards he stilled and frowned.

He knows why we're here. She rode right up to him, deciding for now to stay in her saddle. "Alan Morse?"

"That's my name, my lady."

Did he recognize her? It didn't matter. "My name is Ela Longespée, Countess of Salisbury. We are here to inquire about your wife."

His brows lowered slightly. "What about her?"

"Is she here?" Ela looked behind him into the darkened doorway.

"No, she ain't here." He half-mumbled it.

"Where is she?" Ela disliked asking a question when she was almost sure of the answer.

"She up and left about three weeks ago."

"What do you mean left?"

"Left. That's what I mean. Left her home and hearth and took off."

It was Ela's turn to frown. He was lying. No woman in her right mind would take off in February, especially if she was pregnant.

"Why would she do that?"

"She's a woman, ain't she? Fickle and flighty." He looked directly at her. She was tempted to reach down from her saddle and slap him across the face. Luckily, she was too well schooled to allow such a display of temper.

The guards moved in closer. They hadn't missed his open insolence.

"She was pregnant." Ela wanted to come right out and accuse him of murder, but the process of arresting him would go more smoothly if he somehow confessed it. "Why would a pregnant woman leave her family?"

"T'weren't my baby."

Ela stared at him for a moment, trying to find her bearings. "Whose baby was it?"

"I have no idea. But it weren't mine."

She shifted in her saddle. If his wife was pregnant with another man's baby, that gave her husband a solid motive to kill her and her bastard child.

She didn't approve of the word bastard, or the concept, since her husband could fit that description, but that is certainly how the husband of a cheating wife would see the baby in her belly.

Or was Morse lying?

"How do you know it's not yours?"

He tugged at the front of his grubby and faded blue tunic. "I were injured in battle nigh on ten year ago. Never were able to perform since."

"In the barons' revolt?" The timing was right.

He squinted at her. "Aye." She was tempted to ask which side he fought on, but since he would have been only a hired foot soldier, it was likely of little significance and his answer might upset her own guards or the jurors.

"Do you have—proof of this injury?" She silently prayed that he wouldn't hoist up his tunic and reveal it.

His eyes narrowed. "Never had no children before now, did I?"

"I don't know, did you?" She didn't like his attitude at all. Her guards didn't either. Their irritation was being transmitted to their restless horses. "How long were you married to Katherine?" It was hard to believe that a woman would marry a man who told her he couldn't give her children.

"Seven years."

"Did she know you couldn't sire an heir?"

"Aye. I told her. She didn't care. Couldn't wait to be free of that old bastard what raised her."

"He told me she wasn't living with him at the time. That she lived in the dairy where she worked as a dairymaid."

"Aye. Sending him all her money, though. And what woman doesn't crave her own roof over her head instead of her master's?"

Ela looked up at the deteriorated roof of his grim cottage and wondered. Still, she'd had no say in her own marriage, so she could hardly criticize another woman's choices.

"Why didn't you report your wife missing if she's been gone more than three weeks?" Surely even a murderer would cover his tracks with feigned sorrow.

"Report it to who? When a man's wife runs off with another man, he tends to his wounds. He don't want to shout it all over the countryside."

"You have no idea who this other man was?"

"No." His face grew ruddier, and Ela could feel the full extent of his mortification.

Her mind whirled. If there was indeed another man involved with Katie, he was a new suspect. If he was a married man he might have plenty to lose if evidence of his adultery showed up on his doorstep. He might be tempted to make his problems disappear—permanently.

She decided to stab for the heart and gauge his reaction. "Are you aware that your wife is dead?"

He stared at her for a moment, as if once again he didn't understand. Then he blinked, face still unmoving. "Katie's dead?"

"Her body was found tangled into reeds at a bend in the Avon." She didn't mince words or attempt to spare his feelings.

His eyes darted about, though he stood frozen in place. "She were drowned?"

"Murdered, according to the coroner. We found her body on Sunday." She kept her gaze pinned to him even as her horse shifted under her. "Bludgeoned."

"Oh." He rubbed a hand over his mouth. His lack of sadness should be a concern, but he did look genuinely shocked. Too shocked to even feign sorrow he didn't feel. "He must've murdered her."

"You are also a suspect." She watched him closely.

"Me?" He took a step backward. "Why would I kill my own wife? Do you think I want to prepare my own meals and sweep out my own hearth? Do you think I want to take all these cows to the dairy in the dark every morning? Do you?" Anger rang in his voice.

"If she made you a cuckold, you might do it in anger." Ela found herself growing uncomfortable at the distasteful scenario unraveling in her brain. She told herself to buck up. For all her sheltered life of privilege and luxury she'd had an earful of scandal and debauchery. She just wasn't used to hearing of it among the common folk.

"I didn't kill my wife. I suspected her of sneaking out on me. Like I said, when she took off, I weren't surprised. But I didn't kill her."

Beads of sweat shone on his forehead despite the cold morning air. Evidence of guilt or just of shock?

"You don't seem too distressed to hear of her death." Ela recoiled from the coldness in her own voice. She was starting to realize that the role of sheriff was inimical to the warmth and compassion expected of a woman and a mother.

"I am. Truly I am." He was starting to stammer. "I'm clobbered by it, to be honest. I were angry at her, very angry, but I never wished her dead." He scrunched up his crude features. "She's really dead?"

"For some weeks now." Ela modulated her voice. "We're preparing to bury her. Did you have a particular plot in mind?"

He blinked, clearly confused. "Well, my mother and father are buried in the churchyard at St. Peters. I always figured she and I would end up there as well."

Ela hesitated. Should she offer to bring the body here, as tradition would dictate, or would she be delivering the poor girl's corpse into the hands of her murderer? Alan Morse clearly didn't love her, one way or the other.

"I've made arrangements for her to be buried in the cathedral grounds in Salisbury, if that suits you better."

"The cathedral grounds..." He looked perplexed. "The new cathedral?"

"I spoke to the bishop, and he agreed to find space."

"I'm not a rich man, my lady."

Ela wondered if he would even pay for his cheating wife to have a decent burial. Maybe he'd get final revenge by tipping her back into the Avon or digging a shallow grave in his hayfield.

If Katherine Morse even was an adulteress. They had nothing but his word to go on.

"I've made arrangements for payment. If you're satisfied with the cathedral, then she shall be buried there."

"Yes, my lady. Thank you for your kindness."

Ela had preferred to say goodbye to seven pounds and sleep quietly in her bed knowing that the poor girl's body and soul could rest in the sanctity of hallowed ground. But that was before Katherine Morse was accused of adultery. Though Bishop Poore might refuse the body outright if she were found to have broken her marriage vows.

Ela shifted in her saddle, which now felt rock-hard. She'd come here expecting to take him into custody and have the leisure of questioning him at length back at the castle, but suddenly she found herself doubting everything she'd assumed.

She could hardly arrest Alan Morse now without investigating whether his claims were true. Was he truly unable to get his wife pregnant? And if Katherine Morse had lain with another man, who was her lover?

A light drizzle accompanied her grim realization that they would have to visit the neighbors, one by one, and seek the truth—while considering each one of them a potential suspect.

"Do any of you have questions for Master Morse?" She turned to Haughton and the jurors.

"How did your brother die?" asked Haughton, pinning Morse with a hard stare.

"Broke his insides falling off the roof," said Morse,

without a hitch. "That were nigh on thirty year ago now. What does that have to do with my Katie?"

"Likely nothing." Haughton rode forward a couple of steps. "Did you ever beat your wife?"

Morse shrugged. "No more than any man."

Ela shivered under her cloak. Her William would never lay a hand on a woman. She couldn't even remember him uttering a scolding word. Fresh sadness roamed through her and made her hate this brute for being alive when her beloved husband was dead.

But was he a murderer?

"You are not to leave Wiltshire," she commanded. "Until this crime is fully investigated."

"How do you know she didn't fall in the river and drown?" asked Morse, clearly growing cockier about his own appearance of innocence.

"Because she was dead when she fell in the river," retorted Haughton. "So someone killed her and dumped her."

Morse stood there, impassive as a graven image.

Her guards looked as restless as their horses. They'd come here expecting to make an arrest and transport a prisoner back to the castle. She could arrest him, but that presented the problem of what to do with his herd. His precious cows made flight unlikely, and in the meantime he might incriminate himself in some way. It was prudent to wait.

"We'll return and you shall hear any news." She gathered her reins. "God go with you."

"And with you, my lady," he murmured, his face dark and his brow furrowed.

"Follow me." She commanded the men. She didn't want any discussion until they were out of earshot. Since Morse was still a key suspect she didn't want to inadvertently help him to point the finger of guilt at someone else.

* * *

Instead of heading back the way they'd come, Ela led them on the well-trodden track to the dairy where Morse drove his cows every morning and evening for milking. It was only a short walk away, around a bend in the road, shaded by a cluster of great oaks. A broad stone barn with a thatched roof had a wide doorway that admitted cows to the milking parlor.

Two young girls came out of the doorway as they approached. Their wide eyes suggested that they were not used to the sight of an armed party of officials in their dooryard.

"Good morning." Ela addressed them from horseback. "I am Ela of Salisbury. Are you milkmaids here?"

"Yes, ma'am." The shorter one spoke up. She wore no veil, just a barbette and plain fillet, and her curly dark hair escaped from a bun at the nape of her neck. "I'm Annie Stokes and this is Mary Woods."

"Do you live here?"

"Yes, ma'am. In the loft above the milking stalls." She gestured behind them. This must be where Katie had lived before she married Morse. A stench of dung and sour milk filled her nose even though no cows were visible right now. She couldn't imagine this was a pleasant place to sleep.

"Does Alan Morse bring his cows here for milking?"

"Aye, morn and night, and our master takes the milk into town to sell and turns some into cheese and butter."

"Do you know his wife, Katherine?"

"Oh aye. Katie used to bring the cows every morning and evening until a few weeks ago."

"Do you know why she stopped coming?" She was curious to hear the excuse Alan had made for her absence.

"Sick, I think. At least that's what he said at first. Not a talker, Alan Morse." Her forehead crinkled with concern. "She's not dead is she?"

Ela hesitated. These could be dear friends of Katie's who she'd known for years. "I'm afraid she is, may God rest her soul. We're investigating her murder."

"Murder?" The other girl squealed. Red-gold wisps of hair framed her freckled face below her crudely knotted veil. "Katie?"

"I'm afraid so. Her body was found in the Avon, and there were signs that a crime was committed against her."

Both girls had a look of panic on their faces. Did they know something? "Do you have any idea why someone would want to kill Katie?"

They glanced at each other, then back at Ela. They did know something.

"Girls, you must speak up if you know the truth," called out Haughton imperiously. "Concealing a crime is against the law."

Ela bristled. Browbeating and threatening these girls was no way to get answers. "Were you aware that Katie was pregnant?"

"Of course, how could you not be? She was getting so big." The first girl's face fell. "Oh, that poor baby."

"Yes, two lives were lost. We need your help to bring their killer to justice." She looked from one to the other.

Mary, the redhead, licked her lips like she wanted to say something. Annie glanced at her. What did they know? Pushing them too hard could scare them into silence.

"Were you friends with Katie before she married?" They might have all lived together up in the loft and shared confidences.

Annie shook her head. "I've only worked here a year, since Lucy Hardy left to marry. And Mary's here less than six months."

"But you talked to Katie?"

"About day-to-day things," said Mary. "The weather, if one of the cows were out of sorts. Nothing—personal."

Annie frowned. "But I did hear some gossip." She paused and looked past Ela.

Ela resisted the urge to turn around and look behind her. "Gossip about what?"

Annie glanced at the phalanx of males surrounding them, and Ela prayed they'd stay quiet and let her speak. "About Katie and her husband. That they couldn't have children because he has something wrong with his...his...giblets. So people did talk when they saw she were with child."

"Who did you hear that from? The neighbors?"

"I don't remember exactly. We get customers coming from all over the valley to buy butter and cheese. Sometimes we go to market to tend the stall if the master has business in town. We talk to a lot of folk."

"And did any of the gossip tell you who the father of Katie's baby might be?"

They looked at each other, then spoke in unison. "No."

She wasn't sure whether to believe them. "Who's your master?"

"Philip Nance."

Ela dimly recognized the name. He was a yeoman farmer who'd made a good living from his dairy these past few years and was on the list of local men who could be called as jurors. Was he a candidate as Katie's lover? He had the advantage of proximity. She didn't want to come right out and ask, though. It would sound too much like an accusation.

"Is Master Nance a good man to work for?"

"He's not too bad," said Annie. "I wouldn't complain if he paid more or if we had beds inside the house. Or if we had more wood for our fire since we don't have time during the day to gather any. But he pays on time and doesn't interfere with us." She said the last part as if she knew exactly what Ela was really asking.

Ela nodded, grateful for her understanding. "A good master is a blessing." No doubt these hardworking girls had reason to be here instead of home with their families. She prayed that they'd find good husbands and become mistress of their own homes in due time. A poor girl with no dowry might face a lifetime of loneliness and unrelenting labor. Once again, she counted her own blessings, even in her sorrow.

But she was no closer to knowing who'd murdered Katie. Or fathered her baby. She wanted to ask if they knew more about Katie's relationship with her husband, but, since they hadn't volunteered any information beyond his impotence, that would be tantamount to starting gossip. "Who else lives in this neighborhood?"

Annie looked at Mary, who spoke up. "Widow Nettles, down the lane there." She pointed to a knot of woods. "She won't know anything. Rarely leaves her house, she's that old. We bring her leftover whey and sticks for her fire."

"Good for you. It's important to help neighbors in need." She resolved to visit the old lady to see if she was in need of alms, but not today. This morning she needed to stay focused on the investigation. "Who else?"

"Pat Lesser owns the next farm over. He has twelve milk cows. He has a wife, Ada, and four children. On the other side of the road is Richard Dawson. His wife died two years ago, leaving him with two children, a girl of nine and a boy a little older."

All of these people were close enough to have had regular contact with Katie. Especially if they all brought their cows to the dairy morning and evening.

Mary and Annie rattled off a few more neighbors, families, widows and widowers, and Ela tried to store the information in her mind. Hopefully, those with her were doing the same, as it was a lot to recall. "You've been very helpful." She wanted to reach into her purse and give each girl some coin but worried that might appear inappropriate, as if she was paying them to say something—or not say something. "If you learn more information please come to me at the castle or send word."

They agreed. Ela led her group out of the farmyard and back onto the road. Once they were out of earshot of the farm she turned to the men. "Let's visit Richard Dawson, the widower. A man alone might get lonely and be tempted by a young woman living nearby."

Of course, he was unlikely to come right out and admit it. She'd have to go on his facial expression or movements to determine his likely guilt or innocence.

CHAPTER 6

The drizzle had intensified to a persistent rain, and Ela felt her fur-lined cloak grow heavier by the minute. The road was already deep mud from so much bovine traffic to and from the dairy, and their horses could barely walk, let alone trot.

For a moment Ela wished she was home in front of her fire with some embroidery in her hands and her children buzzing around her, not out here getting chilled and drenched on a potentially futile quest for justice.

Possibly the men wished the same.

As they rode along the narrow road between high hedgerows, Ela turned to Haughton and the jurors. "Your thoughts so far?"

"I think those dairymaids know more than they're letting on," said Peter Howard, the baker. "They're in a position to know a lot of people's business."

Ela nodded. "Possibly, but they didn't give the impression of being guilty or concealing something important. I want them to be our allies, so I didn't like to accuse them of hiding information. They might hear something over the next week or two as word of the girl's death spreads. We'll visit them again."

"Her husband seemed a nasty piece of work," said young Hugh Clifford. "I bet he was on the side of the upstart barons. Probably do anything for a piece of gold."

Ela kept her expression neutral. "He certainly doesn't seem a loving husband and I still consider him a key suspect. But we need to learn more before we accuse him. If he is the killer, it would be frustrating to find ourselves without enough evidence to convict him."

"Agreed." Haughton turned up his collar and pulled down his hat against the rain. "In a murder trial we need to find evidence strong enough to convince the traveling justice at the assizes. I've seen more than one guilty man slip the noose because he was able to sweet-talk his way into the justice's favor."

Ela had as well. A smooth tongue and a fat purse could buy freedom. One of the many reasons she would need to content herself with finding justice for others instead of pointing the finger at her husband's killer. At least for now.

Dawson's cottage was newish and in good repair, in stark contrast to Morse's. A few scrawny chickens pecked at the bare ground outside. One of the guards called from outside to announce their arrival, and a grubby boy with a runny nose answered the door. He stared at the armored guards on their steaming horses and was stunned into openmouthed silence.

"Is your father home?" called Ela. Through the half-open door she could see that the inside of the cottage was dark and not recently swept.

"He went to town to sell a cow."

A little girl with tangled blonde hair appeared beside him. The sight of the guards frightened her and she shrank back inside, tugging on the boy's ragged tunic.

"Do you know when he'll be back?" Ela tried to speak softly, despite having to call through the rain.

"By sunset, he said."

There were numerous villages within a half day's walk so he could be anywhere. They'd have to come back or summon him to the castle and issuing a verbal summons would only scare or confuse his children, who might not even pass on the message.

"Who are you?" The boy asked, curiosity overcoming his anxiety.

"I'm Ela of Salisbury," she said gently, as if talking to one of her own children. "And these men are here with me to keep all of Salisbury and the surrounding lands safe from harm."

"Oh." His nose ran faster than ever. "What harm?"

She wanted to laugh at herself for putting it so obscurely. Of course he was curious. "Any and all harm, but there's nothing threatening at present so don't you worry. Take good care of your sister and mind your father." She smiled at them, hoping this visit wouldn't leave them terrified of unseen evils stalking their fields and woods.

And there were evils. A young woman and her baby lay dead and their killer roamed at large.

The boy closed the door, and they headed back to the deep mire of the road.

"This rain is something, ain't it?" asked Peter Howard. Ela glanced at him. He wasn't a young man, and perhaps he was feeling the cold and damp in his bones.

"Let's head back," she declared. "There's no sense us all catching a chill. This is not such a long ride and we know the way now. We've already spoken to Alan Morse and resolved the question of where his wife will be buried, and that was the most pressing matter." She needed to get the poor girl's moldering body safely in the ground.

Howard looked relieved. They turned their horses around and headed back up the lane toward the path across the fields. Clouds hung low over the hilltops, making stark silhouettes of the leafless trees.

My dear William is dead. The thought crashed into her mind like thunder. Gone forever. He'd never again hold her close just before sleep. He'd never make her laugh in the midst of her anger. He'd never give her that cocky look that said, "I know, but you love me anyway."

Grief rolled over her in a ragged wave just as Freya stumbled in a rut. She caught herself before she could slip out of the saddle, and Freya righted herself. Stay focused. Don't let yourself wallow in grief.

Widows and widowers were all around her. Alan Morse for one and the absent Richard Dawson for another. And they didn't have an entourage of servants or even an extended family from the looks of it. They were forced to pick up the broken pieces of their lives and keep going all by themselves—or starve.

Back inside the outer walls, Haughton and the jurors peeled away from their bedraggled group and headed for their own warm hearths. Ela led the guards back up the steep path into the castle, noting the need for more cinders to lend traction to its slippery surface.

* * *

Back in the great hall, Ela's mother was holding court from William's chair. The children and dogs gathered around her, and Ela could see that she was dispensing gifts.

"My darling, where have you been all morning!"

"Investigating the circumstances of a murder." Maintaining a lie would be too much effort.

Her mother's eyebrows shot up. "Whose murder?"

"A young woman from a nearby farm." It was a relief to be out of the drizzle and free of her heavy cloak. She took a cup of hot spiced wine and sat in a chair a servant placed near her mother's. "Her body was found as we returned from the funeral. Sibel, can you summon Deschamps?"

"Yes, my lady, but let me replace your wet veil, first." Ela let the ever conscientious Sibel remove her damp veil and pin a fresh one in its place.

"Sibel, what would I do without you?"

"Manage perfectly fine, I expect. But luckily there's no need for that."

Alianore looked a little scandalized to hear her daughter's lady's maid talking back to her.

"What do you mean her body was found? Here in the castle?"

"No, thank goodness." She explained the circumstances, avoiding the unpleasant mistake of bringing the body to the armory, where the foul corpse odor still hung in the damp air like a warning.

When Deschamps appeared, she asked him to arrange for the burial to take place early the next morning and—if that was acceptable to Bishop Poore—to notify Morse and the dead girl's elderly father. It would be interesting to see if either of them bothered to show up.

"My darling, you cannot trouble yourself with such awful matters. You're still recovering from a horrible shock and the loss of your husband and protector."

"If anything, it's helping me to get through the greater loss. I prefer to keep my mind and body occupied so I don't have time to brood." Ela petted the head of her favorite greyhound, Grayson, who had sweetly placed it in her lap. She leaned toward her mother and lowered her voice. "The poor dead girl had a difficult husband, who claims the baby in her belly wasn't his." She hoped none of the children overheard. She didn't want the salacious details of the case being repeated.

Her mother's lips pursed. "You are riding around the countryside putting yourself in a path of a killer."

"I went out with two guards as well as the coroner and two jurors."

"This is still no job for a woman. Especially one with children to raise."

"Mother," she attempted a stern gaze, which was hard since Alianore's own look could freeze boiling water. "Please do not attempt to undermine my authority, especially in my own household."

Her mother looked affronted. She whipped out her embroidered linen handkerchief and flapped it about before dabbing at her nose with it. "I shall keep the unfortunate young woman in my prayers."

Ela wasn't sure whether she meant the dead woman or herself. Both of them would no doubt benefit from any extra prayers sent their way.

"Look what Grandma gave me!" Stephen brandished a small dagger, withdrawing it from its tooled leather hilt.

"Goodness. Do be careful with it."

"You know I believe in giving useful gifts." Alianore folded her handkerchief and slid it back into her sleeve.

"She gave me a strip of fabric and all these colored threads," said little Ellie uncertainly.

"To make a bookmark for your prayer book, my dear."

"But I already have one."

"If God graces you with another prayer book you shall be ready with a bookmark for it," said Alianore sharply, but with an indulgent smile. "Needlework is a useful skill as well as a fine pastime for a young noblewoman." She turned to Ela. "Unlike, say, hunting a murderer."

"Can I join the hunt?" Stephen twirled his new dagger. Its blade caught the light through a high window.

Ela lifted a brow at her mother. "No, my love. You're far too young."

"Oh." He sheathed his dagger and jumped to his feet. "I'm going to go find some things to cut."

"Nothing alive or valuable, please," she said, only half-joking. "Why don't you go see if cook needs some things cut in the kitchen?"

"Good idea." He skipped off to the kitchen.

"Where's Will?" He wasn't there. His energetic presence was always highly visible, as if he were surrounded by rays of gold like a painted saint, so his absence was noticeable as well.

"Jean took him out hunting. You know they love the back of a horse better than the warmth of the fire."

"True. That's how he spends most of his time."

"Marriage should settle him. And soon we'll have a new baby to fuss over."

"God willing." Ela didn't take anything for granted lately.

"Don't worry, my dear. Your sweet Will is the late king's grandson. Idonea's family would be fools to eschew such a match."

"I hope you're right." It was hard to predict what Idonea's testy grandmother would do. Ela admired and emulated her salty independence, but she was anything but predictable.

"Oh, their baby will be such a sweet little thing," Alianore exclaimed. "They're such an attractive couple. Idonea has blossomed into such a beauty."

"Looks aren't everything."

"Look who's talking! Your husband drew the gaze of every woman in Wiltshire."

"He was handsome, yes, but a handsome husband is not always the greatest benefit to a wife." She regretted her words as soon as she'd said them. They felt treacherous.

"All men take mistresses, my dear." Her mother had the

tact to whisper the words in her ear. "Just part of life's rich tapestry."

"I know. You prepared me for it well."

"He loved you well."

"I know it. I do. I didn't mean to sound ungrateful. But Will is wild and lusty and the thought of him stepping out on his wife when she's barely more than a child does worry me."

Alianore sighed. "Boys will be boys. It's nature's way of ensuring their finer qualities pass on to the next generation. It's a pity your father sired only you."

"I shall do my best to be enough," she said wryly.

"By becoming sole castellan and high sheriff?" Her mother's imperious eyebrows lifted.

Ela shrugged, a smile tugging at her mouth.

"You are your father's daughter, that's for sure."

Ela felt a burst of pride. "I hope I can do my duty to his memory and to Salisbury."

"Speaking of that, and of life's rich tapestry, my darling…" Alianore gestured at the wall behind them. "These tapestries are filthy. Can they not be cleaned?"

Ela looked up and down the vast—and admittedly grimy —hunting scene that had hung on that wall as long as she could remember. "These tapestries are a hundred years old." She paid no more attention to them than the stones they covered.

"Maybe older. You could commission some new ones?"

"That would be quite an extravagance. Have you noticed how large these walls are?" William had left large debts, some of them to the crown. His will had detailed exactly how his young wards' fortunes should be used to pay them. Which meant keeping a tight hold on those fortunes now he was gone.

"It's part of your duty to make your home and castle an environment that reflects the importance of your family."

"Then how come you never changed them?"

"I did have them cleaned." Alianore surveyed the ones on the far side of the room. "They were given a good scrubbing and never looked quite the same again."

"Then perhaps the layers of soot are doing them a favor."

"There are some fine weavers in Normandy." Her mother took out her handkerchief and blew her nose. "Very fine. You should see the walls of the great houses there."

"I have." Ela had spent more time than she cared to recall in Normandy. She much preferred to be here at home, ancient sooty walls and all.

"So like your father." Alianore smiled. "I told him he should build a new wing with decorative turrets. But he always said that what served his forefathers could serve him as well. He never liked shiny new things. He thought them gaudy. Serve him his dinner on a scarred plate with his father's crest on it, by the light of a bent old silver candlestick, and he was happy as a pig in its sty."

Ela's eyes rested on the rather crooked candlestick, unlit, that sat on a nearby table. "When you have perfectly good candlesticks, what's the point of buying more?"

"Oh, indeed why?" said her mother in a teasing tone. "Perhaps William the Conqueror himself ate by the light of that very candlestick, a hundred and fifty years ago."

"No doubt he read the Domesday Book in its glow. Do you have no appreciation for history?"

"I appreciate tradition. What would that William have thought of a female sheriff at Salisbury?"

"I doubt he would have wasted his time worrying about the gender of his sheriff. I think he would be more concerned about whether peace and justice prevailed in this corner of his kingdom. Let me see how the cook is faring with our meal."

Ela hurried away to the kitchens. Was her mother

warming to her plans? It was hard to tell. She loved her mother dearly but also found her draining.

As expected the cook and her helpers were piling freshly baked rolls on platters and pouring out a big tureen of fish soup into a serving dish. A serving girl dotted butter onto a platter of carrots and leeks.

"Fish and more fish," muttered the cook. "New spring lambs can't come soon enough."

"Or new spring greens," sighed Ela. "Every winter seems longer, but that makes spring all the sweeter when it comes."

Servants carrying plates, napkins, cups and carafes followed her back through the hall, where the family gathered at the main table. Even Will and Jean were there, hose splattered with mud and faces red from the cold.

"How was the hunting?"

"Fine!" exclaimed Jean. "Young Will shot a fat boar in the woods to salt and save for Easter."

"I do hope you weren't galloping too fast," said Alianore to Will, arching a brow. "I know that your father always prided himself on the speed and power of his horses."

Ela felt a pang. William had loved a good gallop and challenged her to races like she were a man. In that instant she felt his loss like a missing limb.

"How could I resist, my love?" retorted Jean. "When my brother-in-law devoted himself to breeding the finest horses in all of England and Normandy."

"Tall, powerful and fleet of foot." Young Will quoted his father's mantra. Ela, like many people, preferred a smaller horse that was easier to mount and dismount and less of a struggle to control. If Will could have harnessed a dragon, no doubt he would.

"Papa said the horses in the Holy Land are some of the fastest he'd ever seen. He promised to bring some back and breed them with his mares and—" Will's face, flushed from exercise, suddenly stilled. He too was hit by the realization that so many hopes and dreams would never come to fruition. Then his face brightened. "I suppose I'll have to go there and get them myself."

"Good lad!" said Jean, raising his cup of wine. "I'll raise a toast to young Will leading a successful expedition to Jerusalem and bringing home some fine horseflesh."

Ela lifted her cup rather reluctantly. She didn't relish the prospect of Will heading overseas, especially on what seemed to be increasingly dangerous and fruitless missions to the far-flung Holy Land. She knew the true Holy Land was inside each of them and was found sooner through prayer than ocean voyages. But now wasn't the time to crush his youthful fantasies.

"Mother, I want to come with you when you ride out to interview suspects again."

Will's change of subject took Ela by surprise. How did he even know where she'd been? Perhaps one of the grooms or guards had mentioned it. Now she felt guilty about riding out without even asking him. He was the future heir to all Salisbury.

"I'd welcome your company. There's a new wrinkle to the investigation." She didn't fancy discussing the woman's potential infidelity in front of her younger children. "Which I shall explain later. Weather permitting we'll ride out again tomorrow."

The porter approached. "My lady, Master St. Germain, the silversmith, has arrived. Shall I show him in?"

"Please do." She rose and looked around for her attendant and found her helping Petronella with her sewing. "Sibel, could you please fetch the drawing on top of the desk in my solar?"

"Yes, my lady." Sibel hurried away. Ela had sketched her plan for her new seal.

St. Germain, a well-dressed man a few years her junior, swept in and bowed. "My deepest condolences on the loss of your husband."

"Your sympathies are appreciated." She ushered for him to take a seat at a table away from the family. "I am taking on new responsibilities in the absence of my husband and need a new seal to—" She paused, not sure how to word it. To make sure I'm taken seriously was not something she could say out loud.

"Indeed, my lady. I quite understand." He sat and pulled out a small leaf of parchment from his bag. "Do you have particular iconography in mind?"

"I do." She looked around for Sibel, who hadn't returned. "It shall show me standing, facing head on, flanked by lion cubs to represent the lions of Longespée."

"Excellent."

"My dress should be natural. Just as I am dressed now, with a simple fillet and veil and no unnecessary ornamentation." She didn't want to look like a merry widow. "Ah, here's Sybil with my sketch."

Sibel placed it in front of her, and she swiveled it around to face St. Germain. "Here's the pose I like. A bird in my left hand and my right hand raised in greeting or offering."

The silversmith surveyed it and looked up at her with amusement. "Your drawing is most accomplished."

"It's mean and unskilled but hopefully provides a starting point." She inhaled. Why did men often look amused around her? It was irksome to the extreme. Why was a woman taking charge of her existence so entertaining? "It should have the Longespée coat of arms on the back."

"Of course." Again he looked up at her with an infuriating twinkle in his eye. "Is the bird a dove of peace or a falcon?"

"A falcon." Ready to hunt down the truth and bring it back home to her. "The seal should have a cross on it somewhere and it should say, Ela, Countess of Salisbury, around the image. The rest of the details I leave up to your skill and experience."

He was busy sketching even while she talked and soon turned his drawing around to face her. It showed a sketch of lozenge-shaped seal featuring a tall elegant woman dressed in a simple gown and cloak in exactly the pose she'd imagined. He'd placed a hexagonal platform under her feet and a cross above her head.

"I'm not sure I'm that tall."

"You are most certainly that tall." He held her gaze, defying her to argue. Had she been fishing for compliments? She fervently hoped not.

"If you insist, then that looks fine. How long until it's ready?"

"I can deliver it by next week."

Ela wanted to protest that tomorrow would be better, but he was a busy man for a good reason so she held her tongue.

"God go with you, Master St. Germain."

"And with you, my lady." He rose and bowed before taking his leave. He'd left her drawing sitting on the table. It looked foolish there so she folded it up and tucked it in her sleeve. "Anyone for a game of Alquerque?"

CHAPTER 7

*K*atherine Morse was buried shortly after dawn in the grounds of the new cathedral. Ela attended the cathedral service partly to offer prayers for the poor girl's soul—and that of her unfortunate baby—and partly to make sure her seven pounds were put to good use. Also to see if Katherine's husband turned up—or if anyone else did.

As expected, Katie's blind father was there, head in hands, in the front row. Ela offered her condolences and he thanked her profusely for paying for his daughter's funeral, with many apologies about his own grinding poverty and misery. Again, Ela silently resolved to make sure he was provided with alms and to check on him regularly. Old age and its wisdom should be a blessing, despite the inevitable infirmities, not a trial to be endured in poverty and solitude.

Katherine's husband was nowhere to be seen, which Ela noted as another black mark against his character. No one else was there, either.

After the funeral, Ela offered to escort the old man back to his smithy, but he politely refused, saying that it was far too mean and humble, and also that it was so close by he was almost home.

She'd intended to bring Will, but he'd been fast asleep when she went to rouse him. No doubt from staying up half the night entertaining their guests. Like his father he was a warm host where she preferred the solitude of her chamber and the solace of her prie-dieu.

She visited the stonemason who was charged with making the effigy for William's tomb. He'd been interred with a plain lid to allow time to make a likeness befitting a great man.

The stone yard was dusty and busy, filled with the clanging of hammers on chisels as carvers worked on details for the new cathedral.

"My lady." The master stonemason hurried forward and bowed. "I've sourced an excellent piece of stone large enough for your lord's tomb. It was no mean feat since it wasn't just his sword that was long."

Ela stared for a moment, surprised by his familiarity. Then she smiled. "Indeed he was quite the tallest man I ever met. I brought a likeness of his face." She reached into her cloak where she'd folded a small parchment sketch. "It shows his features in proportion."

The stonemason took it and studied it. "I thank you, though I hardly need it." He looked up at her. "Everyone in Wiltshire knew William Longespée, and I intend for them to recognize him instantly when they see his tomb."

"He should be in full chain mail, with his longsword by his side and his shield with six rampant lions."

"Yes, my lady. And it will be painted with his heraldic colors."

"He'll be life size?"

"At least life size. He's a larger-than-life figure in these parts, isn't he?"

Ela felt relieved. She'd been assured this stonemason was the most accomplished in all Wiltshire. She wanted to make sure her husband's tomb would be worthy of him. It would outlast all of them and would be the only William Longespée that his grandchildren and their grandchildren would ever know. "Thank you. I look forward to seeing my husband again in your stone carving."

* * *

As she rode back to the castle, a soldier on either side of her, Ela noticed a phalanx of official-looking horsemen riding toward the castle on the London road. "Slow down," she ordered the guards. "Can you see who that is?"

They both demurred. Young and inexperienced, they probably wouldn't know the Ayyubid Sultan if he rode down on them with an army. The men carried no identifying banner but then nor did she. Such things were reserved for official occasions.

She squinted, trying to make out who they were. Her sight wasn't as keen as it used to be, but a sour sensation in her gut began to inform her who her visitor was before she could make out his arrogant visage. Hubert de Burgh.

Startled by her reaction, her horse shied and she had to pet Freya's neck to settle her. How did he have the nerve to show his face here when her husband was barely cold in his tomb? At least he hadn't had the gall to attend her husband's funeral.

She wanted to order him from her castle—from all of Wiltshire—or throw him headlong into the dungeon underneath the castle.

But he was the king's justiciar.

Blood boiling, she spurred her horse forward. She had to arrive back at the castle before he could be warmly welcomed by Will or her mother or Jean, all of whom had no idea what he'd done.

She trotted through the arch and up the castle hill while the party was still approaching at a brisk walk. She'd dismounted and handed her reins to the groom when de Burgh and his retinue of about ten men rode through the gates.

Ela prepared herself to behave with the dignity required of her office as countess and high sheriff of Wiltshire.

De Burgh dismounted and strode up to her with the confidence of a man used to taking what he wanted from life. Something he'd apparently been doing since his birth as a lowly yeoman. He'd risen far and fast on his wits and supposed charm, and she now prayed fervently for the day he'd fall all the way back down.

"Ela! My deepest condolences. His majesty and I are devastated that we were unable to attend the funeral services for his beloved uncle. Unfortunately pressing matters kept us at Westminster."

"The king's condolences are much appreciated," she said stiffly. Could she manage to stay just this side of rudeness? De Burgh could destroy her if he chose.

"His highness charged me with bringing a small token of his affections for his uncle William." He gestured to a rider-less horse, being ponied by one of his companions. The horse wore a pack saddle laden with what looked like a large box. The myth of the Trojan horse stirred in her mind.

Would she ever look at anything without at least a hint of suspicion again? "Bring your men into the hall for some refreshment." She'd have rather offered him a cup of poison out here in the courtyard, but there was no way to avoid the invitation. She prayed he didn't intend to settle in for a long visit. Her castle did house the king's garrison so he could claim to be here on the king's business. She couldn't keep him out without risking the king's ire—something she had no desire to do.

"Thank you, kind lady." De Burgh's honeyed smile churned her gut. "Your hospitality is a credit to your late husband. How is young William bearing up?"

"He's devastated by the loss of his father, as I'm sure you can imagine."

Thank God she'd had the self-control not to share her suspicions with her son. If he thought his father's murderer was about to enter their hall, he'd grab his father's famous longsword and greet de Burgh with it flashing in his hand.

And no good could come of that.

De Burgh cleared his throat. "I must apologize for the unfortunate circumstances of our last meeting." He spoke quietly as they headed through the doorway into the hall. "I'd been told by reliable sources that your husband was lost in the shipwreck. If I'd known he lived I would never have encouraged my nephew to ask for your hand."

Ela felt bile rise within her at the memory. A silly boy hoping to be her husband. And de Burgh had already requested permission from the king!—who'd agreed as long as Ela could be persuaded to say yes. It was a cheap and dirty grab at her lands and titles, and she'd rebuffed it with all the fury and indignation it deserved.

And she'd have to live with the repercussions for the rest of her life.

All rose as de Burgh and his finely dressed retinue entered the hall. Alianore greeted him effusively, and Ela half wished she'd told her mother of his nephew's disgraceful proposal so she could have instead chilled him with one of her haughty stares. Alianore would be aghast to know that a man without even a title of his own had dared to ask for her daughter's hand in marriage. But once again, her mother and Jean were safer protected from information that would inflame their righteous anger and possibly endanger them all.

The servants took their cloaks and fussed over the guests, settling them at a table near the fire with drinks. Ela busied herself with her children, asking them about their morning and telling them about the service at the new cathedral, when she sensed de Burgh's long shadow looming over her.

"Might I speak with you in private, my lady?"

"Anything you have to say to me can be said in the presence of my dear mother and her husband."

De Burgh looked doubtfully at them. "But your children —" He glanced at them, then back at Ela, with more than a hint of menace.

Was he threatening her? Could he destroy her loved ones, one by one?

Fear spurred her to action. "Accompany me into the armory." She rose and led the way, requesting that the two soldiers standing watch should wait outside the door. If he'd come to kill her he'd find her handy with a sword and she'd die fighting.

Seething, she held her tongue until the heavy door closed behind her. "With all due respect to the office of the king's justiciar," she said slowly, "your presence here is an insult to the memory of my husband. William Longespée was alive and well, God be praised, delivered from a terrible shipwreck and a year in exile. Alive and well just days ago!"

"May he rest in peace." De Burgh crossed himself and Ela followed suit, though she would rather have slapped him across his smug face.

"Alive and well until he accepted an invitation to dine at your house, in a supposed apology for your unwise attempt to coerce his wife into an illegal marriage."

"My lady—" She could see him getting ready to ply her with lies, which only added insult to injury and that made her angrier.

"Alive and well until he supped at your table! The next

morning he sickened and by the time he returned here he was feverish and sick unto death." She struggled to keep her voice steady. She had no desire to sound shrewish and shrill. "Within days of that fateful visit he was dead."

"I cannot apologize more, my lady." He bowed his head. "I feel I am to blame."

Ela froze. Was he going to admit to poisoning her husband? This was more than she'd hoped for. And worse than she'd feared. He surely wouldn't let her live with that knowledge at her disposal.

He shook his head, and his distinguished brow wrinkled. "I should never have plied him with such rich fare! A man barely recovered from the privations of a tiresome journey and a long illness." He looked up at her, eyes filled with mock contrition. "I should never have tempted the Lord by breaking the Lenten prohibitions in my efforts to entertain him like a king."

Ela knew they'd dined on meat and milk and all manner of forbidden dainties. William had raved about the transgression during his fevered penance. "Indeed you should not. But I hardly think that rich fare alone was enough to bring a hearty man who'd survived many battles to his deathbed."

"Still, I regret the feast with all my heart, my lady. If I could but bring him back." He let out a dramatic sigh that made her clench her fists. "I've brought a richly illustrated prayer book—the cover decorated with large rubies—to offer to the new cathedral as a gift in his memory."

Did he hope that would buy him a place in heaven? Or win him a place in her heart? On both counts he was sorely wrong. "I'm sure Bishop Poore will appreciate your generosity."

Why had he come here? The king could have sent a troop of soldiers to deliver his gift. Surely he hadn't come all this way for a mock apology? Did he hope that his brazen entry into her dead husband's keep would somehow demonstrate his guileless innocence? Or was he here to gauge her reaction to the events and plan her future accordingly?

It was galling that de Burgh had so much influence with the king. If he chose to wield his considerable power he might even have her driven from this castle and her son deprived of his inheritance.

Or could he? The king was intimate with her husband and had brokered the peace between William and de Burgh after the marriage scandal had enraged William. Perhaps he could be convinced that his justiciar was a stone-cold murderer.

"I don't presume to mention marriage again, Ela." His use of her first name startled her by its presumed intimacy—and pronounced lack of respect.

"I'm grateful for that, at least."

"Although should you change your mind, my nephew was very much taken with your—"

"I will certainly not change my mind." His audacity knew no bounds. "I intend to take the veil when my children are of age."

"Ah. You seek a life of quiet retirement." A look of relief smoothed his features. "No doubt you are anxious to be quit of the responsibilities of castle and garrison."

"Indeed not." She'd seen that coming. "I look forward to serving Salisbury as my husband and father did before me."

He paused, and his lips did an odd twisty thing. Almost like he was trying not to laugh. "That won't be necessary, my lady. I'm sure our master the king can appoint a sheriff to absolve you of the tiresome responsibilities. Then you can retire to one of your peaceful manors and enjoy a life of repose."

Ela felt her father's blood surge within her. He'd raised her from the cradle to hold and serve Salisbury castle. "I have no intention of retreating into the countryside. I have written to the king about my intention to serve as sheriff."

His face creased again, and she wondered if he'd try to pull rank. She braced herself for the onslaught. I am Ela, Countess of Salisbury, and my children are cousins to the king.

"Your desire to serve the people of Salisbury is most admirable, my lady. And quite eccentric under the circumstances. Happily, there are men enough in our kingdom to assume the role of sheriff and castellan, and you need not bother yourself with the labors.

"Service to my king and country is no bother to me, my lord. I consider it my duty. And I will hold the castle until such time as my son William is ready to assume command of it."

De Burgh studied her, his eyes murky with unspoken questions. "We'll see about that. The king is in Northumbria at present. I will be sure this matter comes to his prompt attention." Then he took a step toward her. "Perhaps his majesty will find it needful to wed you to a new husband."

"Perhaps you've forgotten that the Magna Carta, signed by our esteemed king's predecessor, explicitly states that widows cannot be forced to remarry and shall retain control of their own fortunes and estates. I witnessed its signing myself."

"I think we both know that the king signed that document under duress. I assure you that the current king has no intention of making the mistakes of his predecessor."

No doubt he would prefer to raise taxes from his barons at will. Ela held her tongue. "My utmost loyalty lies with King Henry. I look forward to entertaining him here at his earliest convenience." If the king was in Northumbria her letter seeking appointment to the role of sheriff might not have reached him yet.

No doubt de Burgh would have preferred for her to entertain the king here with his snot-nosed nephew installed as lord and master of the castle. Brazen as he was, he might even continue to press his nephew's suit both with her and the king.

However, once Will reached majority, marriage to her would not be the prize it now appeared. Will would be Earl of Salisbury and master of its great estates, and she would be an aging dowager. She smiled at the prospect of cheating de Burgh of his prize by the passage of time.

For now, this charade had gone on long enough. "I'm sure you understand that I am now in deep mourning and cannot offer the lavish entertainments you are used to." So please banish yourself to the bowels of hell, forthwith. "My mother and her husband are visiting, and I've stayed away too long already."

She swept to the door and tugged it open, keen to quit the lingering scent of death in the armory. The two guards outside almost fell in. Had they been listening? No matter. She had no intention of saying anything—ever—that she might later have cause to regret.

She walked back into the hall amidst a clamor of voices. Stephen Hale, the cordwainer, approached her nervously, bowing and stammering. "Apologies for the intrusion, my lady, but there's a commotion in the marketplace here inside the walls. I come to raise the hue and cry."

"Do excuse me," she said officiously to de Burgh. "Duty calls." Deschamps was out collecting rents so she summoned two guards and her son Will—whom she did not want to leave unattended with the scheming de Burgh, donned her cloak, and hurried out on foot toward the nearby marketplace.

They were barely out of the castle gate when Ela heard the sound of a woman shrieking. She quickened her steps, wondering at the woman's strength to continue such cater-wauling. The market square inside the castle walls had shrunk over time, pressed in by the need for more buildings in the enclosed space, until it was barely the width of two ordinary streets.

Ela ducked as a missile flew in her direction—an egg!—and missed her by only a span. The woman pulled eggs from a basket on her arm and threw them at a man while berating him in front of a gathered crowd of enthusiastic viewers. The odd part was that the man just stood there, not attempting to run, barely shielding his face from the sticky, yellow blows. He also held an annoyed-looking red cow at the end of a rope.

"What's she saying?" she asked Will. Sometimes she had trouble understanding the idiomatic speech of the local people. Will, raised on the same courtly French as her, looked confused as she was. One of the guards leaned in. "Begging your pardon, my lady, but she accuses him of laying with another woman."

"She should be put in the stocks for causing a public disturbance," said Will, staring at her.

Ela hesitated. She knew that a woman scolding her husband in public was cause for punishment, but she wanted to know if the woman had good reason for her outburst.

"Silence!" she called. Nervous that the woman would ignore her and undermine her authority, or even throw eggs at her, she quietly ordered the guards to seize her. Then hissed the word, "Gently!"

The two men stepped forward, and each grabbed one of the woman's broad arms. She looked like she wanted to keep shouting but thought better of it. Ela stepped forward. "Madam, speak slowly and tell me why you're causing this commotion in our town square."

Red in the face, her pale brown hair wild beneath her

cockeyed veil, the woman stared at her like she'd grown another head.

"I am Ela, Countess of Salisbury."

"Begging your pardon, my lady," she spoke without a hint of the deference her words might have suggested. "But my husband"—the word emerged with no small amount of spittle— "bedded another woman."

Join the club, thought Ela. Women of the aristocracy didn't expect fidelity beyond their first confinement. She was aware that the local peasant women—to their credit—had more exacting standards for their husbands.

"Is this true?" Ela asked the man, who had raw egg dripping from the end of his nose.

"No, I never!" he protested weakly.

"Then why are you snivelin' because she's dead?" The woman spat her question at him. "You should have seen your face when I told you she was drowned." She turned to Ela. "He's been blubbering like a babby since Widow Crouse told us the little slut was buried this morning."

"Bring them to the castle," Ela said to the guards.

"For what? I didn't do nothin'!" sniveled the man.

"Causing a public disturbance," said Ela stiffly.

"She's causing a public disturbance." He pointed at his wife, who was at least two inches taller than him. "I just came here to sell this cow and buy a few notions."

"Notions!" the wife exclaimed. "Buying her notions for some months now I reckon. Little hussy!"

"You are under arrest," said Ela quietly to the woman. Anger pulsed in her breast, and it was all she could do to retain her calm expression. De Burgh had set her nerves on edge, and she was ready to blow. She couldn't allow some fishwife to rail at her husband in front of her and the guards in full view of the crowd. Two guards took each of the angry woman's arms. She put up a token protest.

"What about my cow?" The man looked at his impassive beast.

"Bring her," said Ela. Another guard took her husband by the arm. He looked like he wanted to protest, then apparently thought better of it. Slimy yellow egg hung in his blonde hair.

Ela hated to return to the castle that she'd just left to get away from de Burgh, but her duty to peace and justice in Salisbury superseded her personal concerns.

They entered the castle, and she instructed a groom to take the cow and bed it in the stables temporarily. She was tempted to buy the beast—which was a likely looking dairy cow with good udders—just to eliminate it as a problem, but she didn't want to be seen haggling with a man who might be a murder suspect in a few moments. The cow could be dealt with later.

Normally she'd have them brought into the hall, but a short spell in the castle's lightless dungeon might make them more biddable—and give de Burgh time to make himself scarce. "Put them down below. I'll talk to them in half an hour."

First she was going to the chapel to resolve another matter.

CHAPTER 8

*I*n the quiet sanctity of the castle's small chapel, Ela pulled out her rosary and said a few decades to clear her mind and invite the Holy Spirit into her heart. Her breathing eased as she murmured the familiar words under her breath.

The burial, a visit by the foul de Burgh, and then having to lay down the law in the marketplace had rattled her. She'd been tempted to yell at the woman to be quiet, which would make her no better than the red-faced harridan and would excite the tongues of all Salisbury.

She needed to remind herself that she was here to represent God's peace on earth, not exert her own authority over all around her. That would be the difference between her and so many other sheriffs, lords, barons and other men in a position of authority.

When in doubt, stop and listen to God's word.

Easier done in a nunnery, to be sure, but she'd have that luxury later on in her life, God willing. She'd pleaded with her husband to heed her advice on many occasions, when his words and actions seemed prompted more by excitement and ire than common sense or piety. She was getting first-hand experience of how challenging it could be to exercise authority and be humble at the same time.

No wonder Richard Poore struggled with arrogance and puffery despite being one of God's bishops.

Ela chastised herself for thinking about the irritating Poore when she'd come in here to cleanse her own mind and heart. It was God's business to judge men like Poore and de Burgh, who were out of her jurisdiction. And indeed God might prefer Poore's grand new cathedral in its quiet and well-watered plain to the old cathedral on the castle mound, buffeted by winds and surrounded by rowdy soldiers.

When she'd quieted her thoughts and strengthened her resolve, she rose from her knees and headed back into the fray. She knew from the burning of the candles that about half an hour had passed, long enough for the coroner and the jurors she'd summoned to arrive, so they could attend when she questioned the unhappy couple downstairs in the castle dungeon.

"The men are waiting in the hall, my lady," said Deschamps, who hovered outside the chapel door. So, he was back. How long had he been standing there?

"Thank you for bringing them here. Have the two prisoners brought up to the hall for questioning." De Burgh and his entourage were nowhere to be seen, thanks be to God.

She sent Sibel to make sure the male prisoner was cleaned of as much egg as possible before entering the hall. She didn't want a spectacle that would make her children titter with laughter. "Isabella, could you take your brothers and sisters outside for a while? Perhaps you can find bluebells to gather." It would be good practice since she'd soon be shepherding her own brood.

Isabella rounded up her younger siblings with a rather sullen expression and headed for the doors with the dogs leaping at their heels. Ela climbed up onto the platform and arranged her skirts in the chair as the guards ushered the man and his wife—redder in the face than ever—in front of her.

"Hold your tongue, woman," hissed the man as they approached.

"I'll hold your tongue, you rogue!"

"Silence!" cried Ela, more shrilly than she would have hoped. "Or I'll have you both clapped in the stocks." She waited for them to be obedient for a moment, then said, "Tell me your names."

"I'm John Brice," the man said so quietly she could barely hear him. "And this is my wife, Lizzie."

Lizzie looked like she wanted to argue, but to Ela's relief she held her tongue.

"Is Katherine Morse the dead woman you spoke of earlier?"

"Aye. Brazen hussy! A married woman." She sucked her tongue in a noise of disgust. The man started to mutter something, but Ela held up her hand to silence him.

"And what makes you suspect your husband was with her?"

"He knew her from when she worked at the dairy. Used to drive our cows there morning and night just to see her."

"I drove the cows there to get them milked," he protested.

"Oh yes? Then how come you had me do it before she turned up there?"

"You were pregnant and needed to rest at home."

"I were pregnant with my fourth child, not half dead!" Her voice rose to a squeal. "While she worked at the dairy he couldn't head there fast enough or return home slow enough. Then when she left to marry, he found other ways to see her."

"What other ways?" Ela wondered how long this woman

had known her husband was committing adultery. And why she hadn't made a hue and cry about it before.

"Fussing over errands to and from the dairy, in hope of running into her while she was there doing her husband's business—bringing the cows in for milking and all—then sneaking off with her and doing only God knows what."

Ela turned to the husband. "Are you the father of Katherine Morse's baby?"

"You son of a she-wolf!" The woman raised her arms as if to beat him, and the man cowered as if expecting to be beaten.

"Silence!" yelled Ela, loud enough to startle the old, half-blind hound by the fire into a volley of barking that reverberated off the high stone walls. "Do not speak unless you are spoken to."

The two jurors gathered behind them, with Deschamps standing off to one side. It was as important to maintain her authority in front of them as with the miserable man and wife in front of her.

"I repeat," she said, daring him to lie to her, "were you the father of Katherine Morse's baby?"

He stood for a second in apparently stunned silence, then started to blubber. "I didn't kill her."

Ela wished she had some eggs to throw at him. "I didn't ask you if you killed her. Did you tup her?" Her crude language cut right to the point.

She watched his Adam's apple bob as he swallowed and fidgeted. He glanced at his wife and flinched. Apparently even her gaze could rain blows on him.

"The Lord is your witness," said Ela, praying to keep her wits about her and not be overwhelmed by exasperation. "He knows and sees all. Will you lie and condemn yourself to eternal damnation?"

She knew plenty of men would and did.

"I did—know Katherine." His face was pale and the words barely audible.

"Know her? You lay with her and—" His wife's voice rose in the air.

"Silence!" Ela's voice cracked. Putting this woman in the stocks grew more tempting with each word that left her mouth. But she knew the pain and shame of learning that your husband stayed with other women and that half the world knew about it before you did.

Ela looked directly at her husband. "When did you last see Katherine Morse?"

"More than a month ago. When I didn't see her at the dairy for a full week, I went to her house looking for her on the pretext of buying a milking stool. But she weren't there and her husband slammed the door in my face."

"Did he know you were the man she—lay with?"

"I don't know. I doubt it. He'd have likely tried to kill me if he did."

Brice was also painting Katherine's husband as a potential killer. Which might be his intention.

"Did Katherine ever tell you her husband beat her?"

"Aye, she did. She sometimes had bruises from where he cuffed her or knocked her to the floor."

Ela felt emotion rise inside her. She regretted not bringing Alan Morse to the castle for questioning and vowed to send guards out to bring him back before dark.

Then she realized that this man in front of her had, if anything, more motive to kill Katie Morse than her husband did. She had been about to give birth to his bastard child, which would cause no end of trouble for him if her husband refused to claim it as his and she wound up on his doorstep seeking money or shelter.

"Did her husband seem concerned about her disappearance?"

"I can't say, as I didn't directly ask about her. She'd told me many times he were a violent man. I just hoped to catch a glimpse of her and satisfy myself he hadn't killed her. I could see from the doorway that there were no sign of a woman's presence in the cottage that day. The fire weren't tended, dirty dishes on the table, the hearth and floor unswept—"

"But he shoved you out of the house? Why would he chase you away if you came there on an innocent errand?" Something about his story didn't add up for her.

"Perhaps he didn't want anyone to know she were gone."

Ela hesitated. If Alan was in fact innocent, and wondering where his straying wife spent her nights, he might be hoping she'd come back and he could save face by not letting on that she ever left.

But if he'd killed her? Might he hope to conceal her absence and pretend she was still alive? That didn't make sense with her being in the river. A man wishing to pretend his wife was still alive would bury her somewhere she'd never be found.

Ela needed time to think. "Do the jurors have questions for this man and this woman?"

"Aye." Thomas Pryce, the thatcher, shuffled forward. He was the oldest of the jurors and his two sons did most of the work on the village roofs these days. "Mistress Brice, you're a strong woman, with a muscled back and arms."

Elizabeth Brice cocked her chin. "Aye, and you would be too, doing three-quarters of the work on the farm as well as raising your children." She shot her husband a dirty look.

"Strong enough, perhaps, to take the life of a young woman who threatened your marriage and family?"

"Never!" She exploded, her face growing bright red. "I never killed no one in my life!"

"Have you ever killed and dressed a sheep or pig or goat?" Thomas Pryce was calm as if he inquired about her laundry.

"Well, aye, of course I have. I'm a farmer's wife. We all have to eat, don't we?"

Thomas Pryce looked at Ela. "It's a possibility worth considering."

Ela nodded. Elizabeth Brice certainly had a temper, and sometimes—or even most times—a murder was the result of a fit of rage. Lizzie Brice was as tall as most men and broader than her own husband. Katie Morse was tall but slight of build and lacking muscle. She probably couldn't have fought off an assault from the older, stronger woman.

She heard a sigh escape her chest. Now she had three suspects, Alan Morse for killing the wife who made him a cuckold, John Brice for killing the girl who threatened his marriage by bearing a child who'd soon be living proof of his infidelity and now Elizabeth Brice, who had motive as much as they did.

Women don't kill with violence. The words echoed in her mind, and she tried to remember where she'd heard them. Her husband, perhaps, while sitting in judgment on a case? She searched her brain and remembered the case of a woman accused of killing her husband over a purse of silver left to her by her father that he'd spent on drink. William had judged that the man was killed by one of the drinking cronies who helped him waste her silver. Women were more inclined to subtle crimes like slipping poison into a man's pottage.

Was de Burgh still somewhere in the castle? He'd committed such a womanly crime against her husband and she imagined for a moment that she might accuse him of such in front of all gathered here.

A flight of fancy. She had to keep her silence and protect her children. And he was nowhere to be seen. Something, at least, to be grateful for.

"More questions?" She knew that each of these jurors had

years of experience considering cases and studying their fellow men and women. They lived among the common people, not in the relatively sheltered enclosure of the castle walls, so they were privy to knowledge of human nature that she couldn't claim.

"Master Brice, did you know Katie Morse was with child?" Giles Haughton asked the question, stepping forward and pinning him with a steady gaze.

Brice hesitated, perhaps wondering how deep in trouble a lie would get him. "Yes." He snuck a glance at his wife, who huffed indignantly.

"And you knew it was your child?"

Brice stared down at the worn toes of his leather boots. "She said it were. I knew she didn't have any children by her husband. But a man never knows for sure, does he?" He raised his eyes and met the coroner's stare.

They'd never know whose baby it was now. The two men looked different enough that a living child might have inadvertently pointed to its true father. Morse was big and burly with dark eyes and graying black hair, whereas Brice was fair, of slender build and had light eyes like Katie.

"How did you come to have an affair with Katherine Morse?" Ela asked the crude question baldly. "How did it start?" She wanted to gain a sense of Brice's character. Right now he seemed the least likely murderer of the three, but appearances were often deceptive.

"Like I said earlier, I drove the cows to the dairy to be milked." He glanced at his wife. "Sometimes my wife would drive them and sometimes I would. Katie always had a kind word and a smile."

"So Katie knew you were married?"

"I don't doubt it, though we never spoke of it. I married young, and I'd been married for eight years by then."

His wife shook her head as if she rued the day. Ela had

a gut feeling that Lizzie Brice had orchestrated their entire marriage from the first glance to the marriage rites. She seemed a far stronger character than her husband.

"I didn't get much in the way of kind words or warm smiles in my home." He spoke quietly, with a sly glance at his wife.

Ela liked him less every minute. If a man wasn't happy with his home life it was his business to fix it, not whine about it in front of the sheriff and jurors.

"I found my heart warming to Katie, and as time went by I looked forward to seeing her."

"Would you say she flirted with you?" cut in Stephen Hale, the cordwainer.

Ela shot Hale a look. She couldn't see how the question was relevant.

"Oh, aye. She acted like she were in love with me. She weren't married at the time, of course."

"And you encouraged her, despite knowing that you were a married man?" Ela spoke sharply.

"To my shame, I did." He had the decency to hang his head a little. Ela wished she'd left the egg on his face. He deserved it.

"When did you first lie with her?" Ela was glad her children hadn't returned to the hall.

"Not that year. Not until about two years later. I wanted to but she didn't. She were looking to catch a husband not a lover."

"So you didn't begin your affair until she was already a married woman?"

"Aye. She didn't work at the dairy anymore, but now, as a farmer's wife, she brought her cows in the morning and evening to milk, much as I did." He hesitated and licked his lips. "And my wife were in confinement and I had opportunity to meet and talk with Katie while our cows were being milked."

His wife's hands knotted into her apron, and if steam could have poured from her ears and billowed her veil out sideways, Ela was sure it would have.

"One day we agreed to meet in a copse between our two farms while her husband was at market and my wife was busy tending to the children. After that we met more often but never very regular. She were unhappy in her marriage. Her husband were rough and cold and—" He glanced at his wife and the look she gave him silenced him.

"Thank you, Master Brice." He was weak, lascivious and ungodly, but that hardly made him a ruthless killer. She could half see what Katie might have seen in him. With his boyish features, soft speech and blonde curls he presented a stark contrast to her brutish husband. "That answers my first question. My next one concerns the last time you saw Katherine Morse."

She stared hard at him, again daring him to fabricate a lie. If he was the killer he'd have last seen her disappearing beneath the cold dark water of the Avon.

"It were some months ago. Before Advent. Once Katie realized she were pregnant she didn't dare risk meeting me. She were afraid her husband would kill her once he found out she were pregnant."

"Did her husband know she was expecting?"

"Not at that time, at least I don't think so, but he was bound to realize sooner or later, wasn't he? Later I wondered if she might have wanted to get pregnant by me since her husband couldn't get her with child."

Ela felt the hairs on the back of her neck prick up. "You think she might have used you just to get with child?"

Brice stared at her. "I thought she were fond of me."

"Do you still think that?" He might have motive for

murder if he were a jealous spurned lover, furious that Katie had left him to go back to being faithful to her husband.

He shrugged. "I think she fancied me. She flirted with me before she was married, after all. If I hadn't been married myself, perhaps things might have been different."

"You swine!" Elizabeth Brice's face was beet red with fury, as well it might be. Ela was half-tempted to clap her straying husband in the stocks to give her the satisfaction of throwing more eggs at him.

But that did not serve the greater cause of finding justice for Katie Morse.

"Silence," Ela commanded. "John Brice, your behavior was reprehensible, as I'm sure you're aware. Your first duty is to your wife and family."

He had the decency to hang his head slightly. Ela couldn't picture this milksop killing anyone, but she knew that almost anyone could kill under the right circumstances. If only she understood the circumstances of Katie's death. She'd sustained a blow to the head, that was sure, but where, when and how?

The pressing question now was whether to detain the couple, or either one of them, in the dungeon or to let them go. Since Brice was a yeoman farmer with land and a herd of cattle to tend he was hardly likely to abscond. His wife had children to care for and was more likely to box his ears and burn his dinner than head for the hills.

Ela had learned much today—that John Brice was the guilty party in Katie's affair and the father of her child—but she needed more time to piece this ill-fitting puzzle together.

"Unless any others gathered here feel that this pair need further questioning, I propose that they return home until such time as we need to speak to them again."

"I need compensation for wasting half the day when I came here to sell my cow." John Brice's high-pitched voice grated on Ela's nerves. "There's no time to sell it now before I must be back for milking."

"Consider yourself lucky that you aren't spending the night in the dungeon for causing a disturbance of the peace." She looked at his wife. "And that goes for both of you. Who's caring for your children?"

"My mother," muttered Lizzie Brice. "She told me to marry him because he had a farm and made a living. She didn't notice that he has all the character of a parsnip."

Ela reflected that a well-seasoned parsnip might take this as an insult, but decided not to dignify her with a response. She looked at Haughton and the jurors to see if they had further questions. Taking their silence as nay, she ordered the guards to escort the couple and their cow outside the walls forthwith.

She needed to talk to Morse again to determine how much he knew about Katie's affair. And to figure out how likely he would be to take revenge on her with his fists.

CHAPTER 9

*E*la spent part of the afternoon in the small room where the castle ledgers were kept safe, along with her stores of vellum and ink and sealing wax, from the depredations of mice and pilferers.

Logs detailing the castle's expenses for food, wages, repairs, etc., were compiled by stewards responsible for ordering supplies and paying wages. For some years now, Ela had taken on the responsibility of comparing the compiled expenses from week to week, month to month and year to year. If she saw signs of waste or worse she was quick to take action. The same was true for her various manors, though their incomes and expenditures were far more modest. Now that she intended to take on the sheriff's duties, Ela reasoned that it would make sense to charge someone else with studying the numbers and providing her with summarized reports.

But the prospect of relinquishing even a little control of the castle's expenditures worried her. Given the vast quantities of—oh, everything—they consumed within these ancient stone walls, there was room for a small leak, a tiny trail of profligacies, to turn into a flood that could drain their fortunes quite rapidly.

She trusted their loyal cook to correctly note down the hundreds of fishes, fowls and sides of bacon, the thousands of eggs, the endless churns of butter and bushels of spices, that passed through her chapped hands, but if there was an intermediary, or two, or three, in between her records and the cook's purchases, would hogs and eggs and flagons of wine start disappearing into the pantries of her staff and their families?

Ela stretched her shoulders, trying to ease the tension building in them. She'd bitten off more than she could chew. Of that there was no doubt.

Her husband would have shrugged his shoulders at such cares. He'd no doubt have calculated the failings of human nature into his household budget like a steady tax. But that was why she'd always managed the accounts, even dismissing two different stewards he'd hired to relieve her during her pregnancies.

You don't trust anyone. He'd chastised her—smiling—on more than one occasion.

I trust the mind God gave me, she'd retorted, also smiling.

Her husband was raised to be a great man. Although he wasn't King Henry's legitimate heir, he'd been raised to wield a sword, win at tournament, command a company of men and shower himself with glory at any opportunity that might present itself. Fussing over quantities of eggs or flour were not in his training.

As a girl, Ela had been raised to run a great household. Her mother was known to give as much attention to the quality of the salt and wine in her cellars as to the wool and furs that clothed her and her husband.

She'd also been trained from birth to delegate responsibilities. She'd never cooked herself a meal, let alone raised and tended the animals or vegetables that graced their table. She'd never swept her own floor or emptied the ashes from the hearth or polished the cups and plates or scrubbed the linen tablecloths. She rarely even pinned her own wimple.

She trusted others to perform those small but important tasks. She really must learn to delegate more responsibilities so her ship didn't founder under its own weight. She must also get ready to handle incoming waves like unexpected taxes and fees from the king and his accursed justiciar, or—God forbid—the loss of one of their wards' generous incomes.

"Ela, darling, are you locked up in here like a pantry mouse?" She heard her mother's voice accompany a rap on the door.

Ela had locked the door from the inside. She guarded these ledgers like the family treasure. She rose and turned the old iron key in the lock. Her mother stood outside with a bright smile and a cup of warm spiced wine, which she offered to Ela.

"Come in, Mama," she said with a sigh. There were two stools. "Do sit down." She locked the door again. "How did you know I was here?"

"Petronella. Your sweet daughter said you spend many hours in here. Were you on your knees in prayer?" There was a hint of mockery in her tone.

"Only if I were praying to the gods of mammon. You taught me well, Mother. I cannot let fifty head of grouse go unrecorded, even if my own son shot them."

"Quite right, too, my dear. Servants are born pilferers. You must watch them out of the corner of your eye at all times."

"But I need to keep my eyes on more important things, like who murdered one of my villagers."

"What about Will?"

"Will doesn't have a head for figures. He finds details dull. If he were in charge of the castle cellars we'd kill the fatted calf every night."

Her mother laughed. "No, my foolish daughter. I meant you should put Will in charge of the murder investigation. As sheriff." She indicated that Ela should sip her wine. Ela put the cup down on the scarred wood table at a safe distance from her ledgers.

"Will is no more suited to be sheriff at this tender age than he is to monitor the dozens of eggs passing through these halls. The course of justice is—as I am learning—a slow and ponderous journey down lots of unlikely dead-end lanes. The pursuit of truth requires patience more than courage. Young Will would likely gallop to conclusions and hang the wrong man in his rush to victory."

"You do have a point." Alianore tented her hands under her chin. Her wimple was pulled tight, as always, to show off her still-youthful jawline. "What about young Richard?"

"He's only twelve!"

"But with the mind and demeanor of a man of fifty and twelve. He could tot up your bushels of oats and kegs of ale."

Ela stared at her. "I want to say that this is the craziest idea I've ever heard—" She frowned. "But he is scrupulous."

"And honest to a fault. If he tattles on your servants the way he does on his sisters, not a penny will slip through your fingers."

"But still, he's only twelve…" She pressed a finger to her mouth, thinking. "Perhaps I could hire a steward and ask him to train him in the management of the household funds. I could tell him I intend for Richard to one day manage the king's privy purse."

"That way he can oversee the steward, while your steward

thinks he's overseeing young Richard." Her mother smiled, showing dimples.

"Did I ever tell you that you're a genius?"

"Not often enough, my dear. Not often enough." Her mother rose to her feet. "Did you open your gift from the king?"

"Yes. It was a chest full of furs and rich fabrics. Very kind of him."

"Perfect to make some new clothes for my grandchildren's weddings."

"Indeed. I want to get Will and Isabella married to our wards as soon as possible." She didn't tell her mother that William's will had designated the wards' incomes to pay his debts. Or that she had a legitimate fear that Hubert de Burgh might decide he wanted to marry those fortunes into his own family.

Her mother didn't blink. "I've already started drawing up an invitation list. Who should be married first, Will and Idonea or Isabella and de Vesci?"

Ela had pondered the same. "Would a double wedding be out of the question?"

Her mother pursed her lips. "I see the enticement of one expensive wedding celebration to secure two fortunes. If their families will agree, why not? We must just make sure that no mortal enemies need to be invited under our roof at the same time."

Ela sighed. "It seems every baron in the kingdom has been mortal enemies of every other baron at some point or other in the last twenty years. Surely they can exchange pleasantries for a few hours."

"The way your William did with Hubert de Burgh right before he died?" Her mother looked at her steadily.

Ela froze. She hadn't shared her suspicions with her

mother and never wanted to. She'd never even told her about the proposal. "What do you mean?"

"I just thought it was so magnanimous of him. When they were on opposite sides during the struggle for power between Louis and King John ten years ago."

"Oh. Yes. True. Well, you know William wasn't one to hold a grudge." She'd forgotten all about that. William could pin someone to the ground at the end of his sword one day and clap a hand around his back the next.

He was too trusting, too brave, too big-hearted, for this cold, cruel world.

"Ela, when was the last time you had that hall floor scrubbed?"

"Uh, never. Why would I? Old and dirty rushes are removed and fresh ones installed weekly."

Her mother sighed. "So like your father! You are as happy to live with the detritus of former banquets as well as earlier generations. At least once a year you should remove all the rushes and have the bare floor scrubbed until it shines. You'll be surprised how it improves the air."

Ela suppressed a sigh. Her mother always had house-keeping suggestions, as if Ela weren't a thirty-nine-year-old mother of eight herself.

And frankly, removing a dead body from your keep did wonders for the air as well.

"Or perhaps you're worried you'll find more dead bodies to burden you with investigations under the straw." Her mother peered over the rim of her wine cup.

"I suspect the dogs would have found anything that exciting by now. But I see the good sense in what you're saying and no doubt the removed rushes would be an excellent mulch for my spring herb garden."

"You're not still growing all those strange plants yourself, are you?"

"Indeed I am." Ela felt her neck stiffen again. "The village apothecaries have all the usual old-fashioned remedies, but there are many that they don't have. If you were to read the Trotula, like I keep suggesting, you'd be aware that they are many efficacious remedies that—"

Alianore waved her hand dismissively. "A lot of foreign rubbish. I don't want to accidentally poison my household with tinctures made from unfamiliar herbs. Do you test them on yourself first? Or do you have a sacrificial taster?" She lifted a plucked brow.

"I don't have a green thumb myself, so my gardener plants the seeds I buy from abroad and tends them for me. His good wife has kindly prepared many potions and pastes from them, which she tests herself."

"On your household staff?"

"Sometimes." Ela had not fully considered the implications of this. Usually a turned stomach or contact rash was the worst someone might suffer from a new herb.

"Did you try any new herbs on your husband as he lay ill?"

"No!" Ela rose to her feet, knocking the ledger and almost spilling her wine, which had crept closer as she sipped it. "I mean, yes, I tried various remedies to ease his suffering, but I didn't kill him with my medicines."

"Rest easy, my dear! I didn't mean to accuse you of murder. Perhaps I've rubbed a sore spot."

"I refuse to close my mind to fresh funds of knowledge, even if they come from the Saracens themselves." Ela hated how closed-minded even educated people could be when it came to new ideas and discoveries. Sometimes she felt that if a concept wasn't mentioned in the pages of the Bible she was supposed to ignore it as if it didn't exist.

Her mother crossed herself as if her soul shuddered at the prospect of Saracen ideas crossing her threshold. "Tread carefully, Ela. As a woman without a protector you must be wary of seeming...odd."

"And wary of using my brain and the powers God gave me as well, I suppose. I should sit by the hearth embroidering handkerchiefs while my children tug at my hem."

"Now, Ela, who taught you to read in both French and Latin before the age of ten?"

"You did. But surely you didn't mean for me to squander that knowledge entirely on romantic verse?"

"I never read you a word of that foolishness. Imagine a true knight spending his days pining for a woman who's married to another man? I intended for you to read the Psalms, not some mystical nonsense from Siena or some such place."

"Salerno. And the Trotula's wisdom is practical medicine, not mysticism, mother. I don't know why you won't at least read the first book before pronouncing judgment. There's such useful advice on managing childbirth and—"

"I've managed to attain this advanced age without reading it and I intend to continue my life in a similar fashion." Her mother rose to her feet—why did she always appear at least six inches taller than her actual height?—and swept out her skirts. "And I suggest you spend at least a few moments embroidering at your hearth and communing with your children before vespers."

"To avoid appearing odd."

"You are no more odd than your father, God rest his soul, though it certainly does look odder in a woman." Alianore leaned forward and kissed Ela awkwardly on her forehead. "I am proud of you, my dear."

Ela's heart fluttered with a mixture of confused emotions. "Thank you, Mama. I think."

She could send Haughton and two of the jurors out to interview Morse again. She could instruct them to report back to her in detail and if necessary bring him in for questioning.

But did she trust them to ask the right questions? To seek the truth even where it wasn't convenient or easy to find? To find justice for Katherine Morse, who was now conveniently buried beneath the thawed ground and could easily be forgotten?

CHAPTER 10

The next day, Ela set out with Will, Giles Haughton and two guards to visit Morse again. He was still the most likely killer, with the motive of wanting revenge on his wife for making him a cuckold. Now they knew who his wife had been sneaking out with, Ela intended to dangle the information in his face and watch his reaction.

Haughton was wary of telling him the identity of his wife's lover for fear of further repercussions, but Ela observed that half of Salisbury knew it already after the performance Brice and his wife had put on in the market-place. Morse was bound to find out sooner or later—if he didn't know already—and she wanted to take advantage of the element of surprise.

Besides, it seemed likely they would bring Morse into custody so he wouldn't be able to kill anyone else.

The day was bright and breezy, with sunlight illuminating clutches of bluebells in the woods and along the shady paths. Hopeful buds swelled on the bare tree branches. Birdsong filled the hedgerows and the world felt heavy with the promise of spring.

Will led the ride at his usual just-short-of-breakneck pace and Ela didn't complain, but let Freya gallop after his mount, mane flying and nostrils flaring. The assizes were due in Salisbury as soon as the traveling justice was available, and they'd be ready to bring Katie's killer to trial. Her responsibilities were to make sure the right person was tried in the first place and that justice was served as swiftly and effectively as possible.

Right now she felt proud of their accomplishments, since in just a few days they'd gone from finding an unidentified corpse to piecing together a picture of her last months. Now all they had to do was figure out who she'd been with on that final, fatal day. Most likely her husband.

Will pulled up his horse as they drew near Morse's fields. Face flushed with exertion, he turned to her. "So we're trying to exact a confession from him, right?"

"We're here to find the truth, though a confession would be ideal. Brice, the man his wife was having an affair with, is also a suspect, though in my view he has less motive. We're here to press Morse harder and see if he cracks. Or if some evidence arises that proves him innocent. We must keep an open mind." She said the latter as much for Haughton, who trotted up, panting and sweating, behind her.

They rode up to Morse's door. It was nearly midmorning so his cows should be milked and back in his fields by now. But they weren't. His bull was there alone in one field, but the other more well-trodden pasture lay empty. "We'll ride to the dairy." She gestured for them to follow her along the lane, which bore fresh hoofprints in its deep mud.

But, as she suspected, the milking parlor was empty except for a few piles of fresh dung and the dairymaids and their master were busy churning milk into butter in the dairy. The dairy's owner approached her and bowed. "Good morrow, my lady."

He didn't look surprised to see her entourage. No doubt the girls had filled him in on the local gossip.

"Good morrow, Master Nance." Ela put a lot of effort into remembering names. Her father had schooled her in the necessity at a very young age. "We seek Alan Morse."

"Ah. A sad business. It appears to involve two of my best customers. I do hope for my own business that neither of them is the murderer."

"That will be determined by the judge, when the suspect is brought to trial." She didn't like the idea that Nance felt he had a stake in the outcome. And his attitude was a little too familiar. "Do you know where I might find Master Morse?"

"I suspect he's out on his patch of common grazing." He jerked his thumb down the road, in the direction opposite from the way they'd come, toward the damp water meadows. "His own grazing's nigh eaten to bare earth."

"Thank you, Master Nance. God go with you." She turned her horse to preempt any more familiar chit chat on his part. Riding down by the water meadows would take them almost half the way home by a different route, which would be good except that she also intended to visit the Widow Nettles that the girls had mentioned on her last visit to the dairy. Perhaps they could drop in on her first, since Morse was hardly likely to abscond while his cattle grazed abroad.

"Annie, could you point me the way to Widow Nettles's house?"

"Aye." Annie pointed down a track that led into a small knot of woods. "She's down that lane a quarter mile." The girl's eyes widened. "Is she a suspect, too?"

"Oh, no." Ela laughed. "I wish to visit her and see if she has any unmet needs."

"Oh." Annie looked relieved. "She's always in need of firewood."

"Thank you." Ela made a mental note to send her a cart-load of wood when the road hardened. She didn't mind Annie talking to her with a degree of familiarity. Why was that? "Good day to you, girls."

"Thank you, my lady." She and Mary both bobbed and bowed their heads politely. Probably the difference between them and Nance is that they seemed genuinely concerned and helpful, whereas there was something…sneering about their master.

Because she was a female sheriff? Or was she being too sensitive?

She shook off her petty concerns. "Will, please lead the way to Widow Nettles's house so we can make her acquaintance."

They trotted down the narrow lane until it became so overgrown that they were obliged to walk and bow their heads, then finally to dismount to pass under the low branches intertwined over the ancient track. A tiny cottage with a steep thatched roof rose out of the forest floor in front of them as the track tapered to an end.

Ela resolved to tell the cart bringing the wood to unload it at the top of the lane and carry it down here because there was no room for a cart to turn around. Or better yet she could send a team of woodsmen to open up the thick growth around the widow's house and turn the burden of brush into wood and kindling for her hearth and space for her garden.

Ela dismounted and handed her reins to a guard. Then she approached the door and knocked. She felt oddly apprehensive as she waited. The wood of the door was black with age and as lichen-covered as the nearby treetrunks.

"Who is it?" A tiny voice called from within. No doubt the old lady was terrified by the sound of strangers at her door.

"'Tis Ela of Salisbury come to visit you." Ela tried to sound friendly and reassuring. "And to see how well you fare."

"Not very well," the voice squeaked. "Not very well at all." Ela heard the sound of feet shuffling across the floor and stiffened with anticipation as the door shifted on its rusty hinges and began, reluctantly, to scrape open across the hard ground.

Two rheumy eyes peered up at her from the darkness inside. The door was still only cracked open a few inches. "What can I do for you?" Widow Nettles looked impossibly old, her face as wizened and creased as the bark of an oak. "It's all I can do to rise from my chair." Ela tried to peer past her into the pitch-dark interior of the windowless cottage but could see nothing.

"You have no fire?"

"Not today." Widow Nettles stared at her. How much she could see through the pale film that covered her eyeballs? At least she had more sight than Katherine Morse's poor blind father. Loss of sight was a terrible affliction of old age. She wondered how long ago this poor widow lost her husband, and if she still felt his loss keenly.

Ela knew she was so blessed to be left with the means to provide for her family after her husband's death. So many women were forced into remarriage or a demeaning job to avoid starvation. Poor widow Nettles was too old to have either of those options left to her. Ela's heart hurt at the realization that this poor woman must have no children left alive to care for her. "Are you lacking wood to build a fire?"

"Aye. As you can see I'm surrounded by it but no longer have the means to cut it."

"Do you have an axe?"

"I do. It's around the back."

Ela looked at Will, who left the reins of his horse on its neck and squeezed around the side of the house, past the brush encroaching right up to the walls.

"What sustains you, mistress?" asked Ela, half-suspecting she lived on acorns and water drunk from cupped leaves.

"The girls from the dairy bring me whey, and Master Nance sends food as well. He's my great-grandnephew."

"I am glad that you are taken care of in that way. Do you get lonely out here all by yourself?" How sad it must be to live long enough for your closest loved ones to have died.

"Nay."

Ela waited for more, but Widow Nettles didn't seem keen to expand. Maybe she worried that Ela would try to pry her out of her home and settle her in an almshouse in the new town. Some people were strangely resistant to the prospect of comfortable new housing that wasn't their own home. Her mother would tease her that she was the same way, preferring the windy castle mound to one of her comfortable manors.

Will returned with the rustiest axe she'd ever seen. He handed it to one of the guards who had already pulled a whetstone from his saddlebag and used it to hone the dull blade. Her son then set to the branches of a gnarled hawthorn starting to crowd the door.

Ela was proud of him for knowing how to do a task that might well be left to servants. Bill Talbot, his tutor in the knightly arts, had insisted that a man must be able to survive in foreign territory and had taught him well. Will chopped the branches into usable-size pieces and set on the next bush.

Many of the branches were dead and already good for a fire. "Would you like me to send a woodcutter to clear the area around your house and stack it for you?"

"That would be too dear. I have nothing to pay."

"It would be a donation in memory of my late husband."

Widow Nettles hesitated. Perhaps she was afraid of being tricked into something or out of her home. If she'd lived long enough someone had probably tried to do that before. "No obligations or recompense due. My husband was always concerned for the welfare of the parish elders."

"If it pleases you." She didn't sound too happy about it. No good deed goes unpunished. That was one of Alianore's favorite phrases.

"Indeed it does please me," Ela tried to sound warm. "I'll have someone come within the week. Is there anything else you need, Widow Nettles?"

The old woman was silent for a moment, and Ela had time to take in the ragged state of her tunic and her old shoes worn almost to vellum thinness. She resolved to send a warm cloak and new shoes along with the woodcutter.

"There is one thing." The woman's tiny voice rose higher, sounding eerie in the quiet of this wooded hollow.

"What's that?" Ela's ears pricked, imagining what she might request. New thatch for her roof? A new broom to sweep her bare floor?

"I'd like a cat. My old cat died a year ago, and the mice are swarming."

"You shall have one." Ela was delighted that her request was so easily fulfilled. Of course, cats weren't as biddable as dogs and were liable to disappear unexpectedly, but the widow's supply of fresh whey was a good enticement, especially if accompanied by a warm hearth. "In fact, one of our cats at the castle had kittens just after Epiphany. They're ready to leave their mother. I'll make sure one is brought to you."

The old woman's thin, dried lips creased into a tiny smile. "The Lord's blessings be with you, my lady."

"And with you, Widow Nettles." Will, who had been hewing away at the bushes, leaned the axe, handle up, against the side of the cottage, and retook his horse. "Good day to you."

Ela rode off, feeling pleased to have brought a little

succor to the elderly widow, if only in the form of promises. They traveled back under the sinister canopy of gnarled branches, then remounted their horses and rejoined the road that led to the water meadows.

Dark clouds gathered above the trees, threatening rain, as they topped a rise and looked down to see Morse's cows scattered across the grassy plain below. "Perhaps you can reveal our news to him, Master Haughton."

"What news is that, my lady?"

"The news that his wife lay with John Brice."

Haughton shifted in his saddle "That's not news a man is like to take kindly."

"He may well know it already."

"I doubt it. Not many will want to tell a man who his wife was tupping."

Ela felt a nasty sensation crawl up her spine. Did he think she was cowardly in pushing the task onto him. Was she? It was surely something a man might take better coming from another man. "Are you afraid to tell him, Master Haughton?"

"Of course not." He looked affronted. "As long as you're sure it's for the best."

"Do you propose that we keep it a secret?" She was growing impatient. Surely Morse could see them watching him from the brow of the hill.

Haughton glanced at the guards. Ela wondered what thoughts were passing through his mind.

They rode down the long, shallow hillside toward Morse's herd of cattle. Morse himself had spotted them and stood staring at them. She could swear she could feel daggers borne on his gaze pricking her skin.

"Good day to you, Master Morse."

"Ye rode a long way to find me."

"Not so far." Ela turned her horse to allow Haughton to come to the front. She hoped Will would keep his mouth shut as she'd gently schooled him before they'd left. He didn't have the experience and wisdom to say the right thing under difficult circumstances.

Haughton halted his horse close to Morse, who peered at him with a mixture of curiosity and insolence. He seemed over-confident for a man still under suspicion of murdering his wife.

"Are you familiar with John Brice?" asked Haughton, his voice low.

"Owns the farm next to mine but one. Be odd if I didn't know him, wouldn't you think?"

"We believe he's the man your wife was visiting."

Morse's whole face darkened. "What're you trying to say?"

"You said your wife might be pregnant by another man."

"Did I?" He sounded confrontational.

"Well, that was the conclusion that we, ah—" Haughton glanced back at Ela, who remained impassive. She knew it would only make things worse if she took control at this moment. "It seems that Brice is the likely father of your wife's child."

The suggestion did sound terrible spoken aloud in the bright midday air.

"Says who?" The words exploded out of Morse in a rush of air.

"Brice's wife accused him of adultery in public yesterday."

Ela couldn't understand why it had taken so long for Elizabeth Brice to explode in rage over his cheating. Why now?

"And John Brice named my wife as his—partner in crime?" Morse looked suitably appalled.

"No, not in public. But later, when we interviewed him in the castle."

Morse looked from Haughton to Ela and then to the rest of the group. "Why are you telling me this?"

Haughton looked at Ela, who rode her horse forward a couple of steps. "We seek your wife's murderer. Do you not think Brice might be a suspect?" That wasn't her reason for telling him, entirely, but it was a good enough excuse.

"You think he killed her?" Now he looked interested. Of course, if Morse himself was guilty, he would leap on the idea of an alternative suspect.

"It's a possibility." Ela fixed her gaze on him. "He seemed upset that she'd broken off with him almost as soon as she learned she was pregnant." She waited for a second, watching his response. "He seemed to think that perhaps you and your wife had planned for her to lay with him so that she could become pregnant and give you a baby."

Morse's face betrayed nothing but astonishment at first, but it morphed into anger as she watched. "You think I would encourage my wife to break her vows in another man's bed?" His voice was deep and carried more than the hint of a threat.

"It would be quite understandable, if you were worried that you might never have an heir."

Morse laughed, then spat on the ground, which made Ela flinch in her saddle. "I'm not the lord of the manor, worried who I'm going to leave my great estate to."

"But every man wants a child to look after him in his old age."

"Not Katie's father! That old cuss don't want no one near him."

"Perhaps he's just proud. Losing one's sight can be humbling to a man."

"So can having his wife's sexual misdeeds broadcast before all of Salisbury." Morse's face was now bright red. "Are you going to arrest me for murder? Because if not I need to drive my cows back home."

Ela glanced at Haughton, who resembled a stone effigy. Ela cleared her throat. "Who do you think killed your wife?"

"John Brice, I suppose. I don't know who else could have done it." He spat the words at her. "Who would want to kill Katie?"

"Except her angry cuckolded husband?" suggested Ela boldly. She'd come here to gauge his reaction, after all. "Who didn't come forward with the information that she was missing." That alone should banish the idea that he and his wife had plotted to use Brice as a breeding boar. "Why didn't you raise the hue and cry?"

"I thought she ran off with her lover."

"But if her lover was just down the lane you'd have still seen her every day."

Morse's eyes narrowed. "I didn't know it was him. Miserable milksop that he is." She watched him closely for signs of rage—tightening fists, lips whitening with fury—but saw none. Odd.

Disappointment spurred her to probe deeper for a reaction. "Did you beat your wife, Master Morse?" The question came out rather shriller than she'd intended.

He looked at her like she was demented. "Only when I had to." His eyes narrowed, and he apparently realized the implication. "But I never hurt her. Why would I injure or kill the woman who cooks my meals and drives my cows for me? If I were going to kill anyone, I'd kill John Brice, wouldn't I?" He shook his head as if unable to believe her idiocy.

Ela's heart ached for poor Katie Morse. It was easy to see why she'd seek a few moments of escape in another man's arms, even a man as insubstantial as John Brice. At least he might be tender. And Katie was a young woman, no doubt with desires that her impotent and hard-hearted husband could never satisfy.

Her husband had motive to kill her for cheating and

becoming pregnant by another man. But would he kill his cook and chambermaid and cowherd and only companion?

And he seemed to have very little emotion about her death or her adultery.

None of this made sense.

Ela drew in a steadying breath. Morse was already whistling commands to his dog and beginning to gather up the cattle scattered across the large meadow.

Should they arrest him? Part of her wanted to, but they had no more evidence of his guilt now than they had before. Will's expression gave her pause. She wanted to ask what he was thinking, but if he expressed a strong opinion she didn't want to feel obliged to act on it or offend his youthful pride. Safer to find out later when he expressed it in private.

Morse turned to glower at her, and Ela shuddered. This was a violent man who beat his wife. Perhaps he'd like to lay his hands on her right now if she weren't guarded by armed men. But he turned and strode away, driving his cows back toward the footpath.

We should arrest him and bring him into custody. But then who would take his cows home and tend to them in his absence? She could have them brought to one of her manors, where she might face whispered accusations of stealing them. The situation was a complex one.

She glanced at Haughton, who now had a troubled look on his face. "Your thoughts?"

"It's a bad business, my lady. He's liable to take revenge."

"On me?"

For a moment Haughton looked dumbfounded. "On John Brice. He'd be within his rights, by the ancient laws."

"What laws are these?"

"The laws in the Bible."

Ela frowned. She didn't remember any passages that sanctioned a man taking another man's life for adultery, but then she was no biblical scholar. She had read enough to know that in those days the woman might well have been stoned to death for her transgressions. She shivered almost as if the dead woman's ghost had laid a hand on her.

Who killed you, Katie?

There was an old woman in the village who claimed she could talk to spirits, but naturally such dabbling in the spirit world was frowned upon by the church. Ela had no desire to run afoul of the ecclesiastical authorities or endanger her own soul.

"Should we arrest him?" One of the guards, a dark, stocky man with a northern accent, spoke up quite loud.

Ela frowned. "I think we should let him drive his cows home." She had no further proof that he was Katie's killer, and she could hardly imagine he'd rush out and strike one of his nearest neighbors dead. Everyone would immediately suspect him, for one thing. "And return to the castle."

CHAPTER 11

"Why didn't you arrest him?" Will accosted her as soon as they rode out of earshot.

"We have no proof that he killed her. It's a grave responsibility to lock a man up in the dungeons, remove his cattle and let his unmanned farm run to ruin."

"You're too soft, Mother. He's a brute beast. A man can see that from looking in his eyes."

"We deal in facts and reason, my son, not gut feelings. His wife was his only helpmate. Killing her would be like cutting off his right arm."

"The facts point to him. Everyone says he beat her. You know as well as I do that a man will cut off his own arm if he's in enough of a passion."

Ela raised a brow. "Name one man who's cut off his own arm." She didn't like Will arguing with her in front of the other men.

"If she was so important to him, why didn't he report her missing?" asked Will.

"Young Will is right," murmured Haughton, riding closer. "Morse is dangerous."

"To who? His wife is dead. Brice already knows to watch his back."

She heard a harrumph of discontent behind her. It stirred some misgivings. Why didn't she arrest him? She set out here with that intention lodged firmly in her mind. But something inside her, something intangible, told her that he wasn't his wife's murderer. And if she didn't trust herself, who could she trust?

* * *

Back at the castle, she devoted the afternoon to spending time with her family and was drawn into an intense game of chess with her mother's husband, Jean. She won the game, and Jean was a good enough sport to be beaten by a woman without sulking all night.

They'd all just eaten their evening meal and Will was loudly wishing for the end of Lent and imagining the roasts and stews they would enjoy—while Petronella and Richard scolded him for impiety—when the hall door flung open on a blast of cold evening air that guttered the fire.

Deschamps strode into the hall, brows lowered. "A word with you, my lady." Ela rose and walked away from the table. Deschamps ushered her out of the great hall and into the passage that led to the armory.

Ela's heart pounded as he closed the heavy wood door behind him.

"Brice is dead." She thought she heard a note of triumph in his voice. She must be mistaken.

"How? When?"

"His wife came back from the dairy with the cows this evening and found him murdered by their hearth."

"Where is she?"

"She's at Widow Lester's being treated with medicinal herbs. She managed to reach the town to raise the hue and cry, then had a fit of fainting."

"I must go to her at once. Send the guards to arrest Morse and bring him to the dungeon."

"I already did. Giles Haughton went with them." Again, that disconcerting suggestion of victory.

Deschamps and her coroner had discussed the situation and formed a plan without consulting her? Fury tightened her chest. She wanted to scold him, but now was not the time for a fight. She had a new murder hanging over her head, one for which she might bear some blame.

"I shall attend the scene and examine the body with Master Haughton in the morning."

"That won't be necessary. I've already sent bearers to bring the body to the castle mortuary."

Ela fought the urge to growl with exasperation. "You should have spoken to me first before disturbing the scene. Did the coroner not ask to keep it intact?"

Deschamps blinked, and she thought she saw some of the arrogance slip from his bearing. "My apologies."

Ela asked Sibel to come with her to Widow Lester's, along with two guards for security. Deschamps stayed behind to wait for Morse to arrive in custody.

* * *

The journey to Widow Lester's house was a short walk through the streets inside the fortified walls, but the moonless night teemed with unspoken threats. Burning braziers lit the walls around the castle, throwing moving shadows in their path. Soldiers from the garrison lolled here and there, some at their posts and some just passing the time. Once they realized who she was they hushed and stood straight to show respect, which was something.

Ela cursed herself for not arresting Morse. Why had she trusted her own instincts over the wisdom of experience and the concerned words of those around her? Was her anxiety about maintaining control of every situation interfering with the pursuit of justice?

And now another murder. A crime committed on her own watch.

They hurried through the narrow passages, beneath the overhanging upper stories. Candles burned in some windows, the light from fires in others. The dark streets were empty save those sauntering to and from a nearby tavern and the occasional tradesman hurrying home late from his labors.

Widow Lester's neat cottage was the first place Ela turned to for common tinctures, ointments and herbal preparations. She could see a light through the small windows that pierced the whitewashed surface. She knocked on the bare wood door, bracing herself for the scene she might find. A girl of about fourteen opened the door and let Ela into the small room where shelves filled with clay jars of spices and leaves and twigs rose from the floor almost to the low ceiling.

Elizabeth Brice sat at the scrubbed table in the center of the room, face angled downward. Her tunic had a dark stain on the front on it, which might be blood but the room was too dark for Ela to see. At the fire, Widow Lester lifted a kettle from the crane and poured hot water into a cup wrapped in a cloth.

No one looked up at Ela or even registered her presence.

"Mistress Brice, it's Ela Longespée. Do you remember me?"

Elizabeth Brice looked up at her. The firelight gleamed in her eyes as she stared at Ela. "I'd hardly be likely to forget the woman that imprisoned me in the dungeon of her castle." Her face looked craggier and older than Ela remembered, but it could be the light.

"Can you tell me what happened?"

Her eyelids fluttered, and she looked like she was about to

faint again. Widow Lester rushed over with her steaming cup and lifted it to Elizabeth's lips. "Here, sip this, it'll fortify you."

Ela watched as she sipped the hot liquid. That dark stain was likely blood. But how did she get it on her? "Did you witness what happened?"

"No." She spat the word at Ela. "I came home from taking the cows for milking and found him there dead! Blood all over the floor." She stopped and made a hiccupping sound, then an odd keening noise emerged from the back of her throat. She tried to go on, but hiccups came out instead of words.

Ella felt her gut clench. Poor Elizabeth Brice. She'd been so angry with her husband only the day before, and now she was devastated by his death. She could sympathize. Her husband had infuriated her on many occasions, but they meant nothing now he was gone forever. "I'm sorry for your great loss."

"It's your fault!" Brice hissed the words so hard that her spittle rained on Ela's hands. "You told Morse that my husband lay with his wife. Did you not know this would happen?"

Ela froze. "How did you know I told Morse?"

"Giles Haughton told me. He came out as soon as I made it to town to raise the hue and cry. I almost lost my way coming across the fields in the dark, but I couldn't stay there until morning, not with his dead eyes staring up at me!"

Ela was at a loss for words. She could hardly believe that Morse would commit this crime when anyone for miles around would instantly suspect him. "I wanted to see what Morse would say or do when I told him about his wife's infidelity. I'm still trying to learn if he killed his wife or not."

"What did he say?" Mistress Brice tilted her head and peered up at Ela with oddly glittering eyes. Her hair had escaped her twisted veil and her voice had a croaky rasp to it. "Was he happy at the news? You already had reason to suspect he was a killer, so you just gave him motive to kill again and rode merrily away?"

Ela inhaled slowly. If Morse responded to her news by committing a violent murder, then it certainly implied guilt in the earlier murder. And made her seem foolishly ill-prepared for the consequences of this morning's visit.

She'd have to make sure Mistress Brice—Widow Brice she would be now—was properly compensated for her loss. Perhaps a jury would decide to grant her Morse's farm and cattle. Morse didn't have any heirs that they knew of and—

Ela realized that Widow Lester was talking to her. The widow wasn't all that old, but she was tiny and had a soft voice that could strain the hearing. "I'm sorry, could you repeat that?"

"Chamomile and valerian root for shock," she said in her silvery tones. "Will you have some yourself?" She offered Ela a clay cup of the liquid.

Ela's throat closed at the prospect. "No, thank you, though I appreciate the offer. God bless you for your kind-ness to Mistress Brice. I shall cover all costs incurred." She turned her attention to the distraught woman. "Soldiers are on their way to arrest Morse. Rest assured that he will hang for this."

Ela supposed it didn't much matter now if she could produce evidence that he'd killed his wife.

"If you'd arrested him sooner my husband would still be alive." Brice's words came out on another keening howl. Widow Lester patted her shoulder and urged her to drink more of the soothing brew.

Ela had brought Sibel along with the intention that she could offer a bed, fresh linens, and succor at the castle. But in Elizabeth Brice's current state of rage that did not seem like a good idea. Ela didn't want the new widow ranting and wailing in front of her children or her mother. Yet she could hardly go home in the middle of the night to her blood-stained hearth.

"Widow Lester, are you able to offer Mistress Brice a bed until morning?"

"I don't need a bed!" shrieked Brice. "How can I sleep when I've held my husband's murdered body in my arms? When my children are left fatherless!"

That explained the stain on her dress, which covered most of the front and part of the forearms. Ela resolved to have Sibel bring her a clean gown, at least. "Rest assured that Morse is likely in custody by now, and your husband's body is being tended to properly. Where are your children?" Ela chastised herself for not thinking of their children sooner.

"They're with my sister."

"Did they witness the murder?" That would be gruesome but convenient for trial.

"No, I sent them to my sister's this morning."

"Why?"

"John and I needed to talk about his infidelities, and I didn't want them to hear it."

Understandable. "And the children can stay with your sister for now?"

"Yes." A big sob erupted from her chest. Ela wanted to press her with more questions—did the children know their father was dead? Who was the first person she told? But those questions could wait.

"Jess and I shall sit with her until morning and do what needs to be done," said the widow, in her singsong tones.

"Morse must hang," growled Mistress Brice. "He murdered my husband in cold blood. Why else would he have come to our house?"

That was damning. If Morse went to Brice's house, it wouldn't have been for a quiet chat. "Did you see him there?"

"He were gone by the time I got back from milking the cows. Just left my husband dead and bleeding on the floor like he were an animal." Sobs racked her substantial frame, and she buried her face in her hands.

Ela's heart ached for her loss. "Justice will be served."

"Aye, but too late for my John!"

Ela could see there was nothing to be gained by staying, so she bid her adieus and tactfully slipped Widow Lester a small purse of money to care for the grieving woman. She ushered Sibel out the door, and the guards escorted them back to the castle in a light drizzle.

* * *

The guards returned with Brice's body on a cart, and it was laid out in the castle mortuary. A much more sensible place than the armory partly because of its distance from the hall and its superior ventilation. Luckily, there were no other bodies laid out there.

Ela knew she could leave examination of the body to the coroner and discuss the situation with him in the morning, but she felt personally responsible in this case and knew she wouldn't be able to sleep if she didn't see it. Dead bodies could change dramatically in appearance even in the course of a few hours, so examining a victim's corpse as soon as possible after the crime was essential.

Morse, however, was safely installed in the dungeon, and she had no intention of facing him on a wet, moonless night. The very idea made her skin crawl. She'd face him in the light of day with as large a retinue of soldiers as possible.

And this time she wouldn't let him loose again. He'd walked his last steps as a free man.

Giles Haughton was there when she arrived. "Bludgeoned, from the looks of it."

Brice was covered in a large sheet of coarse linen, well stained by blood over the torso area, with only his head exposed. His face was white as tallow, eyes staring. Ela was grateful that his wife couldn't see him like this.

Giles pointed to the back of Brice's head, which was turned to one side, revealing hair matted with blood. "Likely hit hard from behind."

Ela stared at Brice's lifeless body. His face was frozen in shock. Had he even seen his assailant? But something struck her as odd. "If he was hit from behind, wouldn't he have fallen forward, onto his face?"

"Quite possibly, yes."

"But his face isn't bruised or swollen like it might be if he fell forward."

Haughton crossed his arms over his chest. "What are you suggesting?"

"I wonder if the fatal blow was to the front, and he hit his head hard on the floor. What position was he found in?"

"He was found curled up like a baby in its cradle, but then he didn't die right away. He died of blood loss from his wounds."

"From this head wound?" She peered at the back of his head. The blood was mostly around his torso.

"Not just the head wound. He was stabbed as well, likely as he lay on the floor."

"Stabbed with what?"

"This knife." Haughton walked over to a scarred table on the opposite side of the room that contained embalming fluids and other items used to prepare a corpse. He unwrapped a length of linen, one of Mistress Brice's aprons from the look of it, and revealed a large wood-handled blade.

"What kind of knife is that? It looks like something the cook would use in our kitchens."

"It could be used for that. Or any purpose, really. A dairy

farmer might use it to cut the throat of a cow he planned to eat."

Ela frowned. "Do you think Morse brought the knife with him, or do you think he found it in the kitchen?" This spoke to his motive for being there and whether he'd planned the murder before he left his home.

"Does it matter? He'll hang either way?" Haughton looked tired.

"True but I do think it's important to know how the crime unfolded. Especially since—" She hesitated for a moment, not wanting to darken her own reputation, but her role in this couldn't be ignored. "Since I had the opportunity to arrest Morse earlier today, and I didn't."

"Ah. You want to know how guilty you should feel?" His penetrating eyes looked sympathetic.

"Nothing so sentimental. I want to know how much recompense his widow might sue me for." She wasn't joking, either. Elizabeth Brice had already proved herself the combative type. "I led the expedition to tell Morse that his wife had lain with John Brice. I wanted to gauge his reaction. I hoped to see the flash of rage you might see in a man who'd beaten his wife to death."

"And did you?"

She paused and drew in a deep breath. She realized she was twisting her hands together. "No."

CHAPTER 12

*H*aughton lifted a grizzled brow. "He didn't show much emotion that I could see, but I suppose if he'd already killed her he'd hardly be sad or angry. He'd wrung those emotions out of himself already." She could hear an attempt at solace in Haughton's voice. "If Mistress Brice blames you for killing her husband, point out that her husband dug his own grave when he climbed into Katie Morse's bed."

"True."

Haughton had years of experience with all kinds of cases and she should rely on his expertise. Still, this was her reputation on the line and she wanted to protect it as best she could. If word got out that she was responsible—even through an act of omission—for a murder under her own jurisdiction, Hubert de Burgh could stir up opposition to her role as sheriff and even whisper against her in the king's ear.

There could be no more mistakes in this case. "So, if he were pushed from the front and banged his head on the floor, Morse could have stabbed him while he was lying there."

"Indeed, though again, it makes little difference. He's dead and Morse is a murderer. And I'm a tired old man who craves his bed."

"I'm sorry it had to happen at night."

"These things usually do. Being roused from my bed is an occupational hazard." He rubbed his mouth. "I'm surprised you want to be sheriff. It's a tough job that requires a strong stomach, long, irregular hours and a lot of difficult decisions."

"Just because I'm a woman does not mean I wish to spend my days at needlework and weaving." She knew her words sounded terse. "I'm sure you enjoy the challenges of your job and take satisfaction in seeing justice served."

"When justice is served, which isn't always." Haughton looked at her. "There's a good deal of corruption in the land these days. Some might accuse you of becoming sheriff so you can fill your purse with bribes or fatten your manors with the confiscated lands of those you imprison."

"While I appreciate your candor, I do hope you're not making that accusation yourself."

"Trust me, I'm not foolish enough to accuse the Countess of Salisbury of misdeeds." He smiled a crooked grin. "If I thought that was your intent I'd have kept quiet about it. But you should know this often happens, so there may be whispers."

She should be shocked that he was talking to his countess as an equal. On the other hand he was talking to her like he might to another man, and that warmed her. She could see how sheriffs might be tempted to appropriate funds for their own purposes. She was already out seven pounds for a funeral and more for the cost of Widow Lester's ministrations.

"There are many reasons I wish to take the role of sheriff.

Not only can I make sure the course of justice is not perverted, but I'll have a deeper understanding of the workings of the justice system that I can share with my son Will. He'll be Earl of Salisbury and I want him to be well prepared for the job."

"Very wise, my lady. Your sense of responsibility is to be much admired."

She wasn't sure if he was sincere or if he felt—as many no doubt would—that she was neglecting her family and household responsibilities. Either way, it didn't matter. What did matter was that she fulfilled her role as sheriff to the best of her abilities.

"May I examine the body?"

Haughton's exasperation was poorly hidden. "Of course, my lady." He tugged the sheet from the corpse in a dramatic sweep that exposed the poor man's nakedness all at once and made Ela gasp. She fought the urge to shield her eyes. She'd rarely even seen her husband completely naked, and the sight was unfamiliar and disconcerting.

She steadied herself—without drawing a deep breath of the room's fetid air—and moved in closer. Blood had dried around several stab wounds in his belly. Each one was a slit, as if Morse had stuck the knife in and pulled it out. "Why would he stick the knife in his belly like this once he lay on the floor. Why not just slit his throat and be done with it?"

Morse must have slaughtered enough cows in his time and surely knew how to kill with one stroke. He was so much larger than Brice that he likely could have accomplished that without even knocking him down first.

Haughton shrugged. "I agree, it is odd."

She looked at the knife, and imagined herself using it to stab him in the belly. Six times from the look of it. "Are there any wounds on his back?"

"None. He might have lost consciousness from the blow to his head, but he died from loss of blood from these punctures. He lay in a big puddle of blood when we found him."

"Then I suppose it was an effective method of murder, if an unorthodox one."

"Indeed."

"Make sure the knife is carefully preserved as evidence. I don't want it disappearing." Ela knew that a good knife was valuable to almost anyone and likely to walk off. "Lock it up somewhere."

"Might I ask why?"

"We need to discover whether the knife belongs to Morse, or whether it was in the Brice's kitchen when he arrived."

"Ah. Yes." No doubt he found this line of inquiry a waste of time. But Ela wanted to know. And the method of murder struck her as odd. A big brute like Morse was capable of killing with his fists, which was likely how his wife had died. Why had he used a knife as well?

Ela needed to think. And to pray.

"I'll bid you adieu, Master Haughton. You must go home to your wife. God go with you."

"God's blessings on you, my lady," he muttered, with a nod. "See you in the morning."

* * *

Ela walked the short distance from the mortuary back to the castle hall, accompanied by the soldiers who'd waited for her outside. From there she climbed the stairs to her solar, where, to her surprise, Sibel stood waiting for her.

"What are you still doing up?"

"Stoking your fire, my lady. And I warmed the water for you to wash."

"You're too thoughtful." Ela let Sibel help her out of her gown, and gratefully washed her hands and face in the clean, warm water. "If only I could wash the stench of death from my nostrils."

"Nicholas has been asking for you." Sibel sounded apologetic. "He can't sleep." She looked at Ela's curtained bed. "He insisted on waiting in your bed for you."

Ela turned and saw the curtains part to reveal Nicholas's curly gold head and big staring eyes. "I had a bad dream, Mama."

"Did you, my love?" She decided to sleep in her shift rather than change to a nightgown in front of her son. "What was it?"

"I dreamed there was a bad man in the castle, who wanted to kill people dead."

De Burgh's hawk-like face swarmed Ela's imagination. It took her a moment to realize her son was talking about Morse.

"He knows?" She whispered to Sibel. How? Deschamps had the tact to pull her away from her family before imparting the grim news.

"The soldiers do natter on, my lady. I told him he's locked up down in the dungeon and can't do anyone any harm," said Sibel softly.

"Sibel's right, my sweet. He can't hurt anyone now."

"Can I sleep in your bed tonight?"

Ela hesitated. She'd intended to spend some time at her prie-dieu before retiring, hoping for some guidance and solace in her prayers. "Just this once." She could rise early and go to the chapel before her rounds. She'd been so busy that perhaps she was neglecting her children. Her new position was so public, and the public life of Salisbury happened right in her home, so there was no way to shield them from it.

She bid good night to Sibel and climbed up onto the bed,

into the cozy cocoon behind the curtains. Her sweet son smelled of milk and honey and she could almost imagine him a baby again, wrapped up in her arms. She lay down next to him. "This castle is the safest place in all England."

"Is it?"

"Of course. All of the soldiers are here to protect us, day and night."

"I thought they were the king's soldiers."

"They are, and the king is our friend."

"I know he's my cousin, or something like that."

"Indeed he is. And he'd never let anything happen to you."

"My daddy died."

Ela's throat clogged and she struggled to swallow before answering. "I know, but that was different. I promise to keep you safe."

"Will says we'll be sent off to war, like Daddy."

"Papa was a valiant knight who fought for the king." She smoothed his hair. "He was very brave. He didn't mind going to fight. In fact, I think he rather enjoyed it." She stroked her son's cheek. "And he didn't die in battle."

"Is Will going to go off and fight for the king?"

"Perhaps one day, but not yet. He's not even a knight yet, though I believe he will be soon."

"Will I go off to fight?" Nicky's worried eyes stared up at her, shining in the dark. Her sweet son was so gentle and preferred her company to that of the boisterous soldiers.

"Maybe one day, a very long time from now. Or you might become a man of God like Bishop Poore, who spends his time leading us all in prayer." She was under no oath to raise her sons to be knights.

"I think I'd like that better."

"Perhaps you could lead us in prayer right now?"

"Can I?"

"If you can remember the words."

Ela watched with amusement and not a little pride as Nicholas scrambled out of bed and knelt on the floor. She followed suit, wincing at the cold, hard wood under her knees through her thin shift. Her gentle son said the words slowly and with so much meaning that her heart was filled with faith and hope.

"…and lead us not into temptation, but deliver us from evil. Amen."

"Amen." Especially that last part. She felt stalked by evil, lately. Though she also had to be careful with the temptation of pride. She prayed that her desire to be sheriff sprang purely from a need to preserve the peace and safeguard Will's inheritance, and not from a desire to puff herself up.

She and Nicholas climbed back under the covers, and she pulled the heavy curtains to keep out the draughts. Snuggled under the covers, with her arms around her last baby, she reveled in the fleeting sense of bliss. She was old enough and wise enough to appreciate what was good about her life and not squander these precious moments in wishing for something else.

* * *

Ela had planned to go to the chapel first thing in the morning, but was so exhausted that she slept far later than she'd intended and was wakened by Sibel, who carried Nicholas back to his own bed before returning to dress her. Ela let Sibel ease her gown over her head, then pin her headdress together. "Let me look in the looking glass."

She usually avoided it as a sign of vanity, but today she wanted to take a look at the face that all the others—including Morse—would be talking to. In her mind she was still a girl of twenty with rosy cheeks and long waves of dark blonde hair tucked under her veil.

The mirror didn't say anything about her hair, which was hidden by her crisp white veil and wimple, but her face looked pale and pinched. The blue of her tunic deepened the blue of her eyes but also some blue hollows around them that she didn't remember. "I look like I was awake all night."

"You look well rested enough to me, my lady," said Sibel tactfully.

"Yesterday was a difficult day. And today promises no different." She turned away from the mirror. "Excuse my complaining. I'm fully aware of how fortunate I am. Do help keep the children busy today. I'd like them to know as little as possible about the events unfolding around us."

"I'm sorry there was another murder, my lady." Sibel spoke softly, almost a whisper, while busying herself tidying the bedclothes.

"What exactly did you hear?" Ela wished her voice didn't sound so sharp. She hated the idea of the servants gossiping.

"That the man who murdered his wife killed her lover as well."

Ela sighed. "That is how things appear."

"I suppose he's done you the favor of signing his own death warrant."

"Indeed." That was certainly Giles Haughton's opinion. "But he hasn't been tried by jury and justice yet." She didn't want Sibel to confirm any rumors and get the people baying for blood. The villagers treated an execution as a festive occasion. While she thirsted for justice as much as the next person, she took no delight in another man's suffering and would prefer to see the people chastened by the awful sight.

"Do you think he's guilty?" Sibel couldn't hide her curiosity.

"It does seem likely under the circumstances, but it's not for me to judge. It's my duty to gather the evidence and any witnesses to the event or the characters of the people involved, and to present the persons and evidence to the court of justice."

"But surely you have an opinion." Sibel looked up from shaking out the bed curtains.

Ela didn't know what to think. She'd trusted her instincts and failed to arrest Morse yesterday, and now another man was dead.

But why would a seasoned cowman with a knife not slit his rival's throat, but instead poke him in the belly with it like an angry child?

"Perhaps I do have an opinion, but for now that is between me and God." Sibel was an intelligent woman with gifts that could likely have taken her far beyond Ela's hall and bedchamber if her circumstances had permitted. Ela considered herself grateful to benefit from them daily. "Pray for justice, Sibel. Because that's my only goal in this difficult situation."

"Yes, my lady." Sibel nodded, chastened. "And I'll try to keep the children out of it. It's hard the way the soldiers gossip among themselves in the hall."

"I'll have a word with Deschamps about that. Please have him summoned to the hall."

With that she swept out on her usual rounds, and Sibel hurried off to stir the chain of command that would summon Deschamps.

* * *

Ela's nerves remained on edge during her uncharacteristically late inspection of the castle and grounds. Wherever she went, people seemed to still their conversation and busy themselves in their work as if afraid to look at her. She tried to conduct herself as efficiently as usual, but it was hard not to be distracted by the pervasive air of unrest.

When she returned to the hall Deschamps was seated at the table, breakfasting near the fire. He rose as she approached, and she motioned for him to sit and continue. "God go with you, Master Deschamps."

"And with you, my lady, as I trust he always does."

She sat opposite him, and a servant brought her a plate of freshly baked bread accompanied by dried fruit and cheese, her preferred breakfast at this time of year. A cup of watered wine slaked her thirst.

Ela whispered that she'd prefer for the soldiers to keep any gossip about the murder outside the hall and grounds and far from the ears of the children.

"I'll do my best, my lady, but short of putting a stopper in their mouths it's hard to prevent them talking. We should congratulate ourselves there is peace and prosperity enough that they're here and not out fighting."

Ela bristled at his lack of deference. "I prefer to save congratulations for something specific. Speaking of which, has the coroner spoken to Morse yet?"

"Not yet, my lady. He's not come here this morning."

Probably sleeping in, like her. "Please summon him and at least one juror, and we can interview Morse together. It's a certainty that he'll be tried for his life now. The more official witnesses to each interview, the better."

"Yes, my lady. Shall I attend the interview?"

"Please do." She wanted Deschamps on her side, not against it. Although he'd done nothing to arouse her suspicions, she knew he was a man of pride and ambition who was quite capable of trying to clamber over others on his way to whatever he perceived as success. "Is there word on whether Morse has confessed to the crimes?"

"He has not. He maintains his innocence." A servant refilled Deschamps's cup of small ale from a pewter jug. "He was fretting over his cows this morning."

"And where are his cows?"

"They are currently being driven to your manor at Marshwood."

Ela paused, bread halfway to her mouth. "Why? Why not install a herdsman at his farm and drive the cows to their usual dairy until justice is served and his property appropriately disposed of?" Once again she could feel the finger of accusation pointing at her.

"Then we run the risk of occupying his property illegally and incurring a suit from his heirs."

"What heirs?"

"I don't know, my lady, but no one will argue that his cows need to be milked and fed, and that they will be safe and cared for at your manor."

"Is there hay and grazing enough for them there? The grass has barely started to grow." She didn't much like the idea of paying for their feed before handing them back to an heir. Would she be entitled to recompense, perhaps in the form of the best cow?

Thinking this way she could see how a sheriff might easily be accused of enriching himself at another's expense.

"I'll visit the manor today myself, my lady, and report back to you."

"There's no need for you to remove yourself from your duties. I'll follow up with the steward." No doubt this was his idea. Deschamps's job was to manage the garrison, not the farms. "I don't much like the idea of the accused's cattle mingling with mine."

Deschamps's mouth tilted. "Afraid they will spread moral turpitude?"

"I'm more concerned about foot rot," she said dryly. "But please do make inquiries into Morse's next of kin."

As she finished her breakfast, the coroner arrived, along with Stephen Hale, the cordwainer, who lived next door to him and was no doubt the most convenient juror to rouse as another witness.

"Hail, gentlemen, will you join us to break your fast?" Perhaps she was procrastinating. The prospect of heading down to the dungeons to meet Morse chilled her blood.

"Thanks, but nay, my lady," said Haughton, who looked a lot brighter after a night of sleep. Or maybe his nose and cheeks were just red from the cold. "My wife has fed me already."

"Mine too," said Hale. "But thank you for your kindness."

Ela rose, inhaling deeply. "Then we can attend to business. As you know, Morse was brought in late last night after John Brice was found bludgeoned and stabbed in his kitchen." She walked out of the great hall and down the corridor that led to the dungeons. The dungeons weren't directly underneath the great hall, thank goodness, but were only accessible through a door in the floor and a ladder heading down into the bowels of the castle.

One sentry stood at the top and one at the bottom of the ladder. Ela descended as gracefully as her skirts would allow and the big, grumpy jailer—who wouldn't be grumpy spending his days down here in the dark?—unlocked the heavy wood door that led into the inner gaol where prisoners were kept chained to the walls.

Ela felt her body tense as they passed through the door. There were two other prisoners down here awaiting the assizes, but her eyes immediately fixed on Morse. There was one tiny slit of a window high in the wall, at least fifteen feet above the floor, but it let in enough light to illuminate his massive form in the far corner.

He stirred when he saw them and struggled to his feet with apparent difficulty. She wondered if he'd sustained injuries resisting the soldiers during his arrest or while being chained. Her eyes hadn't adjusted to the light well enough to see bruises.

Ela found herself shrinking back, even though she knew he was chained to the wall and couldn't reach her. Silence stretched out, punctuated by a steady drip, drip, drip, somewhere overhead, and she realized everyone was waiting for her to speak first.

CHAPTER 13

"*A*lan Morse," said Ela, wishing her voice sounded steadier. "Do you know the reason you're here?"

"I know the reason." He stared at her through narrowed eyes.

"Do you admit to killing John Brice?"

He thrust forward, straining against the chains, which clashed and startled her into taking a step back. "I didn't kill John Brice." His voice rasped and his eyes now bulged like a madman's as he stared at her. "I never killed no one! I'm innocent."

Ela's throat tightened. "Then who killed John Brice?"

"How would I know? I was at home in my own house."

"Was anyone there with you?"

He stared at her like she might be simple. "Who'd be there? My wife is dead. I was alone."

She hadn't really expected him to deny it utterly. She looked to Giles Haughton. As coroner, he had more experience in these situations.

Haughton cleared his throat. "When did you last see John Brice?"

Morse blinked. "I dunno. I don't see him at the dairy. His wife drives the cows there most mornings and evenings. He didn't show his face there yesterday."

"So you're saying you hadn't seen him in months?"

"Not months, no." Morse frowned. "Weeks, though."

"Did you know your wife was having a...liaison with him?"

"Never! Do you think I would have just let it go on?" He raged again, eyes popping. "If I'd known, why I'd have—"

"Killed her?" suggested Haughton.

"No! Of course not." Morse realized his mistake.

"You'd have just beaten her more than usual, perhaps?" said Ela.

"I didn't beat my wife."

"That's not what you said yesterday." Ela disliked Morse intensely. She felt quite sure he was capable of killing both his wife and Brice. She just wasn't entirely convinced that he had.

Her eyes adjusted to the gloom, and she studied his clothes for signs of blood. Given the amount of dried blood on Elizabeth Brice's tunic and sleeves, the victim must have bled profusely when he was stabbed. But she realized with a chill that she didn't see any bloodstains on Morse's clothing.

No doubt he had time to get home and change. "Did the soldiers retrieve any bloodstained clothing from Morse's house?" She asked Giles.

"Not that I'm aware of. I'll ask two of the jurors to search the property."

If he'd cleaned himself up it would have to be in a stream on his property. He couldn't scrub away that much blood with just a bucket and brush. She couldn't remember seeing a stream in his fields, but how else did he water the cows? Dairy cows required a lot of water. She wanted to ride over there herself to examine the place. Soldiers were apt to trample or ignore useful evidence. "I'll go with them."

"You won't find anything because I haven't killed anyone." Morse yelled loud enough to make himself hoarse. "Doesn't anyone hear me? Is there no justice in England?"

"You'll be tried at the assizes," Ela said coolly. "Before a justice and jury."

"Then hanged for something I didn't do! Don't you even care who killed my wife?"

"If you cared, perhaps you'd have reported her missing," said Ela. "You as much as said you thought she'd taken off with a man. There was clearly no love lost between you."

He stared at her, perhaps realizing the truth in her words. He blinked and his lips worked before he spoke again. "My wife and I had a practical arrangement. She knew I couldn't give her children but I could give her a home of her own and a livelihood. She was a hard worker had hopes to open her own dairy in the new town. How many people marry for love in this day and age?" His voice was hoarse with something like desperation.

Ela couldn't claim to have married for love. Nor could anyone she knew. She'd believed it was different among the working people because they weren't bound by obligations to their titles and manors but maybe she was wrong. Perhaps, with limited means, they had even more cause to make their choice for practical reasons.

"She cooked and cleaned for me, drove my cows to the dairy, talked with me, lay with me. My life was a thousand times better with her in it than without it." Morse's voice took on a plaintive tone and Ela found his words affecting her. Who was she to judge him for his lack of poetic ardor?

And if he wasn't passionately in love with his wife, if anything it made him less likely to fly in to a rage and kill her lover.

The stale air in the underground dungeon clogged her nostrils and she longed to quit it. It wasn't her job to be judge, jury and executioner. They had reason enough to suspect Morse and keep him here until the assizes. Her job was done.

But would justice be served for Katherine Morse?

Giles Haughton cleared his throat. "I'd like to ride to the scene of the murder. I couldn't see the details in the dark last night."

"Fine." Ela was glad of the excuse to end this interview. "Morse will remain in custody until the assizes."

Morse's moans and shouts of protest followed them out through the door and up the ladder, until the clanging and locking of the heavy door behind them drowned him out.

"I'd like to come with you," said Ela. "To learn as much as I can about the process of gathering evidence."

"Yes, my lady."

If he was annoyed by the intrusion, he showed no sign of it and they agreed that Hale should come too. The more witnesses to evidence, the better for a trial, especially a murder trial like this one.

* * *

Ela, Haughton and Hale mounted and rode the now-familiar route across the fields, four soldiers behind them. The sun shone on budding trees and new spring grass poked out through the ground beneath their feet. Morse's fields were now empty of cattle, even the lone bull, and his house looked even more derelict and forlorn in their absence.

"We need to find the bloody clothes," said Haughton as they dismounted and tied their horses.

Ela stepped over the threshold into the dim interior of Morse's house. The hearth was unswept and the floor scattered with dirt and refuse like chicken bones. This man sorely needed a woman in his life from the looks of it. "Where might he have hidden them?"

"If it were me I'd have buried them," said Hale. "I'll search the farmyard. It should be easy to see any freshly turned earth. It hasn't rained since yesterday."

"I'll search the house," said Ela. It didn't take long since the house only had two rooms with a few sticks of furniture. Katie Morse's few pieces of clothing lay folded in a simple wood chest, just as she must have left them. Another set of Morse's clothes, all well soiled, lay in a corner of the bedroom next to the unmade bed. "How many sets of clothes would a farmer like Morse typically have?"

"One or two," said Haughton. "Possibly more but not all that likely. We could ask the girls at the dairy. They might be familiar with his clothing since he's had to drive the cows there every day since his wife died.

"Good idea." She turned over the greasy and smelly pile of clothes—a tunic and linen shirt, a pair of torn hose. She lifted the bed cover and grimaced at the stained and lumpy straw-stuffed mattress. Haughton lifted the mattress and they could see there was nothing under it except the crudely made wood bed frame.

"Where would Morse keep his knives?" She hadn't seen any implements except a dirty wooden spoon in the first room.

"Perhaps in the barn? He'd need one for castrating if nothing else."

Ela led the way out of the dank, gloomy house and across the muddy farmyard to the larger and more recently constructed barn. "You can tell he cared more about the roof over his cows than the roof over his wife," she said, peering up at the tight new thatch.

The barn was also neater than the house, its clean

wooden buckets, hoes, hay rakes and a rusted scythe all arranged neatly along the end wall. They found three knives inside an old woven basket, but they were dusty and showed no signs of recent use or cleaning. Another basket contained hooks of the type that might be used to close a barn door or gate and yet another contained stones and a rasp for sharpening other tools.

Manure on the floor indicated recent occupation by the cows, and a pile of rotten hay fenced off in one corner must be the last of the winter food supply. Haughton kicked at the hay, which released a cloud of dust but revealed no weapon hidden underneath.

"Where's the water source he would have washed himself in?" asked Ela, glad to leave the dust-mote filled air of the barn and head out into the fresh spring air. They roamed around the farmyard. A pond in one of the nearby fields seemed the most likely place, and they climbed a stile by the gate and walked around it. The ground was well trampled by the cows, but there were no fresh human footprints anywhere near it.

"Morse was arrested here, correct?" Ela asked.

"Indeed. He was roused from his bed."

"So far we have no evidence that he traveled to the Brice's farm and killed John Brice. All we have is motive."

"Motive can be enough to convict a man," said Haughton. "Especially in the absence of other suspects. And now he seems to have murdered twice—that in itself is damning."

"Unless he didn't commit either of the murders."

Haughton's eyes showed surprise. "You're not thinking of setting him free? Having a suspected murderer at large will cause unrest among the people."

Ela felt the unspoken censure in his words. "I know people are angry that Morse wasn't arrested sooner. They blame me for Brice's death. But we have no solid evidence whatsoever that Morse killed either his wife or his neighbor."

Haughton's eyes narrowed slightly. "Sometimes you have to make difficult decisions to keep the peace."

"Like sending an innocent man to his death?" She was shocked by his callous—or careless—attitude.

"It's up to the judge and jury to decide on his innocence." Haughton's face displayed no emotion. He was a handsome man of fifty or so, his features carved sharper by the passage of time. He gave every impression of being a man of experience and wisdom, someone whose advice and counsel she should heed.

But her conscience pricked her. "Have you ever watched a man go to the gallows when you thought he might be innocent?"

Haughton blinked and took a moment to consider. "No." He spoke with conviction, but she didn't entirely believe him. "I couldn't sleep at night if I presided over a miscarriage of justice."

The diplomatic answer. Haughton was far too sensible of his own position to confess any professional failings. Though his readiness to throw up his hands and head for his bed last night had spoken volumes.

"If everyone in Wiltshire believes a man is guilty," continued Haughton, "and I think him innocent, is it my job to argue with them?"

"Yes," said Ela quickly. "As coroner your duty is to discover the truth."

He looked like he wanted to argue with her but thought better of it. "My duty is to support the sheriff, whose duty is to keep the peace," he said quietly.

This time Ela felt the rebuke like a slap. It stung harder because she respected Haughton. "My duty is to see that justice is served. I live my life in service to the Lord our God, and my duty to him comes even before my duty to the people of Salisbury." The words emerged with a steel edge.

"With all due respect, my lady, surely our Father in heaven is the true judge and dispenses final justice."

Ela inhaled deeply, trying to keep her temper. With that logic they might as well just let the citizens of Salisbury murder each other so they could find their way to heaven or hell faster. "That may be so, Master Haughton, but, as the prayer says. "Thy will be done on earth as it is in heaven," and I consider it our duty to further that cause here on earth."

Haughton's lips moved, but he didn't speak. He was probably considering the wisdom of arguing with God's will. Or with the new sheriff, who also happened to own much of the land and property in the county and who was related by marriage to the king.

"Do you intend to set Morse free?" he asked after a long pause.

"No." She sighed. "I can see the importance of keeping him imprisoned for now, in the absence of other suspects or evidence. And I don't mean to browbeat you. I do respect and value your years of experience and I do truly want you to be frank with your opinions and advice. But I don't intend to knowingly send an innocent man to the gallows, either."

"If Morse didn't murder John Brice and Katherine Morse, then who did?" Haughton's salt-and-pepper brow lifted. The wind tossed his still-thick hair, and Ela looked past him out over the trees and hills behind him. Hale returned, observing that there were no signs of fresh digging.

"Let's visit the Brice house—the scene of the murder—to look for evidence there."

Hale had found no signs of recent disturbance in or around the farmyard, so they mounted and left. Brice's farm was only a short ride away, and they tied their horses in his yard. Like Morse's, the farmyard was trampled with fresh footprints from the soldiers and others who'd come in the aftermath of the murder to retrieve the body.

Ela braced herself for a scene of bloody horror when she opened the door but was surprised to find something entirely different.

CHAPTER 14

"*M*istress Brice?" Ela addressed her from the doorway. Apparently, Elizabeth Brice considered the question answered by her presence because she didn't respond. She looked up from the floor, which she was scrubbing, then returned to rubbing her bristled brush over the flags.

She'd erased all traces of the blood. A bucket of soapy water and one of clean water stood nearby. A pile of wet rags, no doubt already long rinsed of blood, waited nearby for reuse.

"You're tampering with evidence," said Giles Haughton. "Please put down your brush."

"But this is my kitchen! How can I cook in here with—with—" She looked down and seemed about to cry.

Ela felt a wave of compassion, followed by a further wave of annoyance—at herself. She should have thought to forbid Mistress Brice from returning to her house until it was examined. "We understand your impulse to clean, but we need evidence to pursue a conviction in court. Please step aside."

Elizabeth Brice took a reluctant step back. Her gown was tucked up into her belt, but still the brown fabric and the linen shift beneath it were wet and Ela could see a pinkish tinge along the hem of her shift that hinted at the blood she'd scrubbed away.

Ela peered at the stone flags. The blood was gone, though she could perhaps see a shadow of it in the cracks between the stones, or was that just water? "When did you come back here? I left you last night at Widow Lester's."

"I came back early in the morn." She swiped at her nose, which was quite red. "I couldn't bear to think of poor John's blood all over the floor."

"You've changed." Ela glanced around for her blood-stained clothes. "Where's the tunic you had on last night?"

"Hanging outside. I scrubbed it clean."

"Mistress Brice had blood on her clothing last night?" asked Giles.

"Yes, all over the front and on the sleeves."

"From cradling my husband's dead body in my arms."

"May our Lord comfort you," said Ela. But something wasn't sitting right with her.

Red-faced, Elizabeth Brice wasn't wearing a veil right now or even a fillet or barbette. Her long, wavy, sandy-brown hair hung down past her shoulders. Ela was surprised by how much younger she looked. She was a strapping, muscular woman, in contrast to her rather weedy husband. "You've accomplished a lot in a very short time. Did you drive your cows to the dairy this morning?"

"Aye, though I didn't wait there while they milked. I ran home to clean, then went back to drive them home."

"Why the hurry?" asked Haughton with a frown.

Mistress Brice looked indignant. "Would you want spilled blood all over your hearth?"

"No, but I would want my husband's murder thoroughly investigated." Ela's heart missed a beat as she spoke.

Her own husband's death had simply been attributed to a sudden and violent illness. It had all happened so fast and no amount of investigation could bring him back, but it could certainly destroy her family if it ruffled the wrong feathers. She'd buried her husband and now presided over her own scrubbed hearth.

"We know who did it." Elizabeth Brice gripped her brush so hard her knuckles whitened. "The man who should have been in custody already for killing his wife."

"But we have no witnesses who saw Alan Morse here," said Ela. "Even you didn't see him. By your account he was gone when you returned to find your husband dead."

"I saw his big, clomping footprints everywhere." She gestured outside the door.

"Where?" Ela turned to look, knowing that if they ever were there, they'd be long gone under all the feet that came after them.

"Outside the door, then mud tracked inside on the floor."

"And you washed them away?" Ela couldn't believe the woman was this stupid.

"They weren't here this morning anyway. Whoever came to get the body walked all over them." Her tone had a touch of insolence to it. "If evidence was so important, then it should have been looked at last night, shouldn't it?"

It wasn't Elizabeth Brice's business to make that determination. "It was already dark when you raised the hue and cry. There would have been no way to see clearly until morning."

"What time did you find the body?" asked Haughton roughly.

"Right after milking. It was already well dark."

"You're used to driving the cows in the dark?"

"No choice in winter, have I?"

169

"What light do you see by?"

"The moon if it's bright. If it's cloudy I bring a rushlight or taper to see my way. The cows are always in a hurry to go get milked. It's not exactly difficult to get them to the dairy or even back home again."

Again, that tone of mild exasperation.

Could Elizabeth Brice have driven the cows to the dairy last night, then come home and killed John Brice herself rather than discovering his dead body? She couldn't have killed him beforehand because there would be blood on her clothes and she could hardly have gone to the dairy like that.

Ela realized that they needed to speak to the girls at the dairy and discover what time Morse had come and gone himself.

"He was killed here in this spot?" The wet area was quite large, near the hearth, to the left of the front door.

"Yes. Left to bleed out like a dead calf." Her voice shook, making Ela feel bad for her sudden suspicion. "That Morse is a fiend! I hope he burns in hell."

"God will be his last judge," said Ela solemnly. "But he might not be convicted if we can't find solid evidence that he was here." She watched closely for Elizabeth Brice's reaction.

"What?" Brice's eyes widened. They were pale blue, with sparse lashes. "He might go free even though he's murdered two people?"

Ela nodded. "The justice can't convict a man on hearsay." She hesitated for a moment. Did she dare? "They might start to think that you murdered him yourself." She did dare. Though she said it apologetically, as if it was an outrageous suggestion.

"Me?" Brice's reaction was as intense as she'd expected. And twice as loud. "Me kill my own beloved husband?" Her face turned crimson except around her lips, which whitened as they flattened against her teeth.

"You do have motive," said Ela quietly. "After all, you were seen berating him in the market square. Everyone in Salisbury knows he cheated on you." She knew she was twisting a knife. But what if her hunch was correct? "I can't help but observe that you're bigger and possibly stronger than him."

"Me stronger than a man? Never!" Her fingers were now mottled red and white, gripping her scrubbing brush so hard that it suddenly flew from her hand and clattered on the wet floor. Ela jumped back instinctively and realized how tense and on edge she was.

"I never killed him! Never!" Elizabeth Brice let out something between a scream and a roar and rushed past Ela and Haughton to the door, and out into the daylight.

Ela looked at Haughton, whose eyebrows were raised slightly. "Too much?" she said just above a whisper.

"Your words would be offensive and objectionable coming from the lips of a man, but since you are a woman—"

"I feel confident that she still finds them offensive and objectionable. Especially if she's guilty." Ela looked at the open doorway, a bright rectangle of light.

"Don't you find the manner of stabbing odd?" asked Ela. This issue preyed on her. "It still doesn't make sense to me that a big man like Morse would stab Brice in the side and not cut his throat as if he were a calf ready for slaughter."

"I thought the same, my lady," said Hale. "I saw the body before we came to meet you this morning. I don't like to say it, but those stab wounds seem more like something...like..." He hesitated.

"Like wounds an angry woman might make," finished Haughton gruffly. "Stabbing again and again in her fury."

Hale harrumphed. "Her husband broke their marriage vows and made a fool of her in front of all Salisbury."

"You could argue that she made a fool of herself," said Ela. "No one told her to cry her business in the town square."

"Perhaps she couldn't stand to see him get away with adultery and have no one any the wiser," suggested Hale.

"Or perhaps she wanted to see her straying husband accused of Katie Morse's murder," said Ela. "Since no one had made the connection between the two before." People didn't credit women with such artful calculation, but she did.

Ela looked around them. There was a large rusty fire iron by the hearth, and she walked toward it. "She could have bludgeoned him with something like this." She wrapped her hand around the knob at the top. "Perhaps as he walked through the front door. Then while he was down she cut him to make sure he'd bleed to death." Her voice grew louder as the scenario unfurled in her mind, and she glanced at the door and shushed herself. "Would you arrest her for killing her husband?"

"Yes. She has as much motive as Morse." Giles Haughton took a handkerchief out of his sleeve and blew his nose.

"Oh dear. They'll be down in the dungeon together."

"Can't be helped. And we can have the guard listen in on their exchanges."

"One of them is innocent."

"Not necessarily. We have two murders."

"I suppose locking them up is the only way to guarantee that we aren't setting a killer loose." Ela did not take depriving someone of their freedom lightly, but she didn't plan to make the same mistake twice. "I'll order the guards to take her back to the castle, and we can go on to the dairy to talk to the girls."

"What about the cows?"

Ela exhaled. "Let's leave them here. I'll have someone sent from my nearby manor to drive them for milking as usual until we come to some more conclusions."

"That'll cost you money, for the herder and the milking." He looked dubious.

"I shall make sure accounts are settled when guilt or innocence is proclaimed."

"You'd be within your right to keep the cattle." He didn't look at her when he spoke, but was tucking his kerchief back into his sleeve.

"I'm coming to understand that is tradition, but I'm not looking to enrich myself in the pursuit of justice." She swept out of the room. The guards stood in the doorway and she quietly asked them to take Mistress Brice prisoner and escort her back to the castle.

They all looked around. She was gone. Ela wanted to scold them for letting her run right past them, but they were trained to wait for orders.

"Find her."

There was a lot to learn in this job, first of all to be highly suspicious of everyone around you. Second, ask your guards to stop anyone who runs away from you.

She fought the urge to laugh. It would be easy to become a tyrant in this position. She'd have to pray for humility and compassion and the strength to not arrest all the citizens of Salisbury in the pursuit of peace and safety for the half dozen left in freedom by the time she was done.

* * *

Bright midday sunshine illuminated the dairy as Ela and Giles rode into the main yard. Since it was the middle of the day the milking barn was empty, but the milkmaids were hard at work churning milk into cream and butter while a boy of about twelve shoveled manure out of the barn and yard and piled it on the midden.

Philip Nance, the owner, came out at the sound of their horses in the yard. Ela rode up to him. "God be with you, Master Nance. You've heard about John Brice's death?"

"Aye, his widow told me this morn."

"I'm afraid she's now in our custody."

"What? Lizzie Brice a killer?" He rubbed his face. "All this murder is bad for business. I've lost half my custom if they're gone too."

"I'm arranging to keep the Brice's cattle in place and have them driven here for milking."

"And who shall pay me?"

"I'll send my steward to work out arrangements. I presume that the usual payment is in milk for your butter and cheese." Was he hoping to cash in on this tragic circumstance? "He'll look at the Brice's books to determine how things were set up." She doubted the Brices had books of any kind, or that they were even lettered, but she didn't want him making up some new milk-the-countess rate for her.

"Oh, aye." His face had a curious expression. "So we'll just milk them and take the products to market, like always, then?"

"Yes, continue with business as usual until you hear otherwise while we wait for the assizes." Ela shifted position in her saddle. Freya was falling asleep under her. "What time did Alan Morse drive his cows here last night?"

"I don't pay much attention to the time." Nance adjusted his belt. "It was before dark, that's all I know."

"And did Morse come before or after Elizabeth Brice?"

"Elizabeth Brice? John Brice drove the cows here last night. Said she were home with a headache or something."

How odd. "But who was here first? Or were they at the same time?"

"Oh, no, never at the same time. That wouldn't do, would it? All the cows would get mixed up, and my poor maids would have their hands full. Morse is always first at night."

"I see." She turned to Haughton. "In my mind this makes it even more likely that Elizabeth was the murderer. She was at home waiting to set upon him when he returned."

Nance crossed himself. "Well, I never. I heard he was

stabbed in the back."

"In the side," corrected Haughton in his deep voice. "But he was bludgeoned first."

"She is quite a woman," said Nance, eyebrows raised. "I wouldn't want the managing of her."

"Do you have a wife, Master Nance?" Ela was curious. How much did he know about the intrigue amongst his customers?

"Nay, she died giving birth to my last little one. I hired a nurse to look after the baby, and she performs most of the functions of a wife for half the money and trouble." His face creased into a grin, then he remembered who he was talking to—or saw the unamused expression on Ela's face—and wiped his expression blank.

Ela shifted in her saddle again. She needed more padding over the leather if she was to have long conversations while seated up here in her role as sheriff. "Were you aware that Katherine Morse was involved in an adulterous affair with John Brice?"

"No. It wouldn't be good business to meddle in the affairs of my customers." His response was a little too quick to be convincing.

"Or perhaps it would be good business to be aware of the events unfolding in their lives," she said coolly. "Your dairy-maids pondered how Katherine Morse became pregnant when her husband was known to be infertile."

Nance shifted from foot to foot. "I know nothing about that. That's business between a man and his wife."

"Indeed. Thank you for your time. May we speak to your dairymaids?"

"They're very busy right now. They must get all the milk churned before it spoils. On a sunny day like this—"

"My question was a mere formality, Master Nance. I intend to talk to your dairymaids." Ela didn't like to sound imperious, but did he really think they'd just leave? And these were hardly summertime temperatures.

"I see. I'll go fetch them." He scurried away with his tail between his legs.

Giles Haughton muffled a laugh. "You do command respect, my lady."

"And that's amusing to you?" She used a teasing tone of voice. It didn't pay to appear completely humorless, even though she saw nothing to laugh at in the situation.

"Your late husband was a lucky man," said Giles more seriously.

"Nonsense. I was a lucky woman." She fiddled with her reins, suddenly uncomfortable. Would she always be seen a woman and not simply the sheriff? Would she always be William's wife and not Ela of Salisbury? Emotion—or was it simple frustration?—churned in her chest, and her horse rose from its slumbers and grew restless as the girls hurried out into the yard.

They both bowed their heads to her awkwardly. "Good morning, my lady," said Annie. "God be with you. Such shocking news."

"Indeed. Did you notice anything odd in John Morse's behavior last night?"

They looked at each other. "Not that I can think of," said Annie. "He's always a bit of a grump, if you know what I mean."

"What about John Brice?"

"He was cheerful," said Mary, the quieter fair one. "Said his wife was finally in decent spirits today."

"She'd been scolding him something wicked before that, he said," added Annie. "We heard that he was sneaking out with Katie Morse and that she found out when he wouldn't stop sobbing after he learned of her death."

Ela turned to Haughton. "It doesn't sound like John Brice

would have killed Katie Morse if he cared that much about her."

"He wouldn't hurt a flea," said Annie. "His wife on the other hand—"

Ela frowned, still looking at Haughton. Maybe the same person had killed both people. "Could Elizabeth Brice have killed Katie Morse, perhaps in a jealous rage?"

He lifted a salt-and-pepper brow. "It's not impossible."

"But her anger in the market square suggests that she only just found out about their affair. If she didn't know they were together, she'd have no motive to kill Katie weeks ago."

"Unless her rage in the market square was feigned." Ela pressed a finger to her lips. Freya was now getting antsy and dancing under her with impatience. "She must have known Katie was pregnant. And I suspect she would have guessed who was to blame. A woman knows these things."

"And she saw the chance to kill her cheating husband and lay the blame on Morse," exclaimed Annie. Then she clapped her hand over her mouth when both Ela and Giles turned to look at her. "Sorry for speaking out of turn."

"I appreciate your assistance," said Ela.

"Girls! Hurry, the milk is turning!" Nance called from the doorway.

Annie looked apologetic. "He's very upset about all this, you know," she whispered. "Lost business and all."

"Understandable," murmured Haughton. "But I have one more thing to straighten out. Morse came here after Brice?"

"No, Morse was first. He likes to be last in the morning and first in the evening so he gets the best light." Annie looked anxiously at Nance.

"And was Morse directly before Brice or were there other customers in between?"

"Both of the others were in between," said Annie quickly. "Like they always are, morning and evening."

"In the morning Brice is first and Morse is last, and in the evening Morse is first and Brice is last, and the other two are always in the middle?"

"Aye."

Haughton looked at Ela. "Being first he'd have had time to get home with his cows, then make his way to the Brice farm to kill John Brice."

Nance was now walking across the yard. Mary had already started to back away toward him. These poor girls must fear losing their jobs, especially if there was suddenly less work to do.

"Master Nance," said Ela, briskly. "I believe we're done with your girls, but I have a question for you."

Nance shooed the girls off to their work, then turned with a look of considerable annoyance on his face. "What's that?"

"Why did Morse have the best time for daylight both morning and evening?"

"He's my oldest customer."

"Are you sure that's the only reason? He was a large man. Did he ever try to threaten or intimidate you?"

Nance's eyes narrowed and his mouth made a weird shape like it wanted to say something but it wouldn't let him. "No."

His denial was strangely unconvincing. Perhaps he didn't want to admit to being cowed by a customer. That, too, was probably bad for business.

"Thank you, Master Nance," said Ela. "We appreciate your assistance. We shall visit your other two customers."

"Why? So you can scare them off?" He looked angry again.

"We didn't bring this disaster into your midst," said Haughton coolly. "We're trying to restore peace to this hamlet. Do you know their names, my lady?"

"Dawson and Lesser." Once again she thanked God for her excellent memory, honed by the governess who'd drilled her in the Psalms at a tender age. "I tried visiting Dawson last week, but he wasn't at home. Let's ride there now. God be with you, Master Nance," said Ela.

"I hope so. I'll need all the help I can get," he snapped. Then he remembered himself and bowed his head. "God be with you, my lady, and you, Master Haughton."

Ela nodded, and turned her horse rather brusquely out of his yard. When they were out of earshot she turned to Haughton. "There's something about Nance that bothers me. I can't put my finger on it."

"He gives an air of being a bitter man who feels he deserves more than he has."

"Sometimes it seems everyone feels that way these days."

"Do I seem that way to you?" His eyes twinkled with amusement.

"Absolutely," said Ela, with the barest hint of a smile. Then she spurred her horse to a trot.

"And you, my lady?" He trotted after her, fast, and came alongside her. "Do you believe you deserve more than you have?"

He had a nerve. But then she rather liked that about him. "God has blessed me in many ways, sir." She didn't turn to face him. "More than I deserve."

"But?" His horse now trotted in time with hers.

"My husband died under unnatural circumstances and it haunts me." Now she turned to look at him.

Don't!

Internal alarums warned her not to voice her suspicions. Haughton was part of the grand web of justice that spread across the land and spiraled back to de Burgh.

"Unnatural, you say?" He reined in his horse. "How so?"

CHAPTER 15

*E*la's conscience pricked. What if Haughton could investigate the circumstances of her husband's death and find justice for him? She'd love to see de Burgh knocked off his high horse.

"William's illness was strange and sudden, not natural at all."

"Are you saying he was poisoned?" Haughton rode close. Ela was conscious of the soldiers riding behind them.

"I can't help suspecting it. He'd just recovered from his long journey home and was going from strength to strength. He was a man in his prime, as you know."

"What were his symptoms?"

"Vomiting, delirium, bloody flux." It pained her to recall his suffering. "He knew he was going to die. He spent fevered hours in penance with Bishop Poore. When he lost consciousness it was a sleep like death—he could not be roused—and then he died."

"Those are symptoms of arsenic poisoning. And why was I not called?"

"Master DeVere was in attendance. He's a physician to

the king and highly respected. He tried all kinds of draughts and potions to no avail. I was so distraught with grief, and so caught up in managing my children's distress, that the idea he might have been the victim of foul play didn't occur to me until the day of his burial. It hit me like a thunderbolt—and the reasons for it—while we all sat there in church."

"And you never said anything?"

"I'm saying something now." They rode along at a slow walk, speaking in hushed tones. "As you know I am literally never alone. I'm always surrounded by soldiers from the garrison, servants, officials. I have to be very cautious with my words."

His brows lowered. "So why are you telling me now?"

Why indeed? "My conscience goads me. I poured my righteous anger into seeking justice for Katherine Morse, but satisfaction eludes us and now I wonder if I've failed my husband by not seeking justice for him."

"You have a suspect?" Haughton's keen interest shone in his eyes.

"Not one I can name aloud in public."

His stare almost penetrated her skin. "A person of importance?"

She decided to let her silence speak for itself. She spurred her horse back into a trot. She still hadn't decided whether she trusted Haughton with her suspicions. What if he, unbeknownst to her, was an agent of de Burgh told to follow her movements and report back to his master?

* * *

The sight of the farm was a welcome distraction. "This is Dawson's place." This time Dawson himself was outside in his farmyard, seated on a crude wooden stool, hammering at the metal tread on a cart wheel. She didn't see the rest of the cart. He was a scrawny, dark-haired man with pinched features and ruddy skin. Two of his children were chasing each other through a flock of chickens.

He looked up, then rose to his feet, leaning the wheel carefully against a shed wall as she approached and pulled up her horse.

"Richard Dawson?"

"Yes." He looked suspicious and not a little hostile. He clearly had no idea who she was and probably didn't much like the idea of an imperious mounted female riding into his farmyard.

"I am Ela of Salisbury, here in my capacity as sheriff. This is Giles Haughton, coroner. We're here investigating the deaths of two of your neighbors."

His shoulders dropped as he visibly relaxed. What had he thought she was here for? Did he feel guilty of something? Maybe he was a poacher worried she'd find parts of a butchered hog from the king's forest salted away inside his hut?

This job made it hard to think the best of people.

And having two murders to investigate made it hard to know where to start. Starting at the beginning was probably best. "I presume that you saw Katherine Morse almost daily at the dairy."

He frowned and scratched his neck. "I wouldn't say that." He looked at the nearby hillside, covered with his grazing cows. "We weren't there at the same times."

"But did you have a chance to form an impression of her relationship with her husband."

He squinted at her. "That's between a man and his wife."

Ela sighed. "Did you ever see signs of violence on her? Bruises, a blackened eye?"

"Can't say I did." His face had an expressionless look to it that almost passed for arrogance.

"Would you say she seemed—intimidated or cowed by her husband?"

"No." He tilted his chin. "If anything, I'd say he seemed to be the one under her thumb. She were a bit of a shrew if you ask me."

Ela stared. This was new information. "Katie Morse was bossy and demanding?"

"Aye, from what I heard. Always after Nance for a better share of the profits and even talked of opening her own dairy in the new town. We all laughed at her, but she just rolled her eyes and said she'd have the last laugh." He let out a sigh. "She was wrong now, wasn't she?"

Ela felt indignant on Katie's behalf. Somehow it hurt more that a woman of ambition and drive should be cut down so cruelly and left to rot in a river.

Of course, being a woman of ambition was dangerous in these times. As it was in most times. She'd be a fool not to acknowledge that.

"Her...domineering behavior might give her husband cause to be angry with her?" She peered at Dawson.

He shrugged. "Might do, I suppose. I think he were just glad to have a wife and to have her do most of the work. Lazy sod himself." Ela got the feeling he'd never have dared say such a thing to Morse's face—Morse was much larger than Dawson—but felt emboldened by his neighbor being accused and imprisoned.

She decided to scare him a little. "Your farm adjoins his, I suspect."

"Aye. Along the eastern boundary. He and I had a legal dispute over it a few years back. I won." His dark eyes shone with a hint of remembered triumph.

"So you might have motive to want the Morses out of the picture so you could buy their farm, perhaps?"

Suspicions crowded her brain like devils. She shifted in her hard saddle.

Dawson looked appropriately horrified by her suggestion. "Nay, nay, never. I never thought of such a thing." He looked around, shifting as if mice gnawed at his privates. "You think I have coin to buy another man's farm on top of my own? I can barely maintain my own herd and support my family."

Ela let him stew for a moment. "Do you have any suspicions about who might have killed Katherine Morse?" She'd given him motivation to come up with some.

Dawson opened his mouth—which had unnaturally thin lips—as if to speak, then apparently thought better of it. He glanced behind her at the soldiers on their horses. "Nay. I don't know why anyone would want to kill her."

"What about John Brice? Who would want him dead?"

"Morse, from what I heard. Because he tupped Morse's wife."

"And do you believe Morse killed Brice?"

Now Dawson sneaked a look at Haughton. "I don't know. It ain't my business."

"It is your business." Ela readjusted her reins. "The sheriff and coroner of Salisbury are calling upon you as a witness to your neighbor's behavior. Don't think you can't be called to appear at the assizes as well."

"Do you think Elizabeth Brice capable of killing her husband?" asked Giles.

Again Dawson looked reluctant to embroil himself in the local drama. "I suppose it's possible."

"Do you think she knew her husband was sleeping with Katie Morse?"

"No!" He made a half guffaw that startled Ela's horse. "Definitely not. She'd have killed him before now if she did."

Ela looked at Giles. "Motive and method."

He nodded.

"So if the only surviving Morse and the only surviving Brice are going to hang, what will happen to their farms?" Dawson asked, his weasel face taut with curiosity.

"They shall go to their heirs and assigns," said Ela.

"The Brice brats aren't old enough to run a farm."

"Then a wardship can be arranged, but that is none of your concern," said Ela curtly. Those poor children! Were they still with Elizabeth's sister? Did they even know their father was dead? And now their mother being sought by soldiers for murder! She couldn't imagine how distressed and worried they would be. She looked at Haughton. "Do you have any further questions?"

"No, my lady."

"Then we'll bid you adieu. May God be with you, Master Dawson. His presence is much needed in this valley right now."

"Aye." He didn't nod or even murmur "my lady." Ela scolded herself for expecting such niceties.

She and Haughton rode out of the yard, the soldiers following. "I must make sure arrangements are in place for the Brice children." She couldn't believe she'd forgotten them until now. She'd paid more attention to their herd of cows.

"Poor mites, losing both their mother and their father in one night." Giles sighed.

"They're with Elizabeth's sister. I hope she's willing to care for them." She sighed. "If their home were a great manor, friends would be clamoring to take the children on as wards and claim the profits from their lands in the meantime. But the Brice farm likely won't generate profits at all if paid labor is used to run it." She shook her head.

"Aye, such farms rely on subsistence labor. Would make more sense to sell it and put the profits into supporting the children. Perhaps the eldest sons are old enough for apprenticeships?"

They rode on grimly. Ela thought it was cruel that the Brice family might have worked and saved for generations to buy their land, and now a disaster such as this could turn their children and descendants back into landless serfs overnight.

And another situation gnawed at her heart. Ela was painfully aware that she'd half-confessed her suspicions about de Burgh and piqued Haughton's curiosity. Sooner or later he'd come back for more details. At least he had the discretion not to press her in front of the soldiers.

* * *

They rode on to the Lesser farmstead. Their thatched farmhouse was neat and well maintained, with a fresh coat of whitewash and a tidy farmyard. A small woven pen contained two young pigs, and the chickens were similarly contained in a low fenced area where they pecked at the ground. Two of the Lessers' children were busy pulling weeds from the fenced kitchen garden near the door, where perennial herbs put out new shoots and dark, rich soil was turned for seeding.

The children rose to their feet with alarm as Ela and her entourage rode in. "Are your mother and father about?" She tried to make her voice sound gentle, but the sheer volume required made it sound like a command.

"Mama is cooking inside. Papa is turning the ground in the back field."

It was busy planting season. Or at least time to prepare the soil. Scrubby patches of weeds were being plowed all over Wiltshire right now. "Could you please tell them that Ela of Salisbury is here to speak with them?" She attempted a smile. She was coming to understand that her arrival was cause for fear and misgivings and she could hardly expect a welcome.

The Lessers' barn was new and even larger than Morse's, with sturdy wood beams and neat wattle. To one side of it she could see a wide humpbacked field where the herd grazed on the new spring grass. "Nice farm," murmured Ela to Haughton.

"Yes, I wonder how they feel about Morse walking to and fro in the light while they're stuck in the darkness half the year?" Haughton muttered under his breath. Ela looked at him with surprise. Was he seeing murder plots wherever he looked?

He'd been in this job enough years to have born witness to most of man's follies.

"This farm is in between Morse and Brice. By getting rid of both of them they could own quite a manor," she said softly, half-joking.

Haughton raised a brow. "I see you grow as cynical as myself."

"It's hard not to."

Mistress Lesser emerged from the house, wiping her hands on her apron. "My children tell me—" She seemed struck dumb by the sight of the armed soldiers in her yard.

"God be with you, Mistress Lesser," said Ela. "We are here seeking insight into the deaths in this neighborhood."

Mistress Lesser crossed herself. "'Tis terrible. Poor Katie Morse, such a sweet girl and so hardworking. And now John Brice as well, I hear! I'm afraid to sleep in my own bed at night."

Ela climbed down from her horse. She didn't like the idea of looming over this good woman while talking to her. One of the soldiers came forward and took her reins and guided her horse out of the way. "Do you have any suspicions about who might have murdered Katie Morse?"

She looked perplexed. "Why, her husband, of course."

"Really?" Everyone was so quick to put a noose around Alan Morse's neck. "What has he done to make you think he would kill her?"

"Well, I'm sure you heard that Katie was creeping around with another man." She spoke in hushed tones, presumably to spare the children.

"Yes, but he claims that she married him knowing he was unable to give her children. There's even a possibility that the Morses planned to get her pregnant by another so they could have a child."

Mistress Lesser's eyebrows shot up. "And they'd choose their nearest neighbor for that?"

"I doubt Katie Morse had the opportunity to meet men outside of this hamlet."

"She went to New Salisbury often to visit her father and to sell butter and cheese she made herself."

"Why would she make her own butter and cheese when the Morses paid the dairy to do that for them?"

"She said they took too much profit, and if she could manage to build up a market of her own, they could keep more of their earnings."

"She brought milk back home with her from the dairy?" Ela couldn't see how such an unwieldy operation would work.

"Oh, no!" Mistress Lesser laughed. "She kept two or three of her own cows that never went to the dairy. I doubt old Nance even knew they existed. She's been making her own butter and cheese for some years and started selling it when she's in town visiting her father.

"Oh." Ela couldn't see how this impacted on the murders, except for giving Morse even less motive to kill his industrious and forgiving wife. "Do you know how her husband felt about this side business?"

"He was happy to spend the money from it. That's how he built his new barn."

Ela remembered how much finer the Morse's barn was than the house. Did his wife feel resentful of the expenditure when their house was so mean? With this new knowledge Ela wondered if perhaps Katherine Morse also enjoyed the barn more than the house.

"We've heard that Morse beat his wife."

Mistress Lesser shrugged. "I couldn't say."

A man beating his wife was, sadly, not unusual. "Do you think he would kill her intentionally, or that she might have accidentally died during an...altercation."

Mistress Lesser shrugged and glanced over her shoulder. Her children were nowhere to be seen. "I wouldn't know. But who else would kill her? It has to be him."

"Her lover might have motive to kill her when she spurned him," said Haughton. "Could you imagine John Brice taking her life?"

Mistress Lesser stared at him like he was demented. "John Brice?" She laughed. "That man couldn't drown a kitten."

"But he must have killed and butchered cows routinely," said Haughton.

"Ha, that's what you think. If anything got butchered on that farm, his wife did it."

A chill slithered down Ela's spine. She hadn't mentioned that they now thought Mistress Brice had murdered her husband. Haughton caught Ela's glance.

"Who do you think murdered John Brice?" asked Ela, as if the last exchange hadn't already answered the question.

"Morse again, no doubt about it. A big man, angry and resentful, maybe went over there to have words with him about bedding his wife and things got out of hand the way they do."

Again, she was quick to be judge, jury and executioner

where Morse was concerned. Ela glanced back at Haughton, but he still stared at Mistress Lesser. "Why are you so quick to pin the blame on Morse?" he asked.

She looked a bit put out. "Well, it had to be him, didn't it? Or am I a suspect?" She laughed, a piercing cackle with more than a hint of nerves in it. "Where's that husband of mine? I sent the girl to fetch him."

"We can ride out to him," said Ela. She remounted her horse, and they headed to the field behind the house. Mistress Lesser hurried to open the gate for them. "Do try not to trample the ground too much, if you please. It's such hard work to loosen it."

Ela felt a twinge of guilt as they headed across a freshly plowed strip. Lesser was still down the far end of the field, guiding a plow pulled by a sturdy pony. This time she rode up to him, glad to look imperiously down on him from her saddle. "Did you not hear that we wish to speak with you?"

"My wife can answer your questions."

"We seek opinions and you have your own, I'm sure."

"A man and his wife should be of one mind." He was a flat-faced man who probably looked impassive even when he wasn't trying to be obtuse.

"Then you suspect Elizabeth Brice of murdering her husband?"

His eyes widened. "What? No! It was Morse."

Ela didn't want to tell a lie about what his wife said, but she let the possibility sink in. "Would that be inconvenient? Perhaps you're hoping that the Morse property will come on the market cheap and you can buy it to expand your holdings."

"Never!" Now he showed some feeling. "I have more land than I can manage right now."

"So even if the Morse property did come on the market,

you can guarantee that you would never, at any time in the future, seek to purchase it?"

He mashed his lips together, drew in a breath, then tugged at his tunic. "Well, I wouldn't say never. One can never tell what good fortune might come a man's way, if the Lord permits."

"Indeed," said Ela dryly. Master Lesser was a broad-shouldered man who would likely have little difficulty dispatching another man to meet his maker, especially if there was an element of surprise.

Ela's saddle felt harder than ever. "Where were you when Master Brice was murdered yesterday evening?"

"Caring for my cattle." His face settled back into flatness. "The evening is a busy time. They need to be settled in the barn with hay and water for the night. The fields aren't dry enough for them to be out full time, yet."

Ela doubted his words. His fields were on a hill that looked well drained, but she knew that hidden springs could make a field damper than expected so she said nothing further on that subject. "Why did you not come when summoned?"

"As I said, my wife—"

"If you were summoned to appear before a jury you would send your wife?" Ela lifted her chin.

"I'd just hitched my horse to the plough and I have work to do."

"The coroner and myself also have work to do." Ela looked at Giles. "Master Haughton, do you have questions for Master Lesser?" She was beginning to suspect his lack of deference had something to do with her gender.

"Indeed I do. Patrick Lesser, did you murder John Brice?"

CHAPTER 16

*L*esser turned white. "Nay! I never did."

"You may not know I've been coroner in Salisbury for some eight years. Your evasive behavior is the type I've come to associate with guilt." Haughton moved his horse forward a few steps, perhaps to better loom over his quarry. "Perhaps you saw a way to remove two of your neighbors in one night, to reduce your competition and simultaneously expand your holdings and increase your herd."

"Never! I didn't kill anyone. I don't know who did kill them but it wasn't me."

At least they had his attention now. And his respect. Ela resolved to remember that accusation focused a man's mind.

"Well, now we're back to the subject of your opinion. Who, in your opinion, killed Katherine Morse?"

He shrugged. "I want to say her husband, but he was better off with her than without her so I don't see why he'd do it, even if he did know she was cheating. He's not what you'd call a man of strong passions."

"Would you look so kindly on your wife if she was sleeping with a neighbor?"

Ela glanced at Haughton, impressed that he was going for the throat again.

"No! Well, no, I wouldn't. But it's different. I don't have those...deficiencies that he has. We have children."

"Perhaps he thought he could overlook her infidelities, but one day his temper got the better of him?" suggested Haughton.

"I couldn't say." Lesser had realized Haughton's approach was likely a tactic, and his face settled back into its stony repose.

"But you can think of no one else with motive?"

"Nay. Who would want to kill her? She was a kind woman, hardworking and good to everyone."

"Ambitious, we hear. Wanted to open her own dairy."

"So what if she did? Her opening a dairy in the new town wouldn't affect my business."

"It might if it took too much business from the one you supply. What about Nance, would he be afraid of the competition?"

Lesser stared at him for a moment. "I doubt it. It was just a woman's talk. None of us thought she could actually do it. How would she raise the money to buy a milking shed and creamery?" He laughed. "It's the stuff of dreams."

Ela found her horse dancing under her and realized she'd tensed her body. Poor Katie Morse. And she found herself feeling pity for her husband as well. She'd never been convinced of his guilt, despite his strong motive. Was she starting to believe in his innocence?

"What about Brice? Who'd have reason to kill him?" continued Haughton.

Lesser looked perturbed. "If it wasn't Morse, wanting revenge for his wife's affair, I don't know who'd kill him. He was a harmless man, never caused any trouble that I know of."

"Your neighbor Dawson said he'd had a lawsuit with Morse. Have you had any lawsuits with the farmers along this road?"

"No," he said quickly.

"Do you think Brice's wife could have killed him?"

"No. Why would she? Leave her own children fatherless? It doesn't make sense. She can't run the farm alone and her oldest is but ten or eleven."

"Which all rather leaves you as the prime suspect, doesn't it?" Haughton raised a brow, but that familiar twinkle of amusement shone in his eyes.

This time Lesser wasn't taking the bait. "I've no more motive than Dawson. And, no, I don't suspect him either. And I wish you'd catch whoever the real killer is. A man can't sleep sound in his bed these days."

"Alan Morse and Elizabeth Brice are both jailed, so if you find evidence of their innocence or someone else's guilt it's your duty to come to us with it forthwith." Haughton spoke sternly. "Withholding evidence from the sheriff and the king's coroner is a crime."

"I understand." Lesser looked rather cowed.

They were none the wiser. It wasn't even midday yet and already Ela felt exhausted. Her children had likely finished with their tutoring and would be asking where she was. Again she wondered if she should leave all this riding and inquisition to Giles Haughton, who was an experienced master at it.

They rode back to the farmyard and out onto the street.

"Two people are dead and two innocent souls are locked up in my castle," said Ela with a sigh, as they joined the road again. "Or that's the result of this morning's interviews."

"Nay. One of them is guilty. I'm pretty sure Elizabeth Brice killed her husband. We just need to know why."

"Crime of passion? She was furious with him in the town square. Enough to make a scene." Ela was still shocked that anyone would bring such negative attention to their own marriage.

"But Lesser makes the good point that she can hardly run the farm without him."

"Maybe she'd prefer to sell up and be a merry widow?" Ela felt like a traitor to her gender by suggesting it. No doubt some would accuse her of such when she didn't remarry.

Haughton lifted a brow. "I suppose it's a possibility. No doubt many a wife wishes her husband dead on occasion."

"I doubt that sincerely." For a chilling instant Ela wondered if people thought she might have killed her husband. He'd been gone so long—missing in France—that people had started to call her a widow, then suddenly he returned…and then she was a widow. "Most women, myself included, depend on their husband in inexpressible ways. The prospect of life without a protector is a fearful one."

Haughton glanced back at the soldiers. "Should we send these two to make sure that Mistress Brice is safely in custody and on her way to the castle?"

Does he want to be alone so we can talk in confidence? Ela nodded and gave the command. The soldiers turned their horses and trotted back up the lane to the Brice farm, leaving Ela and Giles Haughton alone at last.

They rode along silently for a few moments.

"My husband—"

"Your husband—"

They spoke at the same time. Would Haughton laugh? That would be like him. But he didn't.

"You think your husband was murdered?"

"I do but I hesitate to even tell you the facts of the matter."

195

Haughton reined his horse to a stop, which caused Ela's horse to hesitate. She pulled Freya to a halt as well and called on her courage.

"Why do you hesitate?"

"Because I angered a powerful man. I believe he took revenge on me to further his own aims."

"A man more powerful than William Longespée?" Haughton looked intrigued.

"Unfortunately, yes." Ela felt her courage fail and called upon the Lord to strengthen her. "A man with the king's ear. Someone with the power to make sure justice is never served."

"The king's justiciar?" He whispered it as if it must be impossible. His eyes searched her face. "Why would Hubert de Burgh want your husband dead?"

He didn't believe her. And now the dreaded name had been spoken aloud she couldn't take back her accusation and say it was all a misunderstanding.

Fear clawed at her insides. Fear for her children, for Will's future. "Can you promise me complete secrecy?"

"On my honor." He held up his right hand. His horse stamped and snorted, impatient to continue home.

Ela told him of de Burgh's ill-fated attempt to betroth her to his nephew while her husband was still alive but missing.

Giles's eyes widened. "A bold move, to be sure."

"When my husband returned, I told him that de Burgh had pressed an adulterous marriage. William wanted to tear him apart with his bare hands, and although he'd barely had time to recover from his journey and warm himself at the hearth after his long absence, he rode at once to see the king. He told the king that he demanded apology and redress for de Burgh's shocking insult to me and to himself or he would have to turn the kingdom upside down in his quest for

196

revenge." She spoke so fast her words tumbled over each other. "You know William didn't mince words."

"De Burgh must have been the picture of contrition."

"One would hope that he felt shame. He apologized and made some extravagant presents to my husband. William was never one to hold a grudge—they've been on opposite ends of a sword before—so he accepted de Burgh's invitation to dinner at his home."

She paused, wondering for the thousandth time at her husband's decision to sup in his enemy's hall. He'd probably see refusing as an act of cowardice. "He ate and drank and thought all was well but by the next morning he felt sick to his stomach."

The coroner frowned.

"William rode home at once and took to his bed. At first we thought it was the rich feasting after months of privation —and a punishment for breaking Lenten rules to feast on meat under de Burgh's roof." She cursed de Burgh for laying temptation in her husband's path. She should have known he'd think as little of God's laws as he apparently did of man's.

"Instead of recovering, my beloved husband sickened until he felt death tugging at his sleeve. He begged for the bishop to attend him. They prayed and my husband offered confession after confession—by his own admission he did not live the most Christian of lives—but to no avail. Within days he was dead, taken from his children, who had barely welcomed him home." Tears now flowed freely down her cheeks, and she raised her hand to shield her face. Her pain was so fresh and raw—these events barely a week old.

Protracted silence made her swipe at her eyes with her veil and meet the coroner's gaze. He looked more astonished than anything, frowning at the bank of clouds over the tree-tops. "But your husband is the present king's uncle. And de

Burgh is the king's closest confidant. It beggars belief that he would do something so—heinous."

He didn't believe her. Ela's heart sank, and fresh tears pricked her eyes. "You can see why I didn't dare tell anyone. Who would believe such a thing?"

"Have you shared your thoughts with anyone else?"

"No. Who would I tell?"

"Your family?"

"My mother is my only family left, apart from my innocent children. I don't wish to endanger any of them by burdening them with this news."

"I see." His mouth grew smaller. She could tell he was troubled by this secret she'd laid on him. "And what do you propose that I should do?"

Ela stiffened. Her horse shifted under her. "I have no idea. Honestly. Could justice ever be served? I have no proof."

"We might be able to find proof of poison in your husband's body." He grimaced slightly. "If we were to, say... feed a small amount of his—"

"No." Ela couldn't imagine anything worse than feeding his flesh to some innocent animal in the hope that it would die. "He's already dead. Let him rest in peace. Even if we could prove he'd been poisoned there would be no evidence of who did it. For all I know I might end up accused."

"Who would accuse you?"

"De Burgh." She said it, then lifted a brow. "Attack is often the best form of defense, I've heard. He could accuse me of wanting to maintain my autonomy. He could even use my refusal of the marriage proposal as proof of it."

Haughton let out a long sigh. "I see what you mean. Do you plan to marry again?"

Ela froze. Was this really a question she needed to answer right now? "No. I intend to found a holy order of sisters and join it myself once my children are of age."

He nodded slowly. "If I were you, I'd found it sooner rather than later."

"Why?"

"To avoid the kind of speculation you've just suggested. An unmarried woman is an attractive nuisance in some quarters. Especially if she's as well landed and moneyed as yourself."

Ela's gut clenched. "I appreciate your sage counsel, Master Haughton."

"It's offered with tenderness as much as wisdom. You are a credit to your late husband and do honor to his memory."

"You don't think it bold of me to command the role of sheriff?"

He laughed. Sometimes his laughter really annoyed her. "Bold? Of course it's bold. Why should men only have boldness as a good quality? Perhaps more women should be bold and the world would know less war and strife."

"From your mouth to God's ears, Master Haughton. But I know that many feel a woman's counsel is best whispered in her husband's ear for him to execute."

"There may be some truth to that." He let out a sigh. "Your husband's ancestor Empress Matilda was never able to claim the crown her father left to her."

"I hardly intend to rule as queen, and I study myself daily for the sin of pride." She didn't like being compared to Matilda, though she couldn't help admiring her spirit. "I simply seek to do my duty as Countess of Salisbury, the title and role my father left me." Hmm. Maybe she wasn't so different from Matilda after all.

"You have far to fall. You're right to be cautious."

Ela felt the boldness seep out of her. He wasn't going to do anything. She'd shared her dangerous secret, and now nothing would come of it.

At least nothing good.

She pushed her horse back into a walk. Why had she told him? Had she hoped he'd lead an investigation that would uncover the truth? That he'd seek redress as if his life depended on it?

That was what her big-hearted, brash, brave-to-a-fault husband would have done.

Haughton was too wise for such rashness, as was she.

"If I were to tell my children of my suspicions they might waste their lives in a futile quest for revenge."

"Indeed. Young Will is blessed with his father's courage and daring. I'm sure he would take it upon himself to avenge your loss."

An odd thought occurred to her. "You don't think that would be right, do you? Am I wrong to want his safety at the cost of redress?"

"Some might say so, but I wouldn't be one of them. Your son has a bright future ahead of him as Earl of Salisbury. Hubert de Burgh is the king's right hand, and the king—God bless him—has not yet reached majority, so effectively Hubert de Burgh is in charge of all England, including the courts. It's inconceivable that you could win with an outright accusation in a court of law and quite likely that you might end up imprisoned for treason or worse if you were to accuse him."

Ela felt a trickle of fear at the base of her spine. He could yet do all those things in revenge for her refusal to marry his nephew.

"But if you were to sow the seeds of rumor..." He tailed off. "If word were to somehow travel that William might have been murdered. And that—outrageous as it seems—the king's justiciar might be the hand behind it—"

He turned and looked at her. Her whole body pricked to attention. "Are you suggesting you might be willing to sow these seeds for me?"

His face was grim. "I can't promise any results. And if pressed I will staunchly deny that I heard any suspicion from you. You must remain blameless and above reproach for your own safety and that of your children." He frowned. "But if over a cup of ale, I might happen to mention the strange circumstances of your husband's death to one man…"

He looked ahead. The clouds over the hills had grown darker, threatening rain. "And if Hubert de Burgh's ambition and aspirations were to be mentioned to another man over another mug of ale—"

Ela felt her chest swell. Perhaps her husband's cruel murder wouldn't remain a secret buried in her heart.

"And if, over a cup of wine, two of those men might find themselves talking and might find that two puzzle pieces unexpectedly fit together… De Burgh is an arrogant man and prone to ruffling feathers. His vice grip on power cannot last forever."

"I'm deeply grateful." Ela's voice emerged as a whisper. "And I have no expectations of any kind. God is our judge, and de Burgh will meet him at last. Until then I must content myself with raising my children to bring honor to their father's memory."

"Indeed, my lady. You're wise as well as good."

Ela still felt that the word cowardly might apply. But she could not sacrifice her children on the altar of revenge.

"I just hope you don't find yourself forced to marry de Burgh's nephew against your will. Worse things have happened."

"The Magna Carta permits a woman to remain as a widow. I do not brag if I give myself some credit for that."

"I know you were there when the king signed it."

"And my husband signed it. We keep one copy here in safety in Salisbury. Even the king's justiciar can't contravene the last king's promise to his barons and his people."

"God go with you, my lady."

"And with you, Master Haughton. Forgive me for burdening you with this hard news."

"You do me great honor with your confidence. And I intend to do you and your late husband honor with how I manage it."

* * *

Back at the castle, Ela consulted with the cook about the menus for the next few days. It would be so much easier if the meatless season fell later in the year, when there was a decent array of fruits and vegetables to eat, rather than at the end of winter, when it was hard to find a bushel of carrots that hadn't moldered yet. Her mother was used to the best, and she intended to make sure that she had no reason to complain of her daughter's hospitality.

Ela felt a sense of lightness after unburdening herself from her terrible secret. She knew it might be months, or years, before Haughton could safely get word to spread, but the prospect gave her hope.

Elizabeth Brice was safely imprisoned in the dungeon awaiting the assizes, and arrangements had been made for the Brice cattle to be taken for milking and tended until her fate was determined.

"My head hurts, Mama." Little Nicholas had spent the day running from apron to apron, quick to tears.

"My poor pet." She felt his forehead, and sure enough it was warm to the touch. "You're feverish. Let's tuck you up in a blanket, and I'll sing you a song."

Even that prospect did little to cheer him. They sat in a big chair, with the hounds gathered at Ela's feet, and she told him his favorite stories. Petronella and Richard came over and sang him a song and kissed his hot cheeks and he cheered slightly but wasn't himself.

Ela took him to bed with her again, keeping a damp cloth

at hand to cool his fevered brow. Still raw from her husband's death she couldn't find the strength to trust in providence, and she barely slept a wink.

In the morning little Nicky was still hot, crying piteously whenever he was awake, and now two of her older children were sick.

CHAPTER 17

Sibel and the other maids rushed around with cool spring water and soft cloths, cooling the children's foreheads. Ellie felt too ill to break her fast, and brave Stephen lay pale and still against his pillow.

"I must make a poultice." Ela felt helpless. Her children's fever was now accompanied by a spreading pink rash on the chest that struck terror into Ela's heart. Smallpox? Scarlet fever? They'd sent for the doctor but he was not at home and nor was his servant.

Ela's mother unhelpfully recalled a recent outbreak of illness in her village that had killed a family of eight almost overnight.

All three children were propped up by pillows near the fire in the hall, where they could be attended constantly. Will, tortured by inaction, hovered nearby, fussing. The youngest chambermaid—a child herself—held a candle and murmured Hail Marys. Ela could tell she was scared—as Ela was too.

"Do stop praying like that," pleaded Will. "It's unnerving."

"I'm sorry, sir." The girl's eyes filled with tears.

"Will!" Ela was shocked at him. "Prayer is never amiss. We should all call for God's intercession."

Will loomed in the shadows. "God has shown us little mercy of late. My father was gone an entire year and I prayed nightly for his return—"

"As did we all."

"Then his joyous homecoming is followed hard by an agonizing death. Did God bring him back just to taunt us?"

Shocked as she was by his words, Ela empathized with his anger. But it was her job to counsel him, not just console him. "Every man has his hour on earth. The length of our lives is for God to decide."

"Then prayer is pointless." His voice was almost a snarl. "If our heavenly Father has already decided when our time is up."

"Prayer is our means of intercession. Pray for your father's soul and yours."

"And my sisters' and brothers'?" His voice shook with barely controlled rage and fear.

"Pray hardest for them." Ela could feel tears welling, and she itched to leave the room. "I'm going to my herb cupboard to make a drawing salve for the rash."

She rushed from the room. The hours before her husband's death were so fresh in her mind. How he'd prayed and begged God for forgiveness, sure he was dying and doubting his entry into Heaven after a life with no shortage of worldly pleasures.

She'd felt his agony, his horror at an eternity in the flames of hell that he saw looming before him.

He'd died at peace, thanks be to God, shriven and absolved of his sins. Still, his terror during those last days of fevered prayer and penance was something she'd never forget.

Ela retrieved a small key from her solar, then fetched a

basket from the silent kitchen and headed to the small store-room where they kept dried herbs over the winter. She chose sprigs of chamomile, calendula and lavender, and a handful of rose petals.

In the kitchen she chopped and pounded and added drops of freshly boiled water to grind the herbs into a paste with a pestle and mortar. It was so much easier to keep moving, stirring, doing, than to kneel and pray. A weakness in her character, no doubt. She envied those who could spend hours in stillness and prayer. Perhaps one day she'd be so steady and faithful, but for now each crisis spurred her into action.

She said a prayer over her poultice, that it might bring relief to her sick children, to herself, all the family and servants who would be endangered by fever in the castle.

Despite the bustle of activity, the big hall felt dark and oppressive, its small, defensive windows seemed to keep out the light as much as let it in. "Any change?"

"For the worse." Her mother's voice was taut. "The fever won't break." Little Nicholas was limp and flushed, his eyes glazed. When he spoke it was babbling nonsense that seemed unconnected to his thoughts.

"Let me apply this." She pulled the covers away from his hot, flushed skin and applied the gritty poultice as gently as she could. Nicky stopped babbling and tossing, but his eyes stared, glassy, and his lips moved as if in silent agitated speech with an unseen visitor. Ela said another prayer, and everyone in the room joined her in repeating the familiar, soothing words.

Ela knew how fast a fever could turn deadly, or turn a corner and fade away. She prayed that the Lord intended for her baby, and his brothers and sisters, to live a long, happy life here on earth. She'd been so blessed that she'd never lost a child. Had she counted her blessings too soon?

She also prayed that no other members of the household would catch the illness. You didn't have to be a doctor to know that close proximity to a diseased person placed anyone in danger.

After a long day of worry, her attempt at sleep did not go well. In the wee hours of the morning she visited each of her children, just to watch their chests rise and fall with the breath of life.

In the morning Ela was glad of the distraction of her daily rounds and even small disturbances—a present of dead birds left in the passage by the big tabby cat and a pail of milk half-spilled right outside the kitchen door—provided moments of sweet relief from the ache of worry.

She'd sent word to Westminster that they now had two prisoners to be tried and waited to receive word of when the assizes would take place.

They were expecting a large delivery of wine from Burgundy, and she hoped it would not be as sour as the last batch and that it would last until the next grape harvest.

As the sun rose, she could see that Nicky had turned a corner. His eyes were brighter and though he still seemed listless and weak, he wasn't fevered and babbling. Ellie, however, had entered the more serious stage of the fever and the tearful maid said she'd just suffered a round of convulsions that had scared them all.

Will paced anxiously. "Mama, we must ask Bishop Poore to offer a Mass for their recovery."

"We could have Father Daniel offer a Mass right here in our chapel," she suggested. She wasn't anxious to ask Bishop Poore for any more favors so soon after the last one.

"But the Mass must be in the chapel where father lies interred. His soul can intercede for us!"

Ela blinked. Her son didn't usually show signs of such

deep faith. And yesterday she'd worried his faith was badly shaken. "What do you mean?"

"Father is so recently dead, barely crossed over, I hear that such souls have one foot in this world and one in the next."

"Who said such a thing?" She suspected one of the soldiers, who were from various backgrounds and prone to all kinds of unlikely superstitions, some bordering on heresy. "The Lord hears our prayers no matter which world we are in."

"I know, Mother, but my heart tells me to ask Bishop Poore for a Mass." He looked so earnest.

"All right. I shall ask him. I'll ride there this morning." She was pretty sure Will would offer to do the riding part. He was ten times as restless and energetic as her.

He heaved a sigh of relief. "Thank you, Mama! I promised Ellie I wouldn't leave her side."

Ela was stunned. She couldn't really spare the time to ride there. She'd spent so much time riding abroad lately that she was starting to question her motives when there was much to be done at home. But she didn't want to disappoint her son in his solicitude for his sister and perhaps he was guided by angels or some such thing. "I'll leave at once."

* * *

Ela cursed herself for being glad of the opportunity to stir again even if it meant leaving her sick children. A brisk trot on Freya would blow away some of the worry and fear that dogged her like a cloud of angry bees. She summoned two soldiers to attend her.

The visit to Poore went smoothly, oiled by the application of gold coins from Byzantium. He seemed genuinely concerned about the little ones and took the time to pray privately with Ela, which touched her and made her think more kindly of him. Tierce had just passed but he promised to offer the Masses at Sext, Nones and Vespers with prayers for their speedy recovery, and Ela left feeling lighter.

They rode past two older men yelling at each other. When they came to blows, Ela—as sheriff—called to them to stop. They ignored her and the soldiers jumped from their horses to arrest them. She ordered for them to be placed in the stocks for the rest of the morning to contemplate their misdeeds and left the soldiers there to supervise.

Shaking her head at the never-ending abundance of human folly, she rode back alone through the new town. Despite her misgivings about its creation, and the way it undoubtedly undermined the importance and economic stability of her ancestral home inside the castle walls, Ela admired how quickly the streets had become lined with businesses. Bright new whitewashed buildings with fresh thatch had sprung up along quiet country lanes, turning a sleepy hamlet into a bustling market town in just a few short years. Since she saw it so often she hadn't taken the time to admire the dramatic changes.

She couldn't help but note the rotten thatch and distressed walls of the few remaining older buildings, and one in particular caught her eye. A big iron horseshoe was the only sign announcing the business, and Ela remembered with a jolt that Katie Morse's father—the old blind man—still kept and lived in his ironmongery somewhere in the town.

What was his name? She searched her memory, which was usually good with such facts. Robert Harwich. She'd half-forgotten about him in all the drama surrounding the case. She'd meant to visit him to see what could be done to improve his condition. And perhaps she should ask him what he knew about the Brices and if he thought there was any possibility that Morse killed Brice as well as his wife.

Could this be his shop? It seemed likely. She dismounted Freya and tied her to a ring for that purpose outside.

"Hello? Is there anyone home?" She hadn't much liked the old blind man. He was a rough and crude character, but perhaps her distaste revealed more about her own failings than his.

She heard someone, or something, stir behind the scarred wood door. The area in front of the shop, where horses must have once been shod, was unswept and cluttered with odd-sized pieces of stone and hunks of half-rotted wood, perhaps intended for some project and then forgotten. Being blind he probably had little idea what the place looked like anymore.

"Hello? It's Ela, Countess of Salisbury." Her grand title rang hollow in the dismal surroundings. Perhaps the fact that today she had no retinue made it sound odder. "May I speak with you?"

She heard a piece of furniture scrape against a flagstone floor. "Coming." The low, graveled voice sounded like Harwich. His shop was a prime location near the center of the new town. Rather wasted in its current condition.

The door opened to reveal Harwich, as grimy and disheveled as ever—she scolded herself for the superficial thought—and looking none too pleased at being disturbed.

"Did the scoundrel hang yet?" His white-glazed eyes seemed to see right through her.

"No." His accusatory tone flustered her. "Capital cases must await the traveling justice who comes for the assizes."

"So he's still alive and breathing while my Katie lies in a cold grave?" His voice dropped so low she swore she could hear it rattle.

"He's safely imprisoned in the dungeon and will remain there until his trial." Ela tried to remember why she'd come here. Suddenly it seemed like a terrible idea. Harwich had made it clear from the outset that he was sure Morse was his daughter's killer.

"I don't know if you heard that their neighbor John Brice was killed."

"Stabbed, I heard. Ruthless bastard. I told my Katie not to marry him."

"So you think Morse killed Brice? We have Brice's wife in custody."

"What for?" His upper lip curled with apparent disgust. "Why would you think a woman killed her own husband when there was a violent and greedy man next door?"

"Well," Ela hesitated and—for no good reason—glanced back at the street behind her. She lowered her voice. "Not exactly next door. We don't suspect a disagreement over land or cattle. It turns out that Master Brice was engaged in..." She hesitated, not wanting to cloud a father's memories of his daughter. "In a liaison with your daughter."

"Never!" Harwich hurled his exclamation on a tide of spittle. "My Katie would never do that."

Ela found herself taking a step back. Her horse, tied behind her, pawed and stamped at the rutted ground. "Brice himself admitted it, in public."

"He's a liar. My Katie was an angel, a very saint walking on this earth!"

Ela was already regretting her visit. It hadn't furthered her investigation and now she'd upset a blind old man. If she offered him alms now, they'd be flung back in her face. Still, she'd already stepped in it, so— "If anything, an affair provides a pretext for Morse to kill her."

The old man's eyes narrowed, and her skin prickled. Could he actually see her? "I suppose. Still, he's a murderer one way or the other, ain't he?"

"That's what I'm trying to figure out. Since Morse himself denies both murders we need evidence to convict him at the trial. We don't have any hard evidence and no witnesses. It's his word against—"

"He's a violent man. Used to beat her regular-like." Harwich looked increasingly irritated. "If she sought a little comfort somewhere else, who can blame her?"

Ela blinked. Had he really gone so quickly from denying that she was capable of an affair to sympathizing with her for it?

She peered past him into the dark interior of the blacksmith's forge. "Do you live here in your workplace?"

"Aye." His eyes narrowed again. Maybe he could see her, if not perfectly. "It's not luxurious but it's all I have." She heard the hint of a sneer in his tone.

"It's a fine location now the town has grown around it. Have you considered renting it out and moving somewhere more comfortable for someone with your—"

She groped for less inoffensive words than old age and infirmities.

"I still ply my trade here," he growled, clearly roused. He turned and shuffled back inside and picked up something off a dark and dusty shelf along one wall. Ela peered at it, but had to step in out of the daylight to see it was a crude buckle of the type that might be used on a simple harness.

"You're lucky to have a trade you can follow without your sight." She tried to figure out how she could test whether he could see her. "There aren't many jobs you could do, I'd imagine."

"Aye, and that's why I'm not leaving! Every day folks come to my door and try to make me move. That accursed bishop wants me in his new poorhouse. Well, damn it, I'm not moving." His voice rose, and Ela found the hairs standing oddly up on the back of her neck.

An odd thought occurred to her. "Was Katie planning to open her dairy here in this location?"

He stilled, staring at her with his—maybe—sightless eyes. Ela made a sudden movement with her right hand, snatching it up above her head as if a wasp was attacking her. If he could see, his eyes would involuntarily follow the movement.

But they didn't.

"What are you doing?" He snarled. "I heard you move."

"Swatting at a fly."

"This is no place for a dairy. No room. I'm not moving upstairs when the stairs are rotted and my knees not strong enough to climb the ladder."

Ela's ears pricked up. "She was planning to move here? With Morse?"

"Over my dead body."

His words rang in the air. Ela felt a cold finger of fear scratch at the base of her spine.

His dead body—or Katie's?

But if he was truly blind, he couldn't have killed her and dumped her in the river, could he?

"Come back here, I'll show you how rotten the stairs are." He shuffled back into the gloomy windowless interior.

Ela's nerves sent up a flag of alarum. "I have to go. Thank you." She hurried to the bright doorway. Harwich turned and started moving toward her. Could he be a killer? And she was here by herself like a fool?

CHAPTER 18

*O*utside Ela fumbled with her reins and startled poor Freya, making her jig about while Ela tried to mount. "Thank you for your time, Master Harwich," she called, as she urged Freya out of his yard into the street.

As soon as she was past a cart pulling a load of stones toward the cathedral site, she broke into a trot and kept trotting until she'd left the town behind. On the empty lane Freya stepped up to canter, likely spurred more by Ela's pounding heart than any intentional cues. Ela cantered her all the way back to the castle, mind racing.

But by the time she dismounted she was questioning her own sanity. Why would a blind old man kill the only family member who cared about him?

Unless she was anxious to turf him out of his home. Ela didn't know Katie Morse. Maybe she wasn't the sweet and dutiful girl of her imagination. Maybe she was a greedy harridan who bossed her husband and threatened her old father with seizing his property and ending his livelihood.

Though wouldn't most old blind men rather be taken care of by their daughter in the bosom of their family than left alone to fend for themselves? Why would he refuse her company in his shop and home? None of it made sense.

She trotted up the castle hill and through the arches into the castle, then dismounted and handed Freya to a groom.

"Where are your escorts?" A deep voice from behind made her jump. She spun to face Gerald Deschamps.

"I left them behind to take care of a disturbance in the town. Two men are being attended in the stocks."

"My lady should not ride abroad without protection," he murmured.

"Indeed, I did not intend to." And it was foolish of her to take a detour. She must go check on her sick little ones and reassure Will that the Mass was arranged. And there remained the pressing question of whether Harwich should be arrested for murder. She'd prefer to consult with the coroner, but Deschamps might take it amiss if she didn't speak to him about the situation since he was here and Giles Haughton wasn't.

"I visited Katherine Morse's father while I was in Salisbury."

"The blind man?" Deschamps looked perplexed. "Why?"

"I happened to be passing by what I thought might be his shop, and I wanted to discover his perspective on the Brice murder." She hesitated, not sure how to describe what happened. "It was an odd encounter."

"How so, my lady?" Polite disinterest. She started walking toward the great hall, spurred by anxiety over her sick children.

"He was—hostile. I asked if his daughter had wanted to set up a dairy on the site of his ironmongery. She's been described as having such plans. His reaction was startling."

"Startling?" Again, he sounded bored.

Ela doubted herself. Why had she felt such fear? It was hard to put into words. Harwich had asked her to come look at his rotten stairs, and she'd suddenly felt like her corpse might wind up underneath them. But why?

"I asked him if Katherine and her husband were planning to move there. He said, "Over my dead body." It was unnerving since the circumstances of my visit did involve a dead body."

"Perhaps you're reading too much into it. An elderly blind man could hardly kill anyone. And why would he kill his only caretaker?"

"I had the same thought. But it was odd. I felt—threatened by him."

"You should never ride anywhere alone. What if you'd come upon a thief?"

"It wasn't intended. Next time I'll take more attendants." A guard opened the door into the hall and she swept in, grateful to be back at her own well-protected hearth. Sibel rushed forward to take her cloak.

"How is little Nicky faring?"

"Awake and chattering away," said Sibel cheerfully. "He's turned a corner and is on the mend. I'm sure of it. Ellie and Stephen are still feverish but not worse than before."

"Thanks be to God." Ela crossed herself. If one child had recovered the others should too. She hurried to visit them, pausing as Petronella thrust a prayer she had copied to parchment into her hand for her to admire and stopping to pet her sweet and eager greyhound, Greyson, who jumped at her skirts.

Maybe she'd overreacted about Harwich. He was a rough and grimy character, unsettling to behold. His sightless eyes —for they'd passed her crude test—were disconcerting through no fault of his own. Perhaps, once again, her fear of him revealed a weakness in her own character. A lack of true Christian charity. She would have to pray over it.

Ellie's eyes greeted her as she entered, and a smile played on her pale lips.

"You're awake my sweet," Ela stroked her still-hot brow. "Bishop Poore will send up prayers for your full recovery."

Ela's mother, seated on a chair in the corner with her pearl rosary knotted in her fingers, crossed herself. "Praise God."

"I knew you'd convince him," said Will, who sat on the bed next to Stephen. "I'll attend the Mass myself."

"All of them? He promised Sext, Nones and Vespers."

"You're a wonder, Mama." Will jumped up and kissed her cheek. "The nearest as I need a ride to shake off all the worry." He clapped a hand on poor weak Stephen. "And I know you'll be stronger when I return."

Ela admired her son's faith and youthful energy. Perhaps she could consult him for his views on Harwich?

No, he'd just scold her for visiting him without a retinue. She'd save the news for Giles Haughton, and together they could interview Morse about his relationship with his father-in-law. That might reveal more about both of their characters.

But first her sick children needed her time and attention, as did the cook, her maid and the other castle staff. She did not intend to give anyone, including her mother, cause to scold her for neglecting her womanly duties for her role as sheriff.

* * *

At night, after praying for her children's health and safety, Ela prayed for peace in her own heart and the wisdom to know when to seek justice here on earth and when to allow the Lord to dispense it as he saw fit. She'd sent for Haughton to attend her the next day after Tierce and she hoped his experience would guide them on how to proceed with

Harwich. At the very least they could get Morse's account of his wife's plans and his father-in-law's odd reaction.

Poor Katie Morse, to have been cut down before she had a chance to pursue her dream of owning a dairy. Not that she would have been able to do it anyway, with two hostile men as her nearest and dearest. But if she was wise she'd have found a way to make it their project as much as—or more than—hers and would have enlisted them in her efforts while downplaying her own leadership role.

Sometimes it exasperated her how much a woman had to quell her natural desire to lead, to invent or even to fight. It wasn't unusual for young girls to learn the gentlemanly arts of falconry and hunting, even the skills of swordsmanship, alongside their brothers, but ultimately their role would be circumscribed by hearth and children and their husband's bed.

Widowhood—if horribly unwelcome—was Ela's chance to live on her own terms. She had the benefit of the protections provided by the Magna Carta and by her husband's connection to the royal family, even if the king was still a youth. She'd earned respect locally for her piety and good management of the castle and her household. She wasn't looking to seize power or land or to threaten another's estates, simply to claim control over the estates she'd inherited from her father as a child.

Sometimes she thought her desire to control the estates was a manifestation of the sin of pride. Other days it seemed that God had gifted her with a sense of right and wrong, a talent for administration and insight into the thoughts and actions of those around her. Surely employing such gifts in his service was not a sin?

She knelt at the prie-dieu in the corner of her bedroom and said several decades of her rosary, willing her active mind to still and her willful nature to enfold itself in the

Holy Spirit. When weariness overtook her, she climbed into the bed, her curtained sanctuary from the world, and let her body relax into the well-stuffed mattress.

In her dream she was riding her horse—not Freya but a long-ago dun pony called Tisse—along the edge of a steep cliff. Below her she could see soldiers gathering for battle in long, rectangular ranks, unfamiliar banners waving and armor shining in the sun. She carried a tall lance that was so heavy she could barely keep her grip on it and had to constantly hoist it higher on her shoulder while trying not to steer her mount off the cliff.

She awoke suddenly with a deep sense of unease, missing faithful Tisse and wondering whose armies were gathered below and whether they were friend or enemy.

She rose and Sibel brought her fresh water to splash her face and helped her dress by candlelight. It was still dark as she headed outside on her rounds. Sleepy guards shuffled to attention as she passed and wished them a good morning. The kitchen was already astir with preparations for breakfast. She passed through the herb garden, fresh with morning dew.

The chapel was lit with fresh candles and still smelled of incense from the Matins service. She genuflected before the altar and said a quick prayer before departing to make sure the penned suckling pigs were being attended to and the morning's eggs collected.

She passed a rowdy group of soldiers at the east gate, still drunk to all appearances, who could barely gather themselves to stand to attention as she passed. She'd be sure to mention that to Deschamps. Her husband had been indulgent with the soldiers, saying their loyalty in battle was more important than how straight they stood to attention, but to her mind ill-governed men could be as dangerous as they were useful.

In the shimmering light from the high braziers she observed with displeasure that the main path out the gate and into town had not yet been cleared. Where was the boy with his rake? Then a movement close behind her made her spin about and scan the shadows.

"Who's there?"

* * *

The drunken soldiers she'd passed were out of sight and already laughing about something among themselves.

Her, possibly.

"Show yourself," she commanded as loudly as she could. Then someone grabbed her by the throat and dragged her to the ground in a sudden thrust that knocked the breath from her lungs.

Help! The word formed in her mind, but she couldn't force them to her lips because a big hand clamped tight over her mouth. She struggled, desperate to free herself, but the fiend that held her seemed to have four arms, each like an iron band.

Then she felt the knife blade dig into the skin of her throat even through the linen of her wimple.

"Be careful now," rasped a deep male voice. "This blade is a mite too sharp for safety."

The mocking whisper defied recognition. Had Morse escaped the dungeons? She opened her mouth to speak but found it thrust full of a foul-tasting wad of cloth that made her gag and retch.

Why could those fool soldiers not hear her struggling?

The hard stones of the castle road bumped her right hip and ribs as her assailant dragged her off the main path and in between two great stacks of firewood piled like buttresses against the wall.

What do you want? All she could do was grunt since the rag stopped her mouth, forcing it open.

"It won't do to kill you on the path and leave a big pool of blood now, will it?" The grisly whisper made her struggled harder. "Not when I need to get back out through the gate before daylight."

Harwich. Her assailant's identity assaulted her like a blow. But how? He was elderly and stooped as well as blind, but now his grip was like the forged bonds in the dungeon below. She fought and struggled to free her hands. If he intended to leave her for dead she had nothing to lose.

She used her tongue to push at the filthy rag stopping her mouth. Servants and tradesmen trekked into this castle all morning long, and it was near daybreak. Someone might pass at any moment. If she could just—

A callused hand slapped her so hard across the face that her breath fled her lungs, and she choked on the rag. Unwelcome tears stung her eyes, further blurring her vision.

He shoved her onto her back, and her head hit the stones hard enough to make sparks fly in her mind.

This is what he did to Katie. The blows to her face and head must have come from him knocking her to the ground. Now he intends to leave you dead and your children orphans.

But she wasn't dead yet.

A fierce jolt of energy surged through her, and she managed to jerk one arm free and reach up to pull his hair. All she got was the greasy cap from his head. A futile gesture, but as he struggled to catch her arm she freed her other hand, pulled the rag from her mouth and screamed as he dragged her again across the hard, uneven stones.

Surely someone would hear her? Where was the boy who swept the path? Her veil had slipped to cover her face and, pressed almost face down against the stones, she tried to keep her bearings in the hope that she could gain enough footing to right herself and run. His hand covered her mouth again, and she struggled to bite it through her accursed veil.

But as a door—a door?—closed behind her with a thud, she realized he'd dragged her into a closet within the castle wall.

The door blotted out what wan light bled through her veil from the braziers and the first light of day and now she was trapped in total darkness with a man who wanted her dead.

"What are you doing?" It took her a moment to realize that he'd uncovered her mouth and she could speak. Her words emerged in a rush of shock and fury. She tried to lift her hands to push her veil aside but he held one arm and the other was crushed beneath her while his heavy malodorous weight pressed down on her.

"You aren't as clever as they say if you can't puzzle that out." The cold blade, which she'd almost forgotten about, now dug into her throat again. "Oh dear, there's blood spoiling your fine clothes." His voice sounded oily. "But never mind. Soon there'll be more."

Why hadn't he killed her yet? What did he want? "You'll never leave the castle grounds. There are soldiers everywhere."

"Aye, useless band of loafers in case you hadn't noticed. They take no heed of an old blind beggar. No one does."

Keep him talking. "Are you really blind?" She had to find a way to overpower him. For all his age and infirmity, he was as muscled and strong as an ox drover.

"Been blind nigh on ten years. What they don't realize— those that mock me and kick stones at me—is that losing one's sight sharpens the other senses. I can hear a mouse coming from half a mile away. I know every man, every woman from their smell, before they have a chance to see me."

"Is that how you knew it was me?" Her eyes were adjusting to the deep blackness beneath her veil and she could now make out the thin outline of dim light that marked the door. "What do I smell like?"

"Money!" A raucous laugh made her flinch. "Gold coins and rich meals and fine furs. You don't think they have a smell, but they do."

Her mind raced. "I do have gold. I can give you money. How much do you want?"

His crude laugh made her skin crawl. The knife against her throat made her gag, and his weight on her crushed her spine hard against the uneven dirt floor of the closet.

"Oh, if that were true. I'd be a rich man—for an hour before you arrested me and had me hanged." He sounded wistful. "You think I'm stupid, don't you?" His whisper came hot in her ear, making her shrink from him with revulsion. "A stupid old blind man who'll fall for your trickery. I know all about women and their trickery."

"Did Katie try to trick you?"

"Oh, aye. You all think you're so clever, don't you? With your plans and schemes and manipulations. Coming to take care of me. To keep the place clean and orderly. It took me a while to catch on to what she was really after."

"Perhaps she wanted to live with you so she could tend to you." She could feel his grip on her arm loosening. Any minute now she might be able to tug it free and right her veil. With her sight she had at least one advantage over him as long as she could get that knife blade from her neck.

"She didn't want to live with me. Not even for one day. She hated me. And why wouldn't she? When her mother fell down the well she said I pushed her."

Ela's blood stilled. Another death on his hands made this man a stone-hearted killer who'd think nothing of snuffing out her life.

"I'm sure she loved you. All girls love their father."

"Did you?"

His question shocked her. "Of course. He died when I was nine. I've never forgotten him." She gagged as the knife blade pressed against her skin. She could swear she could almost taste her own blood.

"Lying whore." She heard a rasping sound and felt the hot sting of his spittle on her cheek. "You're all lying whores. Look at that little bitch, letting her neighbor into her bed. I didn't even know about that until you told me. Women are only good for one thing, and I haven't had that in so many years I've forgotten what it's like." He leaned in and his foul breath turned her stomach. "Maybe I should find out."

"One hundred pounds in silver coin," she rasped, her voice shaking. She needed to refocus his mind.

"If you hadn't come by yesterday I'd have left you well alone," he muttered. "You'd have hanged that worthless son-in-law of mine and I'd have peace at last."

"Five hundred pounds in silver coin." She'd offer more but she wanted it to sound believable. Most men in the village would never see that much in their entire working life.

"I may be blind, but I'm not deprived of sense."

"I'm the sheriff. I can guarantee your freedom."

She wasn't legally the sheriff, and she couldn't guarantee anything. The truth of that burned in her blood.

The knife twitched slightly at her throat.

"You'd be a rich man. The law couldn't touch you. I could write you a guarantee of freedom."

His coarse laugh sprayed her veil with more spittle. She tried hard not to swallow as the sharp blade pressed against her throat.

"Oh, sure, I'd live right in Salisbury and you'd ride past

my door on your way to see the bishop and I'd tip my velvet cap to you and you'd wave your ringed fingers."

"You laugh but how do you think the king deals with rebel barons? Does he kill them all? No, they make an agreement and pledge to live in peace. There's a code of honor among the nobles."

His silence suggested that her words had opened a wedge of possibility.

"I'm not a noble. You'd turn on your word and throw me in the dungeon as soon as daylight fell on me."

"My word is my bond." Or so she'd once thought. Now she was lying like the devil possessed her. This man had killed two women, and she was to be the third. "I'm a woman of God. Anyone in Salisbury will tell you that."

"You're a rich man's widow and enjoying your freedom rather too much from what I hear." The knife wasn't pressed so hard against her throat. Ela worked slowly and very carefully to free the hand pinned underneath her. "Some say you killed him."

Her stomach lurched. "Killed my husband? Why would anyone say that?" His words echoed Haughton's and turned her stomach.

His horrible laugh rattled next to her ear. "They say you got used to him being away on wars and jaunts. That you relished the taste of freedom and being mistress of your own home. And that you weren't happy to see him back."

"That's a lie," she spat the words, finding the strength to pull her hand free and rip back her veil. He pressed the knife to her neck, but with her next move she grabbed his wrist and bit hard into it. His hand opened and the knife fell to the dirt floor.

Now she had the advantage. She could see the knife, glinting in the light that fell through the door crack. If she could grab it she could—

What? Kill him? Did she intend to become a murderer? Were people in town truly saying that she already was?

His hands swept over the ground, searching for his knife while his big body still held her pinned.

Then suddenly both of his hands were around her throat. "I don't need a knife to kill a puny maid like you. I never needed one before."

Ela tried again to scream, but his thumbs squeezed it out of her neck. She tried to gasp for air but couldn't get any. She made a frantic grab for the knife, which lay just out of reach.

"Shame about all that money, though. I'd have loved to end my days a rich man." His hands squeezed tighter and tighter. He was trying to kill her in earnest now. She could already see those sparks returning around the edges of her vision.

Hold your breath. Try again. She swept her hand out, and this time brushed the knife handle with her nails. She could feel herself growing heavy, dizzy, her last breath ebbing slowly from her lungs.

Get it. She swiped again, and this time she managed to get some purchase on the blade with her fingertips and shift it closer.

She struggled so hard to draw breath, but his hands crushed tighter and she was sure that any minute he'd crush her windpipe.

Got it! Her fingers closed around the handle. She'd almost no breath left in her body. Her vision had narrowed to a tunnel, and she tried to direct all her energy into raising her hand, with the knife, then she brought it—blade first—down into him as fast and hard as she could. She struck his back somewhere near the ribs.

He yelped and his hands loosed on her neck. She gulped air with the desperation of a drowning man, and as his hands closed back down around her throat, she stabbed again.

"Can barely feel it. A wasp could do worse. You'll be dead soon."

Ela tried to scream, but it just wasted precious breath. Even her stabs seemed to have no effect on this tough, blind beast who felt no remorse for the murders he'd already committed.

Stab his neck. She raised her hand, again feeling her vision narrow and the dazzling sparks of light return. This might well be her last chance. She lifted her fist, inexpertly gripping the unfamiliar weapon, and slashed at his neck with all her might. A spray of darkness splashed across her face.

CHAPTER 19

"*Y*ou bitch!"

The stuff on her face was Harwich's blood. She stabbed again, this time aiming for his eyes, anywhere that she could hit and hurt him.

Blood now spurted from the neck wound like he was a freshly slaughtered calf. He seemed to have forgotten about strangling her, and she took the chance to shove him off her and heaved herself at the door. It flung open. "Help!" she screamed. "Help!" Where was everyone? Anyone?

She crashed along the path, still clutching the bloody knife.

Two soldiers ran up to her and roughly grabbed her, wresting the knife from her hand. Did they not know who she was?

"He's in the wall. He tried to kill me." She didn't want him to escape.

"My lady?" One of the soldiers was holding her hands behind her back but let them go as he recognized her.

"Catch him! He's in the closet between the two piles of

wood." They turned and one ran between the tall woodpiles and disappeared. Ela held her breath.

"He's dead," called back the soldier. "Neck wound. Blood everywhere."

Ela heard a whimper escape her lips. She'd taken a life.

"Are you hurt, my lady?"

"I don't think so." She wasn't entirely sure. Her dress was dark with blood and her hands red with it. "Please have him laid out in the armory and take me to my chamber."

This time, smell or no, she wanted to keep his body close at hand until she learned what the legal proceedings would be. Killing a man was a serious matter, even in self-defense.

Her legs felt weak under her, and she found herself leaning on the soldier. More soldiers rushed around them and past them to where the body lay. As they approached the kitchen door amid shouts and alarums, servants hurried out. Sibel let out a cry at the sight of her.

"It's someone else's blood," she tried to explain. "We need to wash it off." The feel of it on her skin was awful, like a thousand crawling insects that wanted to burrow inside her.

"Mama!" She heard Petronella let out a cry.

"I'm fine, my pet." She looked past Sibel to one of the cook's helpers. "Please keep the children away. I don't want them to see me."

"What happened?" Petronella's face was white.

"I'll tell you later." Her voice was shaky and she couldn't be sure she wasn't about to cry. The immense relief of being out of mortal danger finally hit her. He'd tried to kill her and —thanks be to God—he'd failed.

She wished there was another way to her solar than through the great hall but—for safety reasons—there wasn't. She hung back, waiting for the cook's helper to distract her children, who would be just breaking their fast if they were even up.

"Oh, my lady, what happened?" Sibel was shaking like a leaf.

Deschamps rushed forward. "My lady, are you wounded?"

"I seem to be still in one piece. Please summon Giles Haughton and both of you attend me as soon as I am washed." She tried to sound as coolheaded as she could manage. She reminded herself that the men about the castle saw blood and death in battle and didn't start crying or fainting over it. Or did they?

Up in her chamber Sibel peeled off her bloody clothes. "If I soak them right away, the stains should come out."

"I'll never wear them again." She half-wanted to cast them in the fire right now, but wasn't sure if Giles Haughton would need them as evidence. She and Sibel wiped all traces of the blood from her hands and face, which took repeated changes of water as if the stain of her act of violence couldn't be washed away by mere water.

Washed and dressed, her damp hair tucked behind a fresh veil, Ela struggled to compose herself to face Deschamps, Haughton and all the other men in and about the castle whose scrutiny she'd never felt so keenly.

Haughton was in the hall, breathless and flushed from his rushed journey. "My lady, did you sustain injury?"

"By God's grace, no. Though I admit I'm deeply shaken." She wanted to say she never thought she'd kill a man, but suddenly this seemed a failing on her part. The men around her trained daily in the arts of swordsmanship and riding, with a view to readiness for battle.

"The guards tell me the old blind man attacked you?" He looked perplexed almost to the point of amusement.

"He lay in wait for me. I never had the chance to tell you that I visited him yesterday and laid before him my questions about his daughter wanting to open a dairy in his smithy. He confirmed his animosity to her plan. I wouldn't have thought such a disagreement cause for murder, but he seemed to think I'd pinned him as the suspect and he wanted to silence me."

"Had you told no one about your meeting with him?"

"I told Deschamps about the encounter and that I felt uncomfortable, even threatened, in his presence, but he thought I was overreacting."

Haughton harrumphed. "Clearly you weren't. But how did a blind man gain access to the castle, let alone identify you closely enough to assail you?"

"I'd wondered if he was actually blind or just faking, but he said that his infirmity strengthened his other senses. He also as much as admitted he killed his wife by drowning her in a well and that his daughter witnessed it. How he entered the castle I don't know. The boy who sweeps the path wasn't there. I fear for his safety."

Haughton crossed himself. "A truly evil man. You did well to finish him."

She rejected the pride his praise threatened to raise. "I have no desire to be judge, jury and executioner but in that moment I knew only one of us would emerge alive. I'm truly sorry he will not be judged by his peers."

"No doubt at this moment he faces judgment from his creator." Haughton's face still showed signs of amusement. Or was it amazement?

"His body is in the armory."

"How fitting, since the last person to lie there was the one he killed."

"This time I'd prefer for him to be examined and buried— outside the walls of course—before he has a chance to spread his stench through the castle."

"Shall we examine him now?"

Ela shuddered. "I prefer that you do it without me. I can

answer any questions you have. I stabbed him in the neck with his own knife as I was half-pinned under him."

"You are quite a woman." Again, the rather patronizing amusement.

"I hope that I do justice to my duties," she said stiffly. "And there remains the question of Morse. If Harwich killed his daughter and Elizabeth Brice killed her husband, that leaves Morse innocent of both crimes."

"Indeed. Though we're not sure who killed John Brice so perhaps it's prudent to keep them both under lock and key until the assizes."

"I'd still like to talk to Morse," said Ela. "He should know that he can emerge to freedom. It'll give him the strength to survive the ordeal."

"You seem so sure he's innocent."

"A gut feeling." She frowned. "Like the one I had when Harwich asked me to come deeper into his house and all my instincts recoiled against him. I don't wish to destroy Morse's business and let his land go neglected if he's innocent."

"And I suppose that if he's found innocent he'll inherit his wife's father's property." Haughton's eyebrows lifted.

"In the absence of a will or a closer relation, perhaps you're right."

"Or you could claim it for your estate. Such an action would be considered quite proper."

"I think not. There'll be talk enough once word of Harwich's death gets out."

Might her name might be uttered with a tinge of admiration and fear that could advance her position?

Again, she chastised herself for pride, especially for such an unchristian deed. Thou shalt not kill. Taking a man's life was a grave sin. Did she just sacrifice her place in Heaven?

During his last hours, her husband had prayed and

begged forgiveness for the many things he'd done in life that might be held against him during the final judgment. As a soldier he'd killed many times and—according to his fevered ramblings—he'd broken most of the other commandments as well. She'd prayed and wept with him while he prepared to meet his maker and at the end he did seem to feel ready.

"My lady, are you well?"

"What? I'm sorry." She realized Haughton had been speaking. "I was distracted. Please forgive me." She didn't want to make excuses that might get people whispering that the role of sheriff was no job for a woman. No doubt they were saying that anyway. "I'll come with you to the armory. I'm ready."

Perhaps Harwich's face was less likely to haunt her nights if she dealt with his corpse in the cool light of morning.

"If you're sure—" He looked doubtful.

"I'll be fine." She moved toward the door. Her heart pounded beneath her gown, and she hoped she'd be able to maintain her composure. "I had no choice but to kill him. It was his life or mine."

"Your bravery and quick actions are to be commended."

"There's no need to waste your praise. The entire situation is regrettable." Again she battled a confusing mix of pride and embarrassment. Perhaps the Lord had sent her this trial as a test.

She wasn't sure if she'd triumphed or failed.

They crossed the hallway, and the soldiers outside the armory opened the door for her. She swore she could see a different look in their eyes. Word of the death—and her narrow escape—must even now be sweeping through the castle and the town.

"By God's grace it's him there and not me," she murmured and crossed herself as they walked into the gloomy armory. The only light fell from the small high window. The body was laid out on the table, an awkward bulging form covered by a bloodstained sheet of cloth.

Haughton marched over and peeled the cloth back in a swift gesture. Ela braced herself, half closing her eyes, then opening them slowly so as not to take in the whole grotesque scene at once.

Harwich's black-and-white streaked hair was wild as always, his face pale beneath its veneer of dirt. Blood covered his neck and chest and the lower half of one side of his face. He'd been stripped naked, but Haughton tactfully left the cloth covering the lower parts of his torso.

She seemed to remember stabbing his face but there were no marks on it. The single, fatal wound was to the left side of his neck.

Haughton peered at it. "You severed his artery. A man bleeds to death in seconds from such a wound."

Ela wondered if she should explain that she knew about anatomy from her medical readings and that was why she'd chosen to stab the neck, but decided the information was superfluous.

"A lucky blow." Haughton turned to her. "It's one of the few places where you can kill a man with one cut. The others mostly involved pushing the blade into just the right place between the ribs. Much harder to kill and easier to get your knife stuck.

"I'll remember that for the future," she said dryly. "Though I certainly hope I'll never need the knowledge."

"I've never killed a man myself," said Haughton, "for all the bodies I've studied and handled." He lifted the head and gingerly examined the back of it. "His death was about as quick and merciful as they come. More than he deserved from the sounds of it." He closed Harwich's sightless eyes and pulled the sheet back over the head. "My coroner's report is complete. Or at least it will be when I write it up."

"Will I face trial?"

"Most certainly not. You killed him in the line of duty. If anything you should be rewarded for your services to the crown." Amusement lit his face again. Ela wanted to be annoyed, but she was mostly relieved.

She wasn't officially sheriff yet. There was always the possibility that the king—or, more likely, de Burgh—would appoint someone over her.

"I want to talk to Morse now. Harwich's confession has absolved him of his wife's murder and he should know that." She didn't relish the thought of heading down into the dungeon and the presence of people who cursed the ground she walked on, and Haughton's company would be reassuring. "Will you attend with me?"

"Certainly."

She led the way out of the armory and along the hallway that led to the dungeon. She could see through the open arched doorway at the end that the sun was now well up in the sky and the passages bustling with servants and soldiers.

"I don't understand how Harwich got in." She spoke her thoughts aloud. "It's an armed garrison, for pity's sake."

"An investigation wouldn't go amiss. Find where the fault lies and make sure it can't happen again. And perhaps you should take an armed attendant on your morning rounds."

She sighed. "Perhaps I should have an armed attendant at the foot of my bed all night long."

"I'm sure many a noble or monarch has said the same, and likely had one, too."

"I refuse to live like a prisoner in my own castle, guarded at every step." She frowned. By putting herself in position of power she'd somehow managed to further limit her freedom. It was perplexing. "But I suppose I owe it to my children to guard myself well."

"Yes, my lady. You have a double responsibility."

They descended the wobbly ladder into the grim, airless space of the dungeons. Braziers threw off the only light and the sour smell of unwashed bodies stung her nostrils.

"We're here to see Morse," she said to the jailer, peering into the gloom. Sometimes they moved the prisoners around, for reasons unknown to her. Perhaps to keep antagonists away from each other.

The jailer led them past two prisoners, and she avoided looking at their faces. Morse's massive form was hunched over, facing toward the wall. He didn't stir at their approach.

"Morse," growled the jailer. "Rise and salute the Countess of Salisbury."

"That won't be necessary," protested Ela, though he showed no signs of doing it. "We're here because your father-in-law confessed to killing his daughter, so we know you're innocent of the crime."

He didn't move. Had he lost his wits? Was he asleep?

The jailer kicked him and he flinched, as did Ela. "Attend my lady!" he yelled. "Did you not hear what she said?"

Ela resolved to ask someone else to address the jailer about his harsh manner with a prisoner who might well be innocent. But she knew it wouldn't do for her to scold him in front of the prisoners. He'd likely take it amiss, and she'd have another enemy to watch for.

"We know you didn't kill your wife." Perhaps she hadn't spoken plainly enough the first time.

At last he stirred, his head swiveling slowly and his broad shoulders turning. With his dark beard growing in he looked like a wild man of the woods. Ela stiffened as his gaze met hers.

"I told you that all along." His eyes glinted in the light from a nearby brazier.

"Did you not suspect Harwich yourself?" Haughton

leaned in, speaking to Morse. "You could have saved us time and trouble."

"He's a blind old man. How would he kill anyone?"

"He's a very crafty and capable old blind man," said Haughton. "Who apparently also killed his wife some years ago. Weren't you suspicious of him?"

"Katie never said he killed her mother." Morse looked confused.

"Would you have married her if you'd known?" said Haughton. "Perhaps you'd have thought that murder ran in her blood."

Morse shook his head, obviously confused. "She never said a word against him. Used to visit him almost every day, the ornery old cuss. Why would he kill her?"

"He thought she intended to turn him out of his house so she could make it into a dairy."

"Well, that was the plan." Morse frowned. "Not to turn him out, mind you, but to repurpose the old forge into a dairy and move in with him. He probably didn't have long to live anyway. You'd think he'd be glad of someone to take care of him."

"You would indeed," said Haughton. "But there's no accounting for the ingratitude of some."

"So—" Morse frowned, looking from one to the other. "If he confessed to killing her, why isn't he down here?"

"He's dead," said Ela preemptively. She didn't want to hear Haughton fumbling for an explanation. She also didn't want to elaborate. "But he admitted to the murder before he died. The details are not important."

Morse blinked. She could hear the questions—How? Why? Who?—pulsing in his brain, but he wisely kept them silent. He shifted until he was fully facing them and straightened his back. "Does this mean I'm free?"

Haughton cleared his throat. "There remains the question of John Brice's murder."

"I had no motive to kill him!" Morse rose to his feet. Ela had to fight the urge to take a step backward even though she was well out of reach.

"Cuckoldry is a time-honored motive. Legions of men have killed to defend their honor or that of their wife and no doubt many have been forgiven the deed under the circumstances," said Haughton. Ela thought it was cunning to throw him a lifeline of hope that he might be exonerated even if he was guilty.

"Maybe they have, but I didn't kill anyone."

"He killed my husband!" The screeching voice from a dark corner reminded them all that Elizabeth Brice was down here as well. "He's a murderer."

"I'm innocent. I never touched your accursed husband. I never killed anyone in my life."

"Guilt or innocence will be determined at the assizes," replied Ela. She couldn't let Morse go free while Mistress Brice still protested her innocence. No matter that she now believed Morse's protests. While she could pronounce guilt or innocence in smaller local cases, capital crimes were a matter for the king's traveling justices.

Ela didn't think it was right that men and women were imprisoned together. The reality was that very few women had been imprisoned down here, and then usually just for a night before they—as new-found enemies of the king by dint of birth or marriage—were hauled onwards to the Tower of London.

The assizes were already late and if they were further delayed Brice and Morse might be down here for weeks or months, might even die down here waiting for trial. That was one reason she'd been so reluctant—too reluctant, some might say—to make an arrest in the first place. The prisoners here were ill fed and received no exercise or pleasure in life and that could kill some almost as fast as poison.

"What of my cows?" he asked bleakly.

"They are well fed and cared for in your absence. If you're found innocent they'll be returned to you along with your farm."

The prospect didn't seem to cheer him. He'd already lost a lot of his vigor. A man of his age—not that much older than her but not young either—might not recover from this ordeal well enough to cope with the rigors of running his farm alone. He had no children to help him.

The responsibility of imprisoning him weighed heavily on her shoulders.

"What of my cows?" Elizabeth Brice's high-pitched voice rang out in the darkness. "For when I'm found innocent by the judge?"

"Again, they're being cared for, fed and milked and maintained in your absence."

There was always the grim possibility that the innocent party would hang and the guilty one emerge into the sunlight to claim both herds of cows.

"You shall both be notified when the dates are set for the assizes."

"Not that we even know what day of the week it is down here," mumbled Morse. "And it's calving time when I should be watching over my herd day and night to welcome new life into the world. I've never lost a calf yet."

Never? Unlikely. But whatever lies he told himself to survive a few more weeks were fine with her.

CHAPTER 20

ne week later

Word of the assizes came with barely enough notice to set up curtains in the hall to provide a private sleeping quarters for the traveling justice and his attendants. The lads were still fussing with the poles, and Ela was in the kitchen hurriedly consulting with the cook when the party's hoof-beats sounded on the bridge.

Ela hurried out into the gathering darkness to greet the king's justice in her official capacity as castellan and sheriff. But her welcoming smile soon palled when she noticed the colors of Hubert de Burgh entering the main arch alongside those of the justice.

His boldness both enraged and alarmed her. Had he heard that she'd spread a rumor about him? Had he come for revenge?

The justice, clothed in a long, damp brown cloak and a

leather hat, leaped down from his horse. His name was Alan Fitz-Peter and she knew very little else about him.

"God be with you, Sir." She kept her hands folded together so he wouldn't try to kiss one. "I trust you had a pleasant journey?"

"As pleasant as can be at this time of year, my lady. My deepest condolences on the loss of your most excellent husband." He bowed low and mercifully kept his hands and lips to himself. "His loss could not be felt more keenly by myself or any other knight of the realm." He gave his hat and cloak to a servant, revealing a ruddy face and silvered hair that almost matched his pale gray eyes.

Ela snuck a glance past him to de Burgh, who was fussing over the unloading of some baggage.

"Your kind words are much appreciated. Do come in." She wished she could slam the castle gates behind him. "We have several prisoners awaiting trial."

Had Giles Haughton even told anyone yet about her accusations of de Burgh? It'd been but a week since she'd shared her suspicions with him.

Servants rushed out with jugs of spiced wine, a bowl of sad-looking fruit and a plate of oatcakes left over from this morning's breakfast. "My apologies for our meagre Lenten fare." She offered him a seat at the table. They'd intended to sup on thick pease pottage and fresh-baked bread with butter for supper but the cook was now wrestling some jellied eels and salted cod into acceptable dishes for the party.

Fitz-Peter turned to look for the rest of his entourage. Ela reluctantly watched de Burgh strutting into her hall like a peacock, seizing a cup of wine with one hand and dispensing his gloves with another like he owned the place.

Something that—Ela realized with alarm—might be part

of his plan. She'd still had no word from the king confirming her role as sheriff.

De Burgh walked toward her and held out his hand, clearly intending to take hers and kiss it. She ground her fists together. "God be with you, my lord de Burgh."

Did he fear eternal damnation? Or was he too well-rewarded here on earth to care for his immortal soul?

He took the hint and bowed low. "Greetings, gracious lady. We welcome your hospitality on this unpleasantly rainy day."

"I'm glad the assizes weren't delayed any further. We were worried we might have to wait until summer."

"We hear there are but trifling local squabbles to be dealt with." He smiled boldly. "It shouldn't take long."

"If they were so trifling I would have tried them myself." She bristled at the suggestion she was shirking her duties.

"How? When there is no sheriff named since your husband's untimely demise?" He had the insolence to look amused.

"As countess and castellan of Salisbury I have informed the king of my intent to fulfill the role incumbent upon me." The low, authoritative tone of her own voice surprised her. "Until such time as my son Will gains his majority." She paused a moment. "What brings you here?"

"The cause of justice, my lady. As the king's justiciar it is my greatest goal." He sipped his wine, and Ela praised God that she was too well bred to spit in his eye. "Is Deschamps about?" He looked around, as if intending to answer the question himself.

"No doubt he is. Do you have a question for him?"

"Some dry matters about the management of the king's garrison. There's no need to trouble you with them, my lady."

"On the contrary, as the king's castellan I am most interested in all matters related to his garrison." Ela's stomach churned. If only they could focus on the trials at hand and save this posturing for later. But she could hardly ignore his bold attempts to undermine her status in front of her entire retinue.

The day continued in a similarly challenging fashion. Little Stephen pinched his finger in a door hinge and was inconsolable at one point, which required her to put motherhood first and allow the men to mutter among themselves.

Young Will bravely stepped in and moved among them like a young rooster, which seemed to please—or amuse—them. They plied him with drink and regaled him with tales of his father's exploits that had Will alternately choked with emotion and laughter. Ela's mother had departed for home, so—servants aside—Ela was the only female present and had to carefully steer the conversation to avoid crude male camaraderie intended to jostle her away.

Ela forced herself to stay up late into the night, watching the men slide into their cups until finally Fitz-Peter and de Burgh headed into the curtained bedchambers she'd erected for them in the hall.

With her mother and Jean gone, there were rooms enough to house them elsewhere in the keep but she wanted an ear on them at all times. She quietly asked Will to bed himself down close by them and make a note of anything they said that she should know, and he nodded sagely, clearly pleased by the trust she placed in him. She hoped he was sober enough to comply.

That night, exhausted as she was, Ela murmured the entire rosary on her knees at her prie-dieu. Let justice be served, she prayed. Some would argue that she'd avenged Katie's murder herself, but she didn't see it that way at all. Morse might still hang for the crime and for John Brice's death as well. Perhaps de Burgh had some agenda that might pervert the course of justice to suit his own ends.

He'd tried to fold her castle and title into his own family by plotting her marriage to his nephew. Having failed in that attempt he'd grown bolder and killed her husband.

Who knew what he might try next.

* * *

In the morning, the trestle tables were arranged in a U shape, with the justice, Ela and Haughton and de Burgh seated in the middle, and members of the jury lined up along the sides. Deschamps hovered nearby, ready to command the guards if need be.

Elizabeth Brice and Alan Morse were brought up from the dungeons and stood flanked by guards in the middle of the tables. Ela had instructed that the prisoners be made as presentable as possible before their trial. Sibel had sent two young women down into the dungeon with jugs of water, combs and a clean wimple for Elizabeth Brice, but both prisoners still presented a sorry sight. They looked pinched and harried and had both aged ten years from their ordeal, short though it was.

"Alan Morse," Fitz-Peter looked over his notes. "You stand here accused of murdering your wife, Katherine Morse, and also your neighbor John Brice."

Morse said nothing.

Ela glanced at Haughton, who stood and cleared his throat. "Um, your honor, the girl's father confessed to killing her."

"Then where is he?"

"He is deceased, my lord, but he confessed before he died."

Fitz-Peter looked at de Burgh and the jurors. Ela felt all their eyes burning her skin.

"He died of natural causes?" Fitz-Peter sounded incredulous.

Ela fought the urge to stand and describe the circumstances. She knew it was important that they be described by a third party.

Haughton, still standing, looked about a foot shorter than usual. "Harwich entered the castle unbeknownst to the guards, attacked the countess and—before she slayed him in an heroic act of self-defense—revealed himself as the murderer of his daughter."

Fitz-Peter appeared to be struck speechless. De Burgh sat back in his chair, eyes wide. "The countess killed the suspect?" He glanced at her for a moment, then stared from Haughton to Deschamps. "Why was he not in the dungeon at the time?"

Haughton cleared his throat. "He wasn't a suspect at that time. We had initially thought Morse responsible for his wife's death."

"Why would he attack the Countess?" Fitz-Peter looked confused.

"She had interviewed him in her role as sheriff. The previous day she'd visited him at his home and reported to Gerald Deschamps that she found him menacing and suspicious."

"Yet he still wasn't arrested?"

Frustration surging through her, Ela stood. "We were dealing with illness in the castle. Three of my children were taken ill so I was preoccupied. Harwich was elderly and blind. No one thought him capable of murder." She hadn't wanted to make a fuss. And Deschamps had dismissed her concerns.

"I can imagine that you have your hands full with the management of your family and domestic tasks," cut in de Burgh. "It's entirely unfair that you should have to perform the sheriff's role on top of those most essential duties."

Ela seethed. De Burgh knew that she both wanted and intended to be sheriff. Still, why hadn't she raised the alarum and sent soldiers to arrest Harwich? It was true that her thoughts were with her sick children. She'd doubted her own judgment when Deschamps scoffed at her fears. "I had told Master Deschamps about my suspicions based on a disturbing encounter I'd had with him the day before. Harwich correctly suspected that he would soon be arrested."

De Burgh looked at Deschamps, who had the decency to look flustered. "It's my greatest regret that I didn't send a party out to arrest him immediately." Deschamps shifted from one foot to the other. "He was elderly and utterly blind, so I didn't see him as a threat."

"So he entered the castle in full view of the king's garrison and set upon its lady?" De Burgh seemed to have set his sights on skewering Deschamps.

"It was early in the morning, my lord. He asked for assistance from the boy who sweeps the paths, then sent him off with a coin to buy bread. The boy had seen the old man in the castle before—when he came for an audience with the countess to report his daughter's death—so he had no reason to suspect him."

And the soldiers were drunk. Ela thought it but didn't say it. They'd let him hobble right past them, thinking nothing of it.

"I suppose it's lucky it was just one blind old man, not King Louis and his army." De Burgh looked from Deschamps to Ela. "As castellan of Salisbury you bear responsibility for this breach of the castle walls."

Ela blinked. "Indeed."

"She handled it as a soldier would have!" burst out Deschamps, eager to snatch—something—from the jaws of humiliation. The soldiers' failure to secure the keep lay at his feet. "Killed him dead."

De Burgh surveyed Ela for a moment. "I congratulate you on your knightly response."

He was mocking her.

"I had no intention of killing anyone. I merely acted in self-defense. He knew I had guessed that he killed his daughter and he confessed as much before attempting to slit my throat."

De Burgh stared at Deschamps, then back at Haughton. "Did anyone else hear his confession? Or are we to rely solely upon the countess's assurances that he made it?"

Ela bristled. "Are you accusing me of fabricating Harwich's guilt?" Her words rang out over Haughton's mumbled reply. "Pray tell, why would I do such a thing?"

Was de Burgh hoping to twist this case so that she ended up on trial for murder? He'd already accused her of grave failures both as sheriff and castellan. Now perhaps he intended to sweep her neatly out of the way of his greed and ambition.

"A good question, my lady." De Burgh's oily smile chilled her. "The fact remains that you—the man's killer—are the only soul alive who heard him confess to his daughter's murder."

"How many witnesses does a trial require to prove innocence?" Ela heard the imperious tone of her voice and hoped it covered her fear.

"That is for the justice to decide." De Burgh looked at Fitz-Peter.

Fitz-Peter hurriedly cleared his throat. "And the justice relies greatly on the opinions of the jury." The jurors were looking at each other, clearly startled or excited by this strange turn of events. "We shall adjourn this trial until after lunch while I acquaint myself with these surprising new details."

Ela wanted to protest. It was only half way through the morning. Neither accused had been interviewed. If de Burgh had come to upset the entire proceedings and shape them to his will, apparently he was well on his way to succeeding.

She sent Sibel to the kitchen to see if the cook could send out lunch early. Alan Morse and Elizabeth Brice were sent back to the dungeon. Haughton shot her a helpless look.

Will muttered something in her ear that she didn't catch but he hurried away with Bill Talbot before she had a chance to question him. Probably going hunting to blow off steam. Possibly he couldn't bear to watch his mother squirm under this inquisition.

While the cook fussed and fumed in her harried kitchen, Ela laid out every gruesome detail of her encounters with Harwich, both in his grim forge and in the closet in the castle wall. Ela, Fitz-Peter, de Burgh and the jurors retraced the early morning footsteps that had led her into Harwich's hands and exclaimed over the bloodstains still darkening the earthen floor of the unused storage space. The boy had admitted showing him the closet as a place to rest while he went to fetch the bread.

Over lunch, attended by her children—at another table— since she could hardly exclude them from lunch in their own hall, de Burgh harped on his theme that Ela was far too busy with her maternal role to waste her time policing the county. She didn't waste her breath arguing with him since she had already taken her request over his head and straight to the young king. Still, she now suspected that becoming sheriff would be more of an uphill battle than she'd anticipated

After lunch, Morse and Brice were brought back up from the dungeon and the now-well-fed jurors settled back at their tables.

Fitz-Peter addressed them. "The countess has described her ordeal in great detail, and we have established that the deceased Robert Harwich killed his daughter. We are now trying to determine the guilt or innocence of Alan Morse and Elizabeth Brice in the death of John Brice." He turned to Ela. "Did the deceased utter any words that might indicate the guilt or innocence of either of the parties standing before us?"

"I'm afraid not, my lord. Harwich admitted to killing his daughter because he thought she would turn him out of his forge, but he had no reason to be interested in John Brice, the second victim. Brice's name wasn't mentioned."

"So the two cases are not connected?" Fitz-Peter peered at her.

"Well, no." Ela frowned. Did he really not know? "Katie— the dead girl—was visibly pregnant. It's been established that her husband was not the baby's father, and it's likely that John Brice was. Morse potentially had motive to kill Brice for cuckolding him, and Elizabeth Brice had motive to kill her husband for his adultery."

Fitz-Peter looked from Morse to Elizabeth Brice, who shifted uncomfortably under his gaze.

"Alan Morse, did you kill your neighbor, John Brice?"

"I did not." His voice was rough from lack of use. "I never laid a hand on no man. Not since I was in the battle that left me unable to sire children. I didn't kill Brice any more than I killed my own wife that I miss sorely."

De Burgh sat like a statue. What was he thinking?

"Elizabeth Brice, did you kill your husband for the crime of bedding another woman?"

"Never! Why would I leave his poor children fatherless?" Her plaintive voice pierced Ela's ears. "How will we ever survive without him?"

"Master Morse." De Burgh addressed him in warm tones. "Your anger at your wife's betrayal is quite understandable. No man would blame you for wanting to take matters into your own hands."

Ela glanced at Fitz-Peter, whose impassive face revealed nothing.

"It's a man's duty to defend his honor," De Burgh continued. "In fact some would say you weren't a man if you didn't exact revenge for such a crime."

"I never—" Morse started to protest.

"Silence!" uttered de Burgh. "The prisoner must not speak unless questioned. I'm on your side here. I'm simply pointing out that avenging yourself on the man who stole your wife is something that any of us can sympathize with."

Where was he going with this? Ela was almost sure that Morse—odious as he was—was innocent of the crime. Elizabeth Brice had motive and opportunity. Why would de Burgh seek to incriminate Morse while heaping false empathy upon him?

"Elizabeth Brice seems like the true victim here." De Burgh tipped his head to her. "A poor, simple farmwife just trying to raise her children while her errant husband wasted his working hours in seducing a neighbor. Women are gentle creatures and easily led astray—"

Ela felt her blood start to boil. He was doing his best to undermine her authority while also throwing the facts of the case under his cart wheels where they'd be trampled into the mire and emerge unrecognizable.

Right now he was reminding everyone that Morse had inherited his farm unexpectedly when his brother died. He didn't come out and accuse Morse of killing him, but he was sowing seeds in his already plowed field.

Elizabeth Brice had seemed a strapping woman, a classic shrew, berating her errant husband in the marketplace just days earlier. Here, bedraggled and undernourished from imprisonment, she appeared a forlorn and pitiful figure.

Morse, although whey-faced and thinner, was still burly

and imposing. Ela felt a surge of fear that a miscarriage of justice was imminent.

She was further distracted by Will striding into the hall, pink-cheeked and breathless, clutching a scroll of parchment in his hand. He walked right up to her and whispered in her ear. "May I speak to you alone, Mother?"

"Not right now." Did he really think she could just get up and leave? De Burgh would love that. Her domestic duties summoning her away from official business would feed right into his scheme to unseat her. "You can show me later."

"It's important," Will insisted. His eyes shone in a way she'd never seen before. Bill Talbot hovered close behind him, his usually warm expression absent and a grim intensity hardening his features.

Sure the assembled men would all shake their heads over the pressing call of her domestic duties, she followed her instincts and beckoned for Will to follow her out the door toward the kitchen. She accosted him in the hallway. "What's going on?"

"This." Will rapped on the parchment with his fingers, then unfurled it. It was covered by a closely written hand in somewhat faded black ink.

Ela peered at the broken seal. "Is that de Burgh's seal?"

"It is. This is a contract that he wrote to Robert Harwich for the sale of his forge."

"What?" She peered at the document. "He bought it?"

"No. The sale was never completed. Harwich refused to sell." Will's eyes shone. "We visited Bishop Poore to see if he knew the details. He told us that de Burgh was interested in taking over three properties that abut the cathedral close, possibly to build a residence there. He was able to make contracts for two of them but was unable to persuade Harwich to move."

Ela shook her head. "I'm not surprised that he wouldn't

move. His blindness made him dependent on the familiar. But how does that affect anything here?"

"No doubt he still wants the property," said Talbot softly.

"No doubt. He can just buy it."

"From who, Mama? Morse would be his heir through marriage. And Morse probably knows what it's worth now that New Salisbury has sprung up around it and is growing bigger and faster than anyone expected. Perhaps he hopes to get it cheaper if Morse is hanged and his goods put up for auction."

Ela frowned. "I've taken control of the property, to hold in trust until Morse is tried."

"Thus his attempts to discredit you and push you out of the picture," murmured Talbot. He took a deep breath. "I've never wanted to punch a man so badly."

"Your restraint is greatly appreciated. And so is this document. At the very least it will throw water on the funeral bonfire that de Burgh is piling high for Morse in there right now."

"There is a risk that you could draw more fire to yourself if the only way to the property is through you."

"He'll have to go through Morse and myself since I don't intend to allow this trial to convict an innocent man."

She took the paper from Will, rolled it up and headed back into the chamber. Mistress Brice was busy playing the role of helpless mother, sobbing into her wimple and bemoaning her fate while the jurors questioned her about her husbands' infidelity.

Ela took her seat at the high table, where she sat on one side of Fitz-Peter, with Burgh on the other, and unrolled the scroll.

De Burgh looked satisfyingly discomfited by the sight of his own seal.

"What have you here, my lady?" asked the justice.

"A paper my son discovered in Harwich's forge, my lord. It appears that my lord de Burgh offered him a generous sum to buy the property four years ago, and it was refused."

"Why would he refuse such a thing?" Fitz-Peter addressed de Burgh.

De Burgh simply looked amused. "He said that because he was blind he couldn't adapt to new surroundings. I even donated generously to fund Bishop Poore's new almshouses to provide him with a more comfortable home for his final years."

"And he still wouldn't move?"

"He's a stubborn old fool."

"I half-wonder why he didn't try to kill you instead of Ela," exclaimed Fitz-Peter with a laugh.

Ela stilled. Was there even a shred of possibility that de Burgh had paid Harwich to kill her? Now she knew there was a relationship between them it seemed like a grim possibility. They both wanted her out of the way. The old man needed money and—

No, it was too far-fetched. She needed to stay focused on the trial at hand and save de Burgh's battle against her family for another day when she was better mounted and defended.

"Why do you put this before us now, my lady?" asked Fitz-Peter.

"Oh," Ela tried to look flustered. "I'm not sure, my lord, except that my son just found it in his quarters and thought it might be important." She couldn't risk accusing de Burgh of trying to throw the trial. She'd have to let his own actions do that.

"I fail to see the relevance myself," said de Burgh with his usual smarmy smile. "Indeed I barely recall the event. Though there's no doubt the cathedral close would be improved by the removal of that ramshackle hovel."

Ela glanced at Morse, who looked thoroughly stunned by

her pronouncement, but then his features settled into a morose sadness. As if he could already see his future unfurling as the doormat de Burgh would wipe his feet on as he passed into his glittering property in the heart of New Salisbury.

"May I speak, your honor?" Ela addressed Fitz-Peter.

"Yes, my lady."

Ela felt de Burgh's eyes on her.

"It's my belief, based on conversations with Morse and others, that Alan Morse is innocent. His relationship with his wife was based on practical concerns, not romantic notions. He does not seem to be a man of passions, murderous or otherwise. If he beat his wife it was probably done soberly and out of a misguided sense of duty. Until we informed him of his wife's death he was unaware of it. He thought she had left him for her lover, whose identity he didn't know. He had quietly accepted that fate."

"He didn't report her missing?" De Burgh's voice rang out.

"No. No one was looking for her. Katherine Morse's body was discovered in the river when it thawed." She leveled a cold look at him. "On the morning of my husband's funeral."

"Surely Morse not reporting his wife's absence was cause for suspicion that he murdered her himself." De Burgh turned to Giles Haughton. "How are you so sure he didn't?"

Ela opened her mouth to protest that the real murderer had confessed when she realized that just by raising the question de Burgh was calling the veracity of her statement into question again.

"Naturally that was our assumption," said Giles. "But he protested his innocence and convinced us to keep looking. Similarly, he was an immediate suspect when Brice was killed, but the circumstances turned our attentions to Mistress Brice."

Giles glanced at Ela. "As my lady has stated, Morse does not appear to be a man of strong emotions. He's a practical and hardworking man to all appearances. Plodding, if you will." He glanced somewhat apologetically at Morse. "Whereas Mistress Brice demonstrated to all of Salisbury that she is a woman with a violent and demonstrative nature."

Elizabeth Brice's tears had dried and she peered at Ela through eyes narrowed with hatred.

De Burgh lifted a silvered brow. "And being a woman"—he glanced at Ela, as if implicating her in the crimes of her gender, before looking back at Haughton—"of such violent passions, you think it likely that she slew her husband and the father of her children?"

"Yes." For once, Haughton himself didn't have a gleam of mischief in his eye. "The manner of stabbing, several ineffectual thrusts of the knife, suggest an inexperienced killer. Not a man who's fought in battle."

"A female." De Burgh raised a brow. "Or one who wishes to appear so. Morse might have made such ineffectual stab wounds to confound the coroner."

Ela struggled to hold her tongue. Who was de Burgh to command the proceedings thus?

The king's justiciar. That's who. She reminded herself of the high stakes for her personally, and for her family and her son's future. At least they could all read between the lines of that old contract and see that he might have an ulterior motive.

Was Fitz-Peter struck dumb? His gaze bounced from de Burgh to the prisoners like he was watching a jousting tournament. Ela wondered what the stakes were for him. No doubt he was bought and paid for by de Burgh and only waited to serve his master like a loyal dog.

Was there no justice to be had in England? Ela cleared her

throat. "Will you be polling the jurors for their opinions, my lord?" She addressed Fitz-Peter directly. She had more faith in the solid local men of the hundred than in the king's emissaries.

"Naturally. We'll listen to opinions one by one, starting from the left, if it pleases the king's justiciar." He looked mildly at de Burgh, who nodded in silent assent.

Ela breathed a sigh of relief. As expected the jurors mumbled what they knew of the case and the evidence that pointed solidly at Harwich being his daughter's killer and Elizabeth Brice being her husband's.

Fitz-Peter had been scratching notes for himself. He looked up and around the room. "Does anyone gathered here have any last words to add?" Ela glanced at Morse and Elizabeth Brice but they both looked equally morose and sullen.

De Burgh shifted and Ela felt her nerves prickle. Was he really going to make a last-ditch effort to incriminate Morse when all the evidence pointed to Mistress Brice? Even though they all knew he was interested in owning the property that would rightfully belong to Morse if he escaped hanging?

Silence throbbed in the air as all held their breath. De Burgh leaned back, crossed his arms over his chest and said nothing.

Fitz-Peter stood and muttered a preamble about justice and the kingdom and the good men of the hundred. Then he cleared his throat and Ela held her breath. "I pronounce Elizabeth Brice to be the murderer of her husband, John Brice. She despised him for his adultery and his weakness and saw the opportunity to rid herself of him and blame her neighbor for the crime. The murder was premeditated, which is why she sent her children to her sister earlier that day. She used the element of surprise and her native strength to overpower him, then stuck him repeatedly so he'd bleed to death. For punishment she shall be hanged by the neck until she is dead. May God have pity on her soul and on her orphaned children."

Elizabeth Brice's screams rent the air, and Ela felt emotion rise in her chest. Surely no mortal could bear to see young children abandoned to their fate without mother or father and not feel pity. She resolved to check regularly on the Brices' young brood and find them jobs at the castle or in her manors once they were old enough.

Morse, far from looking happy and relieved, collapsed in his chair sobbing, with his head in his hands.

Ela looked for Deschamps. "Please arrange for Morse to be reunited with his cows, today if possible." She hated that the perverted course of justice had kept him imprisoned during calving season and prayed his herd would still be in milk and no lasting harm done.

She felt Giles Haughton's gaze upon her. He leaned in. "The search for justice is a rocky road and one that forks right when you think you've reached the end." For once his twinkle of amusement soothed her. "Unfortunately, tomorrow there will be fresh crimes to investigate."

"Indeed." She could feel de Burgh's eyes on her as well. "But I'm sure I'll never tire of seeking the truth amidst the lies."

"And you are to be commended for that my lady," chimed in Fitz-Peter. He nodded to her. "As well managed a case and trial as I've ever sat in judgment on."

Looking back she could see plenty of room for improvement, but she'd do her best to learn from her mistakes. "My husband taught me well. He was a great man and will never be forgotten as long as Salisbury stands." She was still waiting with bated breath for a letter from the king pronouncing her the new sheriff.

The jurors applauded, joined by Haughton, Fitz-Peter and

finally a reluctant, and clearly fuming, de Burgh. Her enemy's discomfort gave her almost as much pleasure as the justice she'd worked hard for. John Brice's murderer would hang, but her husband's killer still sat at the king's right hand. She prayed for the day de Burgh would fall from grace and her husband's soul could rest in peace. She intended to secretly further that cause in any way she could.

In the meantime she must learn to find satisfaction in small things, she thought, as she petted her beloved greyhound. "Some wine, perhaps?"

THE END

FOR INFORMATION about upcoming Ela of Salisbury mysteries, please visit www.stoneheartpress.com.

AUTHOR'S NOTE

I first came across the name Ela Longespée while researching a nineteenth century ancestor of mine. When I Googled my ancestor's name, she cropped up on an internet list of people descended from William the Conqueror. As I looked at the line of people in between then and now, I found Ela Longespée and discovered that she'd been Sheriff of Wiltshire in the early thirteenth century.

I was intrigued, partly because she was the first female sheriff I'd heard of, and also because—weaned on Robin Hood—I am used to thinking of the Norman-descended sheriff as the villain. I became intrigued with writing a story about Ela and imagining her life.

Considering that she lived nearly eight hundred years ago, I found a fair amount of information about her, especially in the exhaustively researched *Annals and Antiquities of Lacock Abbey* written by William Lisle Bowles and John Gough Nichols in 1835. Dean of Salisbury during Ela's time, William de Wanda provided crucial dates for the story in his *Historia Translationis Veteris Ecclesiae Beatae Mariae Sarum ad Novam*. Roger of Wendover's contemporary *Flores Histori-*

arum provided some surprising background details, including the suspicion that Ela's husband was poisoned by Hubert de Burgh. When William Longespeé's tomb was opened in 1791, a rat was found curled inside his skull, with traces of arsenic in its body. There is no record of anyone being accused of or tried for the crime, so his murderer remains unpunished.

The mysteries Ela solves in this book are entirely a product of my imagination. The details of her life and family are, insofar as is possible, researched and represented as I found them. Speech in this era would have been a mixture of Norman French, spoken by Ela and her noble cohorts, and middle English spoken by the local people. By today's standards Ela might seem excessively snobbish or pious. Her impulses to manage her own life and castle, however, and to be a leader as well as a mother to her eight children, are very relatable to us in the twenty-first century.

If you have questions or comments, please get in touch at jglewis@stoneheartpress.com.

SERIES BOOKLIST

CATHEDRAL OF BONES

BREACH OF FAITH

THE LOST CHILD

FOREST OF SOULS

THE BONE CHESS SET

CLOISTER OF WHISPERS

PALACE OF THORNS

A SURFEIT OF MIRACLES

THE D'ALBIAC INHERITANCE

UNHOLY SANCTUARY

AUTHOR BIOGRAPHY

J. G. Lewis grew up in a Regency-era officer's residence in London, England. She spent her childhood visiting nearby museums and watching the mounted regiment ride down her street. She came to the U.S. for college and stayed for the sunshine and a career as a museum curator in New York city. Over the years she published quite a few novels, two of which hit the *USA Today* list. She didn't delve into historical fiction until she discovered genealogy and the impressive cast of potential characters in her family history. Once she realized how many fascinating historical figures are all but forgotten, she decided to breathe life into them again by creating stories for them to inhabit. J. G. Lewis currently lives in Florida with her dogs and horses.

For more information visit www.stoneheartpress.com.

Cover image includes: detail from Codex Manesse, ca. 1300, Heidelberg University Library; detail from Beatus of Liébana, Fecundus Codex, 1047, Biblioteca Nacional de España; detail with Longespée coat of arms from Matthew Parris, *Historia Anglorum,* ca. 1255, British Museum.

Made in the USA
Las Vegas, NV
20 July 2024